Maelstrom
Robert G. Griffin

Little One Publishing—Hurst, TX
ISBN: 978-1-7374582-1-0
Title: *Maelstrom*
Author: Robert G. Griffin
Digital distribution | 2021
Paperback | 2021

This is a work of fiction. The characters, names, incidents, places, and dialogue are products of the author's imagination, and are not to be construed as real.

Dedication

To Rochelle, the love of my life and to Caitlin Gomez, a real life Abbie Preston.

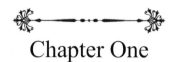

Chapter One

It was a half hour after sunset in the central Florida town of Delaney and middle school teacher Olivia Preston was home alone grading her student's papers. As one classic, soft rock song after another echoed through the house from the Bluetooth speakers, the widow of six months worked at her desk in her home office. When her cell phone chimed straight up at seven, she got up and walked down the hall to the kitchen. She picked up the cookie sheet with chunks of raw, chocolate chip cookie dough arranged on it and slid it into the preheated oven. She set the timer before heading for the front door, smiling to herself how happily surprised her sixteen year old daughter would be for her favorite treat. Her heart swelled with pride as it often did when she thought about the gift from God that was Abigail. Born premature, Abbie, as she was affectionately known, was afflicted with Cerebral palsy, which left her muscles stiff and awkward, especially on her right side. As if an IQ of 131 wasn't impressive enough, Abbie's life loving attitude endeared her to everyone who knew her. Even the horrifying death of her beloved father couldn't extinguish the love she felt for her mom and her friends, her teachers and her art. Olivia unlocked the front door and turned on the porch light expecting Abbie to arrive home in the next fifteen minutes or so from watching a movie with friends. Even though Abbie had a key, it was easier for her if the door was unlocked. Until recently, Olivia wouldn't have hesitated to leave a door unlocked but this once relatively tranquil small town had recently experienced a shocking trend of violent crime. But it was the still unsolved murder of her husband that prompted her to take the extraordinary step of buying a gun to protect Abbie and herself. She kept the Ruger LCP II .380, loaded and on her nightstand where she could get to it in a hurry. The small gun fit her hand perfectly and it could be concealed almost anywhere. As she walked back down the hall toward her office, she gazed at the plethora of pictures that adorned the walls. Suspended moments in time chronicling her

1

family's happy lives together. Most were of Abbie at almost every age and important event in her life but there were pictures of her dad and Olivia as well. Back at her desk, Olivia tried to hurry and complete the grading of her student's papers before the cookies were ready. A few minutes later the front door slowly opened and someone stealthily stepped inside. In between songs, the carpet muffled the footfalls that made their way toward the kitchen. Just beyond Olivia's peripheral vision a dark figure passed across the far end of the hallway as Bryan Adams began singing 'Everything I do, I do it for you.' In the kitchen, a large butcher knife was quietly pulled out of its wooden block sitting on the countertop. A few minutes later Olivia completed the last grading and slipped the reading glasses from her face and tossed them on top of the stack of papers. She got up and walked out of the room, down the hall, and into the kitchen where she stopped dead in her tracks. She froze when she was confronted by a person dressed in all black clothing, a black ski mask, and black gloves. Olivia forced herself to tear her eyes away from the large butcher knife the intruder held in their hand to unbelievably now making eye contact with someone who was obviously there to kill her. Her adrenaline surging, she suddenly bolted back down the hallway desperately running for the master bedroom and the gun that could save her life. She was tackled from behind and landed in the bedroom doorway, her face smashing into the doorframe. Dazed, she suddenly felt the intense, searing pain of a stab wound to her upper back. Olivia shrieked in overwhelming fear, knowing she was in a fight for her life. She frantically tried to get up and turn over but the attacker was straddling her lower back. Another stab. Olivia screamed in pain and terror causing blood to spew from her mouth. Another stab. Olivia flailed her arms and legs in sheer panic as another thrust of the knife sliced through her right lung. Another scream was accompanied with a mist of bright red globs of blood spraying on the bedroom door. Another thrust pierced her middle back. Olivia tried to scream again but only a guttural cry escaped her mouth. Two, three, four more blows rained down on her back- the assailant now in a frenzy. After so many more deep gashes and gaping puncture wounds were inflicted on her, Olivia could now only utter helpless grunts. Her fingers clawed at the carpet, her body in more paralyzing pain than her brain could compute. She began coughing and choking on bright red blood and Olivia knew she was about to die. It was just a matter of whether she would die of blood loss or drown in her own blood as it filled her lungs. The blows finally stopped and the attacker got up off of Olivia and rolled her over on her back. With her nervous system totally overloaded, her blood soaked body twitched violently. With blood bubbling from her mouth, Olivia was now too weak and too badly in shock to get up. She looked up at the black clad assailant and watched them pull the mask away from their face. Olivia knew who this person was and it was incomprehensible that they would want to kill her. The attacker's eyes were ablaze with rage and hate and the mouth contorted into a cruel sneer before spewing a terrifying taunt. "I am going to murder your daughter too!"

Olivia helplessly lay there, drenched in blood, unable to breathe anymore or able to comprehend why this person would want to kill her daughter. As she began to lose consciousness, the last thought Olivia had in life was absolute terror for her daughter's life.

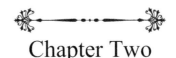

Chapter Two

On Wednesday, September 15th, nine days after Olivia Preston's funeral, Delaney Chief of Police Samantha "Sam" Taylor, sat in her patrol car at the Arcadia Municipal Airport, the closest airfield to Delaney. She was waiting on a plane carrying an F.B.I. agent who she understood would evaluate her request for assistance with a horrifying series of unsolved murders. At forty-two years of age, the tall, lean, redhead watched as a twin engine Beechcraft appeared from a partly cloudy sky and lined up for a landing on the single runway at the airport. Once the wheels were down for a textbook landing, the aircraft idled down the adjacent taxiway and pulled onto the parking tarmac reserved for planes.

Taylor got out of her patrol car and stood beside it so the agent couldn't miss seeing her. She was hoping he would be an older and more experienced agent rather than some young hotshot.

The plane parked, the door opened, and the staircase extended to the ground. The man that disembarked was about six feet tall, with an average build and he was wearing khakis with a blue dress shirt. He spotted Taylor and began walking toward her from roughly a hundred feet away. As he neared her, Taylor was relieved that he looked to be in his mid-fifties with short brown hair that was just beginning to gray at the temples. He carried a suitcase in his left hand so he extended his right hand toward her, "I'm Special Agent Michael Evans."

She managed a smile and shook his hand, "I'm Police Chief Sam Taylor."

"Oh," he tried not to look surprised.

She waved him off. "It's alright, I get that all the time. It's short for Samantha."

"Ah, okay. Call me Michael."

She opened the trunk and Evans placed the suitcase inside. They climbed into the car and Taylor pulled out of the parking lot onto the road that led out of the small airport.

"How far from Delaney are we?" Asked Evans.

"Thirty five, forty minutes."

"How long have you been the chief there?"

"Six years, but I've been on the force for twenty. My first and only job right out of college."

"Impressive."

"Thanks, how bout you?"

"F.B.I. agent is the only thing I've ever been or wanted to be. Forty one years now and I retire in ten months."

She glanced at him with a surprised look. "You don't look old enough to retire."

"Thanks but I'm sixty four."

"You don't look it."

"I appreciate that," he thought she seemed open and friendly so he decided to offer her a nugget of truth about himself to see what she'd say. "These are the days I've feared for quite some time. My fatalistic streak is warning me not to get killed right before I retire."

"Well, I'm afraid I'm dragging you into a lion's den."

"How so?"

Despite thinking about it for quite some time, she didn't even know where to begin. "How much do you know about our situation?"

"Virtually nothing. I was in Miami, about to fly back to Washington when I got redirected here at the last minute."

She sighed, "I guess it all started with a career criminal named Kyle Stanton. Does the name sound familiar?"

Evans shook his head, "I don't believe so."

"He was born and raised in Delaney. The story goes that his mother took off and left him with an abusive, alcoholic father. By the time he was ten years old he was already getting in trouble with the law. Theft and vandalism, arson and fighting. He dropped out of school in junior high after he was expelled for setting fire to the school office after hours. He went on to graduate to adult crimes. Burglary, drug dealing, gun running, and indecency with a child. He treated the town like it was his own personal criminal playground. He was a huge guy and he would threaten or intimidate anyone who

5

tried to press charges against him, especially for anything serious. During my time as a patrol officer he was locked up numerous times but rarely convicted. He did several stints in prison but he always came back to Delaney to bedevil numerous residents there. In addition to being a criminal, he had several out of wedlock children. He preyed on lonely housewives, drug addicts, or women down on their luck. During my fourteen years as a patrol officer and the first two years as chief, we only had three murders in Delaney. All three were solved relatively quickly. Then four years ago a body was found in some brush on a farm just outside of town. Turned out to be a prostitute from Miami, over a hundred miles away. She had obviously been tortured for days before she was killed. Horrific. We had never seen anything like that before. We couldn't even determine how she ended up here. A year later, a college girl from Gainesville turned up dead in a field on the opposite side of town. Raped and strangled. Although there were some similarities, there were also dissimilarities. The evidence was gathered up and sent off to the state crime lab. After a year of investigations that failed to produce an arrest, politics reared its ugly head."

"It always does."

"Especially in a small town. A man named Travis Reynolds won the town's mayoral race. He owns the town's only fitness center and is a leading member of our local good ole boy network."

"Let me guess. He doesn't appreciate a female Chief of Police."

"Especially considering I arrested him for DUI when I was a patrol officer."

"Ah, yeah," Evans nodded knowingly. Although he had just met her, he felt sorry for Sam considering what she was up against and he had little doubt he'd heard only a tip of the iceberg.

"It wasn't long before he was secretly working with my Deputy Chief of Police Brandon Holt to have me replaced. The reason they claimed it was necessary was because the two murders had not been solved. Brandon had wanted my job for years and Travis used that to push for a no confidence vote to have me removed. It failed by one vote."

"Unbelievable."

"A year ago, the state crime lab matched up DNA found on the college student and the prostitute to Kyle Stanton."

"I could see that coming."

"We started looking for him immediately but word travels fast in a small town and several people spotted him walking in the Beechnut Tree Mobile Home Park and called us but before we could get there a mob of people had attacked him with rocks, garden tools, anything handy. The first officer on scene had to draw her weapon to get through the crowd. Stanton was found beaten and unresponsive. EMS managed to restart his heart and he was transported to the county hospital. He's been there in a coma ever since."

"Good lord, vigilante justice."

"Big time. Years of his bullying and criminal behavior finally caught up to him."

"Anybody charged with the attack on him?"

"No. The first officers on the scene only saw a crowd of people around him. No actual violence. The people at the scene, identified by our officers, were all questioned but each of them claimed to have arrived after the assault had taken place. A year later they are all sticking to their story."

"Is there any video of the assault?"

"Not of the actual assault. A number of people have submitted videos that they took out there but it was after Stanton was already down."

"What is his prognosis?"

"Well, that's a point of contention within the medical community. My understanding is there is just enough brain activity to prevent the state from pulling the plug, so to speak. We have identified three children he fathered but never had any contact with. None of them want to have anything to do with him. The general belief is there are others but tracing them has been difficult. Not too many women want to admit being with him sexually."

"I can understand that."

"Three months after his assault, one of the leading suspects in his attack was hit on his bicycle as he crossed over a bridge one night. If the impact from the vehicle didn't kill him, landing thirty feet down on the rocky creek bed surely did. No one saw it happen and no one came forward but it was generally believed to be an accident. He was a veteran cyclist and had almost been hit a couple of times over the years. We tested the bike but the paint analysis never led to the right vehicle. Three months later another man, who we know was working on the power lines near the trailer park when the attack

7

happened, was gunned down on the job just outside of town. An elderly couple found him slumped over in his cherry picker on the side of the road, shot six times. He was married to a lifelong friend of mine. Rumors began to fly…"

"Is she a good enough friend to confide in you about whether or not he told her what he witnessed out there?"

"She did but she was murdered two weeks ago."

"Good lord, this is out of control!"

Taylor nodded, "It's a powder keg about to explode. People are pointing fingers at each other, threatening each other, gun sales are through the roof, and there's even armed civilian patrols popping up in some neighborhoods. We may be one accidental shooting away from needing the national guard."

"I can understand why F.B.I. assistance is needed."

"Of course Brandon and Travis think it's because I'm not doing my job. There's talk that they're planning another recall vote, pressuring the rank and file to join them because they're going to be in charge soon."

Evans felt profoundly sorry for this woman. He was a good judge of character and she seemed to be a smart, dedicated law enforcement officer that had an unimaginably horrible situation thrust upon her. "I'm sorry about your friend. What happened to her?"

"Stabbed over two dozen times in her own home, only minutes before her teenage, disabled daughter came home and found her. Broke my heart for that beautiful child," even though she felt like it, there was no way she was going to cry in front of this F.B.I. agent. "I've watched her daughter Abbie grow up so I took her in. With no other family, I felt like I owed it to Abbie and her parents. Besides, even though a lot of people offered to let her live with them, how could I trust she'd be safe anywhere else? I sure don't want the state to take her. She's grown up here."

Even though Evans didn't have enough knowledge yet to determine if Taylor was a good Chief of Police, it was obvious to him that she cared deeply about her town and the people in it. "What was your friend's name?"

"Olivia Preston. We were classmates and friends and have been ever since. Her husband Cameron was a couple of years older, from a neighboring town. He took a job here as a lineman. They met at a dance and they instantly hit it off. They were married in no time and a couple of years later, Abbie came along. She was born with Cerebral palsy and at first they were crestfallen but determined to give her the best life possible. It didn't take long for them to realize they had a special child. She has an almost genius IQ, an unquenchable thirst for learning, a true gift for painting despite her disability, but most importantly, she has always had an amazing love for life."

"How is she doing now?"

"She's heartbroken, of course, but God has blessed her with an indomitable will."

Evans smiled at her warmly, "And obviously with someone who cares deeply for her."

"Yeah," Taylor was now struggling even harder not to become emotional. "For her to have such a great outlook on life despite everything that has happened to her- it is truly the most awe inspiring thing I've ever witnessed."

"I look forward to meeting her. How full is your house now?"

"It's just me and her. I was married once but not for long. No kids."

"Law enforcement can be hard on a relationship."

Taylor wondered if he was referring to himself so she asked him, "How bout you?"

"Married thirty-seven years and my wife can't wait until I retire."

"Well, I'm sorry you're getting dragged into this Hellish situation."

"Oh, I've seen some bad ones in my day. What is your best guess of what's going on?"

Taylor thought for a moment, "I think Stanton killed the prostitute and the college student. I originally thought Aaron, the cyclist, was an accident and even Abbie's dad was a one off crime of opportunity. Someone passing through town killing a defenseless person who was working by himself. But when Olivia was murdered, I knew then we were in the grip of a frightful evil. She was a middle school teacher, a sweet lady who never had an enemy in her life. If Aaron and Cameron were killed because they were at the scene of Stanton's attack, why would anyone target Olivia with such viciousness? I don't think Kyle Stanton ever had a friend in his

9

life. Who would want to avenge his assault by murdering innocent people? It makes no sense."

"No, it doesn't," Evans agreed. "You said Olivia told you what her husband saw that day?"

Taylor nodded, "She confirmed he told her exactly the same thing he said in his statement to us. He was working on the power lines on the road that leads into the trailer park. All of a sudden he noticed a lot of people showing up on foot and by car so he followed to see what was happening. When he got to the crowd of people, he said Stanton was already beaten to a bloody pulp and lying unmoving on the ground. He never saw anyone raining blows on him."

"Was anything stolen from Olivia's house?"

"Only one thing was taken. A gun that Olivia bought for protection when Cameron was murdered. They didn't have any valuables to speak of. They were modest and frugal people."

"So we can probably rule out robbery as a motive," Evans thought for a few moments, "Which means she was targeted, especially considering her husband was murdered six months ago. And the only connection between these three cases is the attack on Stanton?"

"Only Olivia had nothing to do with it," Taylor hoped her tone didn't come across as too acerbic.

"Cameron didn't either, really. But he may have been perceived as being involved. My experience tells me the motivation of someone that violent can be hard to ascertain sometimes."

"Anyone who can do that to Olivia has to be psychotic or totally evil, or both."

"I agree, and yet the crimes are so different..." his voice trailed off when Taylor's phone rang.

"Chief Taylor," she answered.

Evans watched as Taylor's expression hardened.

"Oh, God, who is it?" She listened for a minute, then said in a voice that trembled slightly,   "Alright, I'll be there in about twenty minutes."

Evans considered asking her the obvious question but the stunned look on her face made him decide to let her tell him in her own time.

"As if things seemed like they couldn't get any worse, they just did," Taylor slowly shook her head in disbelief. "They've found another body. His name was Darius Kelly. He was rumored to have been one of the main instigators in Stanton's assault."

10

"That's definitely worse alright."

"It could be catastrophic. Darius was black. He was found hanging from a tree on his property."

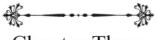

Chapter Three

Darius Kelly lived at the end of a road with older, wood framed houses and mobile homes set on huge lots. When Chief Taylor turned her patrol car onto the street they could see dozens of vehicles of all kinds lining both sides of the road. She pulled forward as far as she could and parked behind another police vehicle. As they got out of the car, Taylor and Evans could see a crowd of at least a hundred people at the far end of the street.

Taylor pointed to the houses on the same side of the road as Kelly's and said, "Let's cut through the backyards so we don't have to run through the gauntlet."

Evans gladly followed Taylor on the circuitous route rather than wade through a potentially unruly crowd demanding answers to obviously difficult questions, none of which could be answered yet without an investigation. They had to scale two chain link fences and circumvent an agitated rottweiler tied to a tree to get to the yellow crime scene tape blocking off Kelly's tree lined property. As they emerged from the trees a tall, slender uniformed officer saw them and hurriedly strode up to them. As he approached, Evans could read his nametag, 'B. Holt'. He took stock of the Deputy Chief of Police. Early thirties with a somewhat prematurely weathered face and longish hair under a Delaney Police Cap.

Holt sputtered, "We've got a shit storm brewing out front..."

Taylor interjected, "Brandon, this is Special Agent Michael Evans with the F.B.I."

"Good! We need all the help we can get," they shook hands.

"Where's the body?" Asked Taylor.

"This way," Holt led them toward the back of the property where a dozen or so people huddled around a body covered with a white sheet on the ground. A man who appeared to be in his mid-seventies wearing white scrubs with the words 'Raymond McDevitt, Coroner' written in blue cursive on his chest, saw them and walked over.

Taylor spoke up, "Raymond this is Special Agent Michael Evans with the F.B.I." They shook hands. She asked him, "What do we have?"

"Unfortunately the decedent's family cut the body down before the police got here…"

Holt interrupted, "The crime scene has been completely compromised."

"Oh, God!" Taylor exclaimed. She couldn't believe things just kept getting worse.

Holt continued, "When we got here, there were a dozen of his relatives already here and in the house. We got them cleared out as quickly as we could. Travis is talking with them in the front yard right now."

Taylor had noticed Officer Elena Acevedo, the town's only crime scene technician, dusting for fingerprints on a three foot tall, metal step ladder sitting directly beneath a four foot long section of rope hanging from a tree limb. Taylor asked Holt, "Is that where the step ladder was found?"

Holt shook his head, "Darius' brother said it was lying on its side a couple of feet away but he used it to step up on to reach high enough to cut the rope."

"Dammit!"

"The worst part is any tracks that were here have been completely trampled on," added Holt.

With a sick feeling in her stomach growing by the second, Taylor asked, "Raymond what is the condition of the body?"

The Coroner began, "I estimate the time of death at about thirty-six hours, so probably the night before last…"

Taylor interrupted him with an incredulous tone, "You mean he hung here all day yesterday?"

"Looks like it."

Holt spoke up, "Darius lived here alone and when a couple of his family members couldn't reach him last night or this morning his brother came over to check on him and found him here."

The Coroner motioned for them to follow him, "Look at this," with Taylor, Evans, and Holt crowding around him, the Coroner lifted one side of the sheet to reveal Darius' hands zip tied together behind his back.

"I guess we can eliminate suicide," speculated Holt.

"Not so fast," the Coroner told him, "I've seen many instances where people committing suicide have tied their hands behind their back so they don't panic and try to free themselves. If the step ladder was where his brother said it was, Darius could have kicked it aside himself. Although it will take an autopsy to know for sure, my preliminary examination of the body revealed no bruises or signs of a struggle."

Taylor exhaled a long sigh, "Brandon, have Darius' family transported to the station. We'll interview his brother first," she turned toward the Coroner, "Raymond, we'll need an autopsy as soon as possible obviously, but make a note of any little thing. There's going to be a lot of scrutiny on us."

Both men acknowledged their assignments and Taylor turned to Evans. "I think we better go back the way we came."

Evans noticed the chief looked paler in the face, which made the sprinkle of freckles on her nose and cheeks stand out a little more. With his knowledge of human behavior, he was fascinated to stand back and watch the interaction between these people. His initial positive impression of Taylor had not changed although he felt even sorrier for her now. Deputy Chief Holt seemed understandably nervous but Evans didn't detect any overt disrespect from him toward Taylor. That could be attributed to such a brief conversation or to the fact he was just nervous about the whole situation. It was hard to picture him as a Chief of Police though. As for the Coroner, he hoped his medical skills were still sharp because the man was clearly past his prime. As they made their way across the backyards Evans told her, "With your permission, I'd like to request an agent with a medical background to get here as soon as possible to conduct a second autopsy. It would lend a degree of legitimacy and transparency to the process."

"Oh, that is a good idea. I think I would have thought of that, I'm just a little rattled right now."

"You have every right to be. This would be a major challenge even for a much larger town. By the way, what's the population of Delaney?"

"Roughly seven thousand."

"How many officers do you have at your disposal?"

"Fifteen, including three part time flex officers."

"I'd also like to see if one of the F.B.I.'s Florida offices can free up a couple of additional agents to help us."

"That would be great."

As soon as they got back into the car, Evans was on the phone attempting to rally reinforcements.

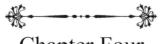

Chapter Four

The Delaney, Florida Police Department was housed in a relatively small, two thousand square foot stand-alone building on Main Street. Both Taylor and Evans were surprised but grateful there were no citizens already gathering there when they arrived. They pulled into the adjacent parking lot of the red brick, law enforcement building, parked in the closest available space, and quickly walked inside.

Christina, the young woman sitting at the front desk, seemed relieved to see Taylor and with a slightly harried tone said, "The phone is starting to ring off the hook."

"Call Maria and see if she can come in early and help with the phones," Taylor told her, barely slowing down. She turned left into a short corridor, with Evans right behind her, and opened the first door. The room was semi-dark with a single computer screen illuminating the face of a thirty something year old woman with brown hair. "Jessica, call all three of the flex officers. Tell them it's an emergency and we need them up here for crowd control."

"Yes, ma'am."

They heard the bell ring at the front door so Taylor left the dispatch office to head that way. Before they reached the lobby, a female uniformed officer whose name tag read 'L. Thorson,' met them. She was probably in her late twenties with dark brown hair and big, dark eyes. "Chief, I just saw a Channel 4 news crew from Gainesville drive into town."

Taylor turned toward Evans and shook her head, "Shit, the media is going to congregate and demand answers we don't have yet."

"What most municipalities do is issue a press release setting a time for a press conference when you'll at least have the autopsy results," Evans advised.

Taylor was so grateful for Evans' experience and calm demeanor. He was right of course. She nodded and turned toward the uniformed officer and said, "Leah, I need you to watch the front door. Brandon is bringing the Kelly family up here for questioning any minute now. Don't let anyone else from the public inside."

"Yes, ma'am."

Before the officer could get there, a large, muscular man in jeans and a red, short sleeve, Under Armour shirt came storming through the front door. He took one look at Taylor and barked, "Sam, what the fuck are we going to do about this?"

With surprising calmness Taylor said, "Travis, this is Special Agent Michael Evans with the F.B.I. Michael, this is our Mayor, Travis Reynolds."

"Good! We finally have professional law enforcement on hand!" Reynolds' voice echoed in the lobby. Neither man offered to shake the other's hand.

Evans' experience told him not to make a snap judgement about someone when you first meet them but he already didn't like this man. He said, "Mayor, the Chief is very busy as you can imagine. Can I have a word with you in private?"

Taylor offered, "You can use my office."

Without saying another word, Reynolds walked off down the hallway. Evans exchanged glances with Taylor and he flashed her a reassuring smile before following Reynolds.

Taylor was so appreciative of Evans presence. She was certain he would make a world of difference for her in what was shaping up to be one of the worst days of her career. At that moment, Deputy Chief Brandon Holt came through the door, leading the members of the Kelly family inside. Taylor told Holt, "Brandon, let's put Darius' brother in interrogation room number one and the rest of the family can wait together in the conference room. Let's make sure they have bottles of water and plenty of tissues."

He nodded, "Alright."

Reynolds had bypassed Taylor's office and walked into the break room at the end of the hall and Evans followed him inside. "Mayor, I have a lot of experience in cases like this and I can tell you, especially with this latest death, everyone in a position of authority needs to rally around each other."

"I see she's already talked you into siding with her on our dispute."

Evans sized up this thirtysomething year old bodybuilder and noticed he had acne, unusual for a man his age, unless he was using

17

anabolic steroids. It would also explain his apparent anger management issues. "No sir, she hasn't. I just arrived and I'm not in a position to gauge the quality of law enforcement here in town yet. Give me time to evaluate the situation. If I believe a change is in order, I'll lend my voice to yours. I can tell you however, these cases would be difficult to solve for a much bigger town with considerably more resources."

Reynolds exhaled and nodded, "Alright. It's just...this is my town and it's about to come apart at the seams."

"I understand," Evans tried sounding agreeable, "I've got an F.B.I. medical specialist arriving tomorrow to conduct a separate autopsy on Mr. Kelly and I've requested additional agents as well."

"Thank God!"

"I'm sure you have things you need to do so I'm going to assist with the interviews now."

"Yeah, thank you for your help," he extended his large, calloused hand and Evans shook it.

With the Mayor at least temporarily placated, Evans headed back toward the lobby and approached Officer Thorson, who was watching the door, "Can you tell me where Chief Taylor is?"

"She's in interrogation room number one," she pointed across the lobby toward a different hallway, "First door on your left."

"Thanks."

When Evans entered the room, Taylor turned around from the table she was seated at, across from a middle aged black man and said, "Tevaughn, this is Michael Evans with the F.B.I."

Evans extended his hand and Tevaughn Kelly shook it. "First of all let me express my deepest sympathies for the loss of your brother."

"Thank you," he had obviously been crying.

While Evans took a seat next to Taylor, the Chief said, "This is how seriously we take this, Tevaughn."

Kelly nodded his head.

Taylor turned toward Evans and said, "I've already read Tevaughn his rights and he's agreed to talk with us. Feel free to jump in if you have something," after he nodded an acknowledgement, she turned back toward Kelly. "Tevaughn, when was the last time you talked to Darius?"

"The night before last. At my house."

18

"How late was he there?"

"I'd say...eleven."

"What were you guys doing?"

"Eating and drinkin. We get together once a week to do that. He ain't workin so he comes over and we eat barbecue and drink beer. He doesn't have a lot of money so it's a big treat for him. He and I are the only males left in the family. Dad is dead, so it's just mother, us, and our three sisters, not counting a few cousins.

"When did someone realize he was missing?"

"Mother tried calling him last night but his phone went to voicemail. She says that happens sometimes cause he drinks and passes out but when she couldn't reach him this morning, she called me to go check on him."

"Walk us through what you did when you went over there."

He thought for a few moments, "I parked in front of his house and went up to the front door and it was unlocked..."

"Was that unusual?" Asked Evans.

"Not really, I mean, he would lock it at night but during the day it might be open. So I opened it and called out for him. Nothing. I got this funny feeling something was wrong. I thought he might be lyin in there unconscious or something so I started looking room to room, calling for him. He just wasn't in there. I looked out the back window to see if his car was parked under the carport and I saw him..." he started to cry. "Hangin there."

"I'm sorry, Tevaughn, take your time," Taylor said in a consoling tone.

"I couldn't believe it. I just started running and screaming for him. When I got to him, I could tell he was long dead. I just lost it. All I knew was I had to get him down from there. I grabbed the ladder and set it upright, took out my pocket knife and cut him down. I felt so bad because I tried to hold him up but he was too heavy. I just fell to the ground with him and hugged him."

Evans and Taylor exchanged looks and he could see tears welling up in her eyes and indeed, despite his vast experience of forty years conducting interviews with countless victim's families, he felt heartache for this man. He was willing to bet his retirement money that Tevaughn did not kill his brother.

Kelly continued, "As soon as I could talk, I called my oldest sister and they called 911."

19

Taylor asked as gently as she could, "Tevaughn, we know Darius was there when Kyle Stanton was beaten. He told me he got there after Stanton was already unconscious on the ground. That's not true is it?"

He shook his head, "I guess it don't matter now. We got cousins who live in that trailer park. He was over there visiting when he heard a big commotion outside. Darius told me he went out there and Stanton was fightin with some dudes. Everybody knows who Stanton is. People in the crowd was saying he was looking for a girl to nab and we got a fourteen year old cousin who lives there so Darius grabbed a rake and went after him. He said Stanton had already knocked down two dudes until Darius whacked him in the back of the head with the rake. Then everybody started wailing on him, even a couple of women. Darius said that was the only time he hit him. Said he didn't need to anymore. Everybody beat him to a bloody pulp. He said police was there in like, two minutes and he threw the rake under the trailer."

"Obviously it's not Stanton who did this to your brother...can you think of anyone else who would?" Asked Taylor.

He shook his head, "No. Darius ain't had a beef with anybody in years. He lived alone, didn't have a job, and he didn't go anywhere or bother anybody."

Evans had to ask, "Tevaughn, this is a difficult question but we have to ask. Is there any chance he would commit suicide?"

Kelly sat there motionless and quiet for a surprisingly long few moments, obviously running the question over in his head. He finally asked, "Is what I say going to be known by everybody?"

Taylor answered, "The only way what you say in here would become public is if there is a trial and your statements come out in court."

He slowly nodded, "I would say no he wouldn't. But he has been more depressed lately and if he was going to do it, this might be a way he would do it. But I honestly don't think he would."

Evans asked, "Why might he choose this way if he was going to do it?"

Kelly snorted, "I don't know. If he was going to, it would be just like him to go out stirring up some shit."

Taylor and Evans exchanged looks and the Chief spoke up, "Tevaughn, give us a minute," they stood up and left the room. In

20

the hallway, once the door was closed, Taylor asked, "Are you as sure as I am that he's not involved?"

"Totally. I've had forty years of learning interrogation techniques, human behavior, body language- there's just no red flags to indicate any sort of deception."

She was relieved that he concurred with her. "Now the hard part, was it suicide?"

Evans nodded, "Since the crime scene was compromised to the extent it was, the autopsy is going to be critical."

Taylor was torn between the two bad possibilities. "If it's murder, our problem just became worse. If it was suicide, I don't know if the black community is going to believe it."

"All we can do is keep an open mind and let the evidence take us where it will. Hopefully interviewing the rest of the family might shed some light on something."

"I can't thank you enough for your help so far."

"You're welcome," Evans could tell Taylor was an intelligent, caring law enforcement officer with a genuine, likeable quality. He knew she would like a touch of humor, "All of my knowledge and experience tells me something else. Mayor Reynolds is an asshole."

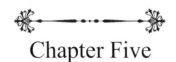

Chapter Five

The press release had set the news conference, later that same day, for 5:00 P.M. Right on time, Chief Taylor, Mayor Reynolds, and Agent Evans walked out of the Delaney Police Department and stepped up to a cluster of microphones set atop a podium. A part of the parking lot for the police department had been sectioned off and was now filled with not only townspeople but half a dozen news crews from as far away as Miami and Tampa. As per prior arrangement, Reynolds stepped up to the podium and spoke first. "Good afternoon ladies and gentlemen. My name is Travis Reynolds, I am the Mayor here in Delaney. To my left is Chief of Police Samantha Taylor and to my right is F.B.I. Special Agent Michael Evans. I'm going to make a short statement and then the three of us will take a few questions. This morning police were called to the home of one of our longtime residents, Darius Kelly. Darius, who was black, was found deceased and hanging from a tree limb in his backyard by members of his family. His hands were zip tied behind his back which we acknowledge is suspicious. An autopsy has been completed by our local coroner and while toxicology results are pending, there were no other injuries to Mr. Kelly. It's early in the investigation so no final determination has been made about whether this was a suicide or a murder. I can assure the Kelly family that everything that can be done will be done to determine the answer. With that, we can take your questions."

Several media members tried asking questions at the same time so Reynolds implored, "One at a time please."

A female reporter asked, "Mayor, how can you say it could be suicide when his hands were zip tied behind his back?"

Reynolds turned to Evans and asked, "Do you want to take that one?"

It didn't surprise Evans one bit that Reynolds would want to pass the baton when the tough questions started. He stepped up to the podium and said, "Let me start off by expressing our sympathy for

Mr. Kelly's family. It is extremely important to the town of Delaney, the police department, and the F.B.I. to get to the truth. I'll explain why it's sometimes difficult to determine whether a death is suicide or murder. First, hanging or suffocation, is the second leading method of suicide. Many people secure their hands behind their back when they hang themselves because they know they'll panic and try to free themselves. Having said that, the use of zip ties is rather unusual but not unheard of. That's why we have to gather and analyze all of the evidence and come to the right conclusion. With that in mind, an F.B.I. forensic pathologist will conduct a separate autopsy tomorrow to double check the findings of the local coroner."

Another reporter asked, "Sir, there are rumors circulating around town that Darius Kelly was killed because he was on a hit list of people involved in a mob that attacked Kyle Stanton a year ago."

"Let me take that one," Taylor spoke up and took Evans' place at the podium, "I can assure the public that law enforcement has no proof such a hit list exists. The rumor is probably the result of the hit and run death of Aaron Driscoll and the unsolved murders of Cameron and Olivia Preston. Cameron came upon the scene of Kyle Stanton's assault after it happened. Aaron was there to see a friend, Darius was there visiting relatives, and Olivia was never there so we still don't have any evidence that there is a connection to the assault."

A reporter from Miami asked, "Chief Taylor, you mentioned the murders of Cameron and Olivia Preston. Do you believe their murders are related and are you close to solving them?"

"First of all, I knew Cameron and Olivia very well. I went to high school with Olivia and we were close friends right up until her death. They were very good people. No drugs, no legal problems, no apparent reason for either of them to be murdered. I don't want to go into any details that haven't been released to the public but there is no evidence to suggest they are related. While they presently remain unsolved, I can tell you the investigations are making progress."

A reporter from Tampa said, "Chief Taylor, you said there's no evidence linking the cases together so whether there's one perpetrator or four, don't you think it's safe to say there's a violent crime wave here in Delaney?"

Taylor fought the urge to be snippy and responded, "One murder is too many for a small, tight knit community like ours so let me detail the timeline for you. During my first fourteen years as a patrol officer here in town and then my first two years as the Chief, we only had three murders, and they were all solved relatively quickly. Then four years ago the body of a young woman from Miami named Carmen Bustamante was found here. A year later, the body of a young lady from Gainesville, named Lauren Spencer, was discovered. DNA eventually linked the two murders to Kyle Stanton. Those cases are considered to be solved and closed. Nine months ago, Aaron Driscoll was hit by a car and killed while cycling one night. Six months ago, Cameron Preston was shot and killed just outside of town. Two weeks ago, his wife Olivia was killed at their home here in town. As I said, the investigations into their murders continue. The cause of death of Darius Kelly has not been determined yet. The safety of our citizens is my primary job, that is why I requested assistance from the F.B.I."

Another reporter asked, "Chief Taylor, the Kelly family spokesman has told the press they intend to have an independent autopsy done. Is that a sign of a lack of confidence in the police department?"

Taylor felt her face flush but she kept her cool and replied in an even tone, "Absolutely not. We are aware of what they intend to do and they have every right to take whatever measures they deem prudent to ensure justice is done. It has become a common practice across the country for families to do that. I am proud of the diversity of our police department and their interaction with the public. For instance, we have twelve full time police officers, three of them are black and four of them are Hispanic. Five of the twelve are female. We all live here with our families and we're all committed to keeping everyone safe."

A video producer from Miami with a true crime YouTube channel, who had a reputation for being snarky asked, "Chief, a couple of years ago a recall effort was made against you, led by Mayor Reynolds, that just barely failed. Are you concerned that in light of recent events another effort against your leadership will occur?"

Taylor thought, "What an asshole," and she resisted the urge to glance at Travis to gauge his reaction but instead replied, "No, I'm not. That is all of the information we have right now. We will have another press conference tomorrow at 5:00 P.M. Thank you."

Several of the media members shouted questions but Taylor, Reynolds, and Evans left the podium and headed for the police department doors. Once inside the lobby, Reynolds bellowed, "I hate the fucking out of town media!"

Evans thought, "Figures, now he's willing to talk," but he ignored the man and directed a question to Chief Taylor. "I don't suppose there's a car rental company in town?"

Taylor shook her head, "I'm afraid not. There's just not a big demand for it in a town as small as ours."

Reynolds wasn't finished venting, "They think we're a bunch of fucking rubes in a podunk town!"

Taylor kept her attention on Evans and continued, "Plus, there's only two small motels in town and they're usually almost full with down on their luck locals. With out of town media here, they're probably all booked up."

To no one in particular Reynolds blurted out, "I'm going back to my office!"

As Reynolds stormed off, heading for the back door, Taylor and Evans exchanged wry smiles but it was Evans who spoke up first once Reynolds was out of earshot, "Narcissists have a hard time accepting they're being ignored."

Taylor laughed out loud. It was the first time in a long while since she'd been able to laugh at anything. She didn't expect a federal agent to have a sense of humor. She told him, "Please come stay at my house. I have a couple of extra bedrooms and it would give us time to go over some of the case files together. Besides, I want you to meet Abbie."

Evans didn't have to think about it for more than a moment. It had already been a long day for him and the thought of driving forty-five minutes to start looking for a rental car and a hotel room sounded tiring. Plus, he liked Taylor and he didn't want to rebuff her kind offer. "Sounds good."

On the way home, Taylor made two phone calls. One was to tell Abbie they were on the way home, and the other was to order pizza. Only three minutes after leaving the police station, Taylor pulled her patrol car into the driveway of her ranch style house. Much to her chagrin, there was Abbie, sitting on the front porch swing all by herself. As much as she adored this kid, she could be a little frustrating sometimes. So incredibly smart and yet seemingly oblivious to the current level of danger, especially considering the violent murders of her parents. She would make a point of bringing it up to her when she could get her alone. She parked the car and popped the trunk lid so Evans could retrieve his suitcase.

When Evans had his luggage in hand, he briefly assessed the sixteen year old girl walking over to greet them. She was about 5'3" with an average build, shoulder length, light brown hair and green eyes, but it was her jerky, awkward gait that garnered the most attention. She had a big, warm smile on her face and he couldn't help but think that anyone who would brutally murder this child's parents must be pure evil.

Taylor introduced them, "Michael, this is Abbie. Abbie, this is Agent Michael Evans with the F.B.I."

"Abbie, it's a pleasure to meet you," Evans extended his hand.

"Nice to meet you," she shook his hand. "I've never met an F.B.I. agent before."

He was surprised at how firm her grip was but he found it easy to reciprocate her infectious smile. "Oh, we're just people too."

"You look just like what I would think an F.B.I. agent looks like."

Taylor spoke up, "Abbie, you okay with pizza?"

"I'll always eat pizza."

Taylor was carrying a bankers' box full of files relating to Abbie's parents so she had made sure the box was unmarked. "Let's go inside, the pizza should be here soon."

During the pizza dinner, the three of them got to know each other better and Evans came away quite impressed with Abbie for several reasons. One, she was friendly and engaging but surprisingly, she didn't show any outward sadness for the devastating loss of her parents. Two, he learned she was taking the toughest courses the high school could offer including some college courses and she was still getting straight A's. Three, she proudly showed him some of her paintings and although he wasn't very knowledgeable about art, he was stunned. The use of colors and the level of detail showed extraordinary skill despite her disability. Evans now knew why Taylor was so complimentary about Abbie. She was indeed a remarkable young lady.

After dinner, Abbie's friend Lily came over and the two of them retreated to teenager's bedroom, supposedly to catch Abbie up on school work, having missed a week after her mother's death. Even though Taylor didn't think Abbie needed any help, she knew her friends were more important to her than ever. Evans and Taylor sat in the dining room with files strewn all over the table for a couple of hours, reading and comparing notes, when she wanted to know what he thought about the evidence.

Evans looked up to the ceiling, thinking for a few moments and told her, "Well, with regards to Aaron Driscoll, it could easily be classified as an accidental hit and run, if it weren't for the fact that he was known to have been at the scene of Kyle Stanton's attack. Some of the rumors say he was one of the first people that physically attacked him. Regarding Cameron, he was shot with a .38 calibre pistol, which doesn't leave shell casings, which could suggest preplanning and at least a rudimentary knowledge of crime scenes. He was shot up close, which means Cameron apparently didn't fear the person who got that close to him. They emptied the gun into him which means they definitely wanted to make sure that he was dead. And at least four of the shots could have been fatal which might indicate they're proficient with firearms," he let out a weary sigh, "As for Olivia, several things stand out. The murder weapon was almost certainly a knife taken from Olivia's kitchen, which makes it seem like it was a spur of the moment crime but the killer took it with him. Why? It's dangerous because he could be caught red handed with it. There were no unidentifiable fingerprints but there were bloody finger smears which look like they were made by gloves, which suggests premeditation. The bloody shoe prints were estimated to be a size 9, which suggests a short man, 5'6" or even shorter. The topper is, Olivia either let this person into her home, or, as Abbie explained, she left the door unlocked for her. Which could mean someone who knew their routine."

Taylor asked him, "Do you think it's the same person or persons?"

Evans thought for a moment, "The crimes are totally different which would led you to believe different killers but, Aaron Driscoll aside, a husband and wife from a small town where murder is rare, that's too much of a coincidence. There's one other thing that seals it for me. In both of those cases there was overkill. Whoever did it wanted to make damn sure they didn't survive. Why? Again, because it's a small town, Cameron and Olivia knew their killers."

Taylor felt a little sick to her stomach. "I was afraid you were going to say that. I think so too. That means… I know them too."

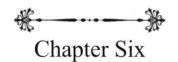

Chapter Six

It was mid-morning the next day, Thursday the 16th, when Taylor and Evans were waiting in the small lobby of the coroner's office. Evans sat in an uncomfortable plastic chair watching Taylor nervously pace back and forth. He thought she had every right to considering the results of the first two autopsies performed on Darius Kelly. The local Coroner, Raymond McDevitt, had issued a preliminary autopsy report citing no evidence of homicide with the final report pending until the toxicology results came in. A doctor hired by the Kelly family determined the death was likely a homicide. He cited the primary reason was how tight the zip ties were around Kelly's wrists. His assumption was that Kelly simply wouldn't have been able to get them on as tight as they were from around his back. The Coroner ruled the tightness was likely caused by bloating of the body. Evans kept talking to Taylor to try and keep her mind occupied. "I've got higher ups pushing for the lab to put the DNA tests on Mr. Kelly's zip ties to the top of the list."

"Thank you, that helps," she continued pacing like a tiger in a cage. "It's frustrating. Even the toxicology report could take a few weeks."

"That shows the volume these labs are dealing with."

The door opened and F.B.I. Special Agent Michelle Fitzgerald, a forensic pathologist, came into the room. The middle aged woman in white scrubs spoke first, "Well, first things first. This man would have died of cirrhosis of the liver within six months to a year had he not died of asphyxia. Having said that, there were no cuts or bruises on the body that would indicate he fought with someone or vigorously resisted being hung. Then again, his brother stated that Mr. Kelly drank a twelve pack of beer which could have made it easier for someone to murder him in that fashion. As for the marks left by the zip ties, they were unusually deep which means they were on very tight. Whether someone would have put them on themselves that tight or not would be mere conjecture. The DNA and the toxicology results will be crucial but for now there's no definitive evidence to prove it was a homicide."

Taylor looked at the ceiling and exhaled a frustrated groan. "The Kelly family is not going to like this."

"You might tell them we aren't saying he wasn't murdered, there's just no evidence to prove it yet. Hopefully the DNA and toxicology reports will shed more light on it."

"I hate to do this to you but unofficially, what does your gut tell you?"

She nodded slowly, "Unofficially, I would lean toward that he was murdered. Officially, I'm listing it as indeterminate, pending the lab work."

Taylor nodded and shook hands with her, "Thank you for your work and for getting here so fast."

"You're very welcome," she then looked at Evans with a smile and joked, "Do you request me on all of your cases?"

He answered her as Taylor's phone rang, "C'mon Michelle, you know I do. You're the best."

He watched as the color seemed to drain from Taylor's face.

"We'll be right there," she made eye contact with Evans and shook her head, "We have another one."

Evans stood up and asked with a tone of disbelief, "Another body?"

Taylor nodded, "Only this time there's no doubt it's a murder."

"Why?"

"His head was beaten in with a hammer."

"Good lord!" Exclaimed Evans. "Who was it?"

"His name was Jonah Sutherland. He was known to be at the scene of Kyle Stanton's attack."

"Well that seals it," Evans concluded, "These have got to be acts of revenge, and brutal ones at that."

Taylor looked at Agent Fitzgerald and said, "It doesn't sound as though we'll need your expertise on this one."

"I'm based in Miami so if you need me, I'm not far away."

"Thank you," Taylor turned toward Evans, "If we hurry we can beat the media there."

It was only a five minute drive and surprisingly there were only four vehicles in front of the mobile home or in the driveway, and two of them were police cars. Officer Leah Thorson stood outside of her patrol car with a man Taylor recognized as Shane Dodson, a coworker and friend of Jonah Sutherland's. The other officer, DeAndre Turner, who was built like an NFL linebacker, stood on the front porch like a sentry. As Taylor and Evans walked up the footpath toward him, Taylor could tell by the look on his face that the officer was a little shaken. Taylor asked him, "Are you okay?"

Turner shook his head, "It's not good in there," he then pulled a handful of disposable booties out of his pocket and said, "You're going to need these."

Taylor asked him, "Who all has been in there?"

"Just me, when I cleared the house."

Taylor and Evans began putting the booties over their shoes to preserve the crime scene and she asked, "Who called this in?"

He pointed at Shane Dodson. "His friend there said when Jonah didn't show up for work or answer his phone he came out here to check on him. He called us when he couldn't get an answer at the door. He gave us the phone number to Jonah's parents in Alabama and they gave us permission to force entry to check on him. I kicked the door in."

"Has anyone informed them yet?"

Turner shook his head, "No."

Just as another patrol car pulled up in front of the house, Taylor said, "Okay, we're just going to take a quick look. Don't let anyone else inside, of course."

The front door was pulled to but not closed so Taylor pushed it open with one knuckle. She stepped inside with Evans close behind. Taylor stopped after one step, stunned at what she saw. There were literally hundreds of dried blood droplets splattered all over the living room. On the carpet, furniture, walls, even the ceiling. Jonah Sutherland lay face down on the floor, covered in dried blood. His head looked like a pumpkin that had been dropped on a sidewalk from the top of a five story building. Taylor uttered, "My God, I've never seen anything like this before."

"Overkill again," Evans added.

Taylor pointed, "Look, the bloody hammer," the obvious murder weapon lay beside Sutherland's body. The foul odor of dried blood and the early stages of decomposition hung in the air.

Evans looked the body over and asked, "Was he married?"

Taylor shook her head, "No, he was one of those single, beer drinking, good ole boys who worked as a mechanic. I saw him just the other day driving past the shop."

"He's wearing pajamas so he must not have been expecting company, and apparently he didn't see it coming."

"It must've been someone he knew," Taylor said as if she still couldn't believe it.

"It's pretty obvious the people at Kyle Stanton's assault are being targeted."

"Yeah, but it doesn't explain Olivia."

"Considering the level of overkill in these cases, we're obviously dealing with someone filled with hatred and anger. Maybe enough that they would even target the spouse of someone who just happened to be there."

"Whew, that's a crazy thought," she still couldn't imagine who they were dealing with. "I guess I'd better call Jonah's parents for the death notification."

When Taylor and Evans stepped out of the trailer, Crime Scene Technician Elena Acevedo, wearing a full body Tyvek suit, was just walking up to the porch. Taylor warned her, "You've got your work cut out for you, Elena."

Acevedo nodded, "Raymond should be here any minute."

Officer Turner spoke up, "Chief, Leah wants a word with you."

"Okay," Taylor and Evans pulled the booties off of their shoes and started walking toward Officer Leah Thorson standing beside her patrol car with Shane Dodson, who looked like he'd just seen a ghost. As they walked over to them Taylor said, "I'm sorry about your friend, Shane."

"Thanks. I still can't believe it."

"Officer Thorson is going to take you to the station so we can get an official statement from you, okay?"

"Yeah."

Thorson spoke up, "Chief, there is something I need to tell you."

"Step over here," Taylor led Thorson and Evans out of earshot of Dodson and over a dozen neighbors now gathering around the entrance to Sutherland's driveway. "What's up?"

"I'm not saying it has anything to do with this but last night I was on patrol about 10:00 when I made the u turn at the city limits out on the highway, and as I was coming back in, I passed a red pickup truck heading out of town. The fact that it was an older model is what caught my eye and that's when I recognized it. Tommy Dalton."

"Tommy Dalton?"

Thorson nodded her head, "It was dark and I haven't seen him in years but it looked like he was the person driving. I don't think I could swear to it in court though."

"Who is Tommy Dalton?" Asked Evans.

"It's a long story," Taylor sighed, "I'll have to fill you in."

"I'm pretty sure it was his truck though," Thorson added.

Taylor nodded knowingly, "It's suspicious because that particular location is less than a mile from here. Especially since it was last night."

Evans asked Thorson, "I don't suppose your dash cam was on?"

"No, sir, it's activated by lights or sirens."

"I was afraid you were going to say that."

"Thank you, Leah," Taylor said, "I'll let you know if we need a statement from you."

"Sure thing."

At that moment the first news van pulled up in front of the house. Taylor said, "Let's get out of here while we can."

Before they could leave the small housing edition, they passed by the Coroner, two more patrol cars, and another news crew.

Evans asked, "Tommy Dalton?"

Taylor jumped right in with the story. "Thomas Dalton was a senior in high school when I was a freshman. Seemed like a popular guy, had a pretty girlfriend, and was on the baseball team. Came from a well to do family. They owned real estate, car dealerships, and other companies. After high school he wouldn't go to work at any of the family businesses or let his parents pay for his college. He surprised everybody when he went into construction. Over the years he learned carpentry, got his electrician's license, his plumber's license, even learned welding. It was when he was twenty-four that his life took a turn for the worse. I was in college at The University of Florida in Gainesville at the time, but I heard all about it on my trips back home. He began secretly dating a local girl named Vanessa Godfrey who was sixteen years old. When it became public knowledge, some people were understanding because she looked older and was mature for her age but her parents were not in that camp. Despite their daughter's pleas, they pushed for charges against him and he was arrested and went to trial. Even though Vanessa testified for the defense and even cried and pleaded for an acquital, there was enough evidence that he was ultimately convicted of statutory rape. It caused a split between Vanessa and her parents that continues to this day. She moved out and my understanding is she hasn't talked to them since. Tommy did three years in prison and when he walked out, Vanessa was there to pick him up. The next day, they went to the Justice of the Peace and got married. Tommy was faced with being a registered sex offender for the rest of his life and perhaps for that reason they moved to a five acre island in the middle of a lake on one of his family's ranches. They've lived there for eighteen years and have two children. The only times I know of that he's been into town was when he accompanied his wife to doctor's appointments and the births of his children. They have everything they need delivered to the ranch out there, about a half hour east of town."

"Wow! How well do you know him?"

Taylor shook her head, "Not very well. Didn't really know him in school and since he got out of prison I've exchanged pleasantries with him maybe two or three times. And that was years ago."

"Do you think he's capable of such violence?"

"No, I wouldn't think so, but I can't see anyone in our town committing these horrible crimes."

"The higher ups have told me there's going to be a delay getting additional agents here to help because the bureau is so busy. Maybe this latest murder will motivate them to expedite some help for us."

"I hope so," she sighed, "Let's interview Shane Dodson, then we'll pay Tommy a visit."

"We just have to be back for the news conference at 5:00."

"I'm already dreading it."

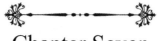

Chapter Seven

Without a current phone number for Tommy Dalton, Taylor and Evans drove a half hour east to the entrance of the Dalton ranch. A short, metal pole off to the side of the large, steel gate had an intercom on it so Taylor got out of the patrol car and hit the button. About thirty seconds later a female voice said, "Hello?"

"This is Delaney Chief of Police Sam Taylor with F.B.I. agent Michael Evans. We'd like to talk to Tommy if we could?"

After almost a full minute of silence the gate began to open and Taylor returned to the car. Evans pointed to a telephone pole about thirty feet inside the entrance. "See the camera?"

"Yep."

"If all of the exits are covered by cameras, it could prove if it was him or not."

"True. Let's see if he brings it up first."

"That's what I was thinking."

Taylor pulled the patrol car through the open gate and they made their way along a sandy, gravel driveway that wound its way through moss covered trees. Three quarters of a mile later, the road opened up into a large clearing that backed up to a lake. Parked on the far right hand side was a white SUV and an older model red pickup truck. There was a thirty foot long wooden dock that jutted out into the gentle swells of the water. As Taylor pulled the car to a stop near the dock entrance, a white ski boat was approaching them from what must've been the island located about a hundred and fifty yards out in the middle of the lake. Evans and Taylor got out and stood beside the car as Dalton cut off the motor and the boat bumped up against the rubber tires encasing the dock. He tied a rope to one of the dock poles and then climbed out of the boat.

Evans took stock of the forty-five year old man who approached them. He was about six feet tall, lean, with light brown hair that just covered the tops of his ears and he was wearing dark shorts, a white t-shirt, and tennis shoes.

Taylor was surprised that Dalton didn't look as though he had aged much in the several years since she'd seen him last. "Hello, Tommy."

"Hello, Chief Taylor."

"This is F.B.I. Special Agent Michael Evans."

The two men shook hands and Dalton said, "I'm not surprised to see you."

"Oh?" Asked Taylor.

"We've seen the news about what's going on in town."

Evans asked, "Why would you think we'd come talk to you?"

"When bad crimes occur, don't they always go around talking to the area's sex offenders?"

Evans noticed that while Dalton's face was expressionless, his voice betrayed a tone of bitterness.

Taylor told him earnestly, "Tommy, I don't consider you a sex offender."

"The State of Florida disagrees with you," Dalton said.

"We're not investigating sex crimes," Evans explained.

Dalton's eyes narrowed as he looked at Evans, "I'm being nice by allowing you on my property and answering your questions."

"Believe me, Tommy, we know that," Taylor assured him.

"What do you want to know?"

Taylor thought she would work in reverse order. "We had another murder today."

"Jesus, who was it?"

"A man named Jonah Sutherland. Does the name ring a bell?"

Dalton shook his head, "No."

"Did you know a man named Darius Kelly?"

"He was the guy found hanging, right?" He watched as Taylor nodded and then he answered, "No. I heard his name on the news."

"Cameron or Olivia Preston?"

"No."

"Kyle Stanton?"

"I've heard his name in the news a lot lately. Even way back in the day, I'd heard of him. He had a really bad reputation. I'm pretty sure I never interacted with him though. I would remember that."

Evans watched Dalton closely as he answered these basic questions. While he rattled off answers easily enough, his body language indicated he was somewhat defensive.

Taylor thought this was a good spot for a big question. "When was the last time you were in Delaney?"

Dalton thought for a few moments, "Uh, back in March I took Charlotte, that's my daughter, to the doctor for an ear infection."

"How old are your kids?"

"Charlotte is nine and Aiden is seven."

Evans wanted to go ahead and jump right to the point. "When was the last time that red pickup truck was driven to Delaney?"

Dalton glared at Evans and replied, "I see. Someone saw a truck that looks like mine and since I'm a registered sex offender I would logically be at the top of the list to investigate."

Evans now knew that Dalton was quite bitter about being considered a sex offender, not that he didn't have a reason to be. "Again, like I said we're not investigating sex crimes."

Taylor didn't like the way the interaction between these two men seemed to be going. She quickly interjected, "Tommy, the truth is an older model, red pickup truck was seen not far from our last murder scene."

"That's all you had to say," he shot Evans a contemptuous look. "I use the truck to move things around on the ranch or to pick up items at the front gate that we order online. If we travel anywhere we take the SUV."

Evans knew Dalton was going to love this next question. "Are all of the exits on this ranch covered by cameras?"

Dalton hesitated, as if contemplating his answer. Finally he replied, "Yes."

"Could we get a copy of the video for the last twenty-four hours?" Asked Evans.

A slight smile crossed Dalton's face before he answered, "Sure. All you need is a warrant."

Evans wasn't deterred, "Would you have any objection to us talking with your wife?"

"Yes, I would," he answered indignantly.

Evans could tell by Dalton's tone and body language that the questions were beginning to push his buttons. He decided to press ahead. "With all due respect, Mr. Dalton, we have an alarming string of brutal murders in Delaney, and you are not being entirely helpful."

"I can appreciate your dilemma, but you've approached this very badly. I'm done talking with you."

Evans nodded and turned to Taylor and said simply, "I'll wait in the car."

Taylor activated her car's remote start system so he would have some air conditioning. When they were alone she said, "Sorry about that, Tommy."

"The next time you want to ask me some questions, don't bring a federal agent with you."

"Point taken."

"I'm sorry for what you're going through, I know it's an awful situation."

"Yes it is. We just have to run down every lead, as you can imagine. I just wanted to eliminate you as a suspect."

Dalton nodded, "Well, I haven't been into town since March and my truck hasn't been there since last year."

"Alright," she pulled her phone out of her pocket, "Mind giving me your phone number?"

"Not at all," he took her phone and typed his number into it.

Taylor took her phone back and extended her hand, "If I need anything Tommy, I'll call you."

"Okay, bye."

"Bye," Taylor got back into the car and she added Tommy as a contact.

Evans spoke up, "Sorry, I didn't intend to be the bad cop, it just sort of developed that way."

"Oh, that's okay. It was clear that he's not a big fan of federal law enforcement."

"Well, you know him somewhat. What do you think?"

Taylor shook her head, "I just can't see him being violent. There's not a single instance of it in his background. You might have a different opinion."

Evans smiled and said, "This may surprise you, but I agree. Now, we were only able to ask him a few questions but he displayed no signs of deception whatsoever. It's clear he has a problem with law enforcement but considering his experience with the criminal justice system, I think that's understandable."

"It's entirely possible that Officer Thorson saw a red pickup truck that looked like Tommy's."

"Especially considering it was dark. Canvassing Jonah Sutherland's neighborhood for any security cameras might show the killer's vehicle."

"We're already on it. We need some kind of a break, on any one of these cases."

"We'll get one, it's only a matter of time. One thread could begin to unravel the whole thing."

While she steered the patrol car along the driveway, Taylor checked her watch, "We have enough time to check on the latest crime scene information before the news conference."

"I wonder if Mayor Reynolds will be there."

Taylor snorted, "He will. He may not want to answer tough questions but he definitely wants to be seen."

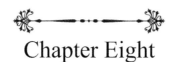

Chapter Eight

The news conference began on time with Chief Taylor, Agent Evans, and Mayor Reynolds walking out of the police station right at 5:00 P.M. The bevy of news media had grown considerably since the previous day. Taylor stepped up to the podium, flanked by Evans and Reynolds, and noticed how the microphones had multiplied as well. She took a deep breath and began, "Good afternoon ladies and gentlemen. I am Chief of Police Sam Taylor, to my right is F.B.I. Special Agent Michael Evans, and to my left is Mayor Travis Reynolds. I'm going to issue a statement and then we'll take some of your questions. As it's been widely reported today, we have suffered the loss of another one of our citizens. This morning we were called to initiate a welfare check at the residence of Jonah Sutherland. He was found deceased inside his home, the victim of an obvious homicide. We are withholding the cause of death as well as other important information as a way of proving whether or not someone has knowledge of the crime.

An update on the Darius Kelly case is the Coroner and the F.B.I. forensic pathologist have issued preliminary autopsy reports listing the cause of death as indeterminate, pending the results of DNA and toxicology reports. The doctor hired by the Kelly family determined the cause of death to be likely a homicide, pending the lab results. Now, what I'm about to say is very important. It amounts to a public service emergency. In the last six months, we've had three murders and two other deaths that are potential murders, and three of them have occured in the last two weeks. Four of the victims were at the scene of Kyle Stanton's assault, in the Beechnut Tree Mobile Home Park a year ago. The fifth, Olivia Preston, was the wife of Cameron, who was one of those people at the scene. It is apparent now that people who were there are being targeted. If you were present at the scene or if you are closely related to someone who was there, you need to take extra precautions. I think a lot of those precautions are pretty obvious, but if you need a security review the police department is ready to provide that. One last thing. In each of these last four cases, if Darius Kelly is included, someone got close to the victim, apparently without raising any suspicion. Be careful who you trust, especially if you are alone. We will now take your questions."

Several reporters shouted questions at once which caused Taylor to raise her hands up, "One at a time please," she pointed to a female reporter from Tampa.

"Chief Taylor, is there a working theory as to why someone would murder people for being at the scene of an assault of a career criminal?"

Taylor was expecting that question, "It would appear to be revenge, but like you said, why would anyone target innocent people for the assault on someone like Kyle Stanton? As far as we have been able to determine, Stanton never operated with an accomplice. That is obviously a major line of inquiry for us."

An unfamiliar reporter yelled out a question, "Chief, we've been digging around town and have heard from numerous people that Kyle Stanton had several illegitimate children. Has there been any thought that one of them may be the killer?"

"I'm glad you brought that up. That is something we've worked on since the beginning. We have identified three children that Kyle Stanton fathered here in town. Two of them have moved away, including one who now lives out of state. The one that is still here in town has been thoroughly investigated and we know that person has airtight alibi's and couldn't have been involved in any of the murders. However, we suspect there may be others out there who don't know he was their father or the mother is understandably reluctant to admit it. We are asking anyone who had one of Kyle Stanton's babies, or who knows of someone who did, to please contact us. You can remain anonymous."

A Miami reporter shouted a question, "Chief Taylor, my cameraman and I have already filed a complaint with your department because we were going around taking stock footage of each of the murder locations and when we came to Mr. Kelly's neighborhood we were stopped at the entrance by a group of eight or ten armed men who wanted to see our identification and then wouldn't let us through. Are you aware of that?"

Taylor sighed and hoped it wasn't audible, "No, I'm not, I've been busy out in the field. My message to our residents is, I understand you're scared and frustrated, we all are. But, armed vigilante groups are not the way to go. Things can go wrong in a hurry and then you are the one in trouble. Please leave law enforcement to the professionals."

Another reporter asked, "I have two questions for the F.B.I. agent. Sir, what is the role the F.B.I. is playing in this investigation, and secondly, have you personally ever seen a case like this one before?"

Evans took Taylor's place at the podium. "The F.B.I.'s role is strictly supportive. We have laboratories and technical skills a small municipality like Delaney cannot possibly have. These cases are local and Delaney PD has the jurisdiction. As for cases like this, each one is unique, and this one certainly is. Murder cases, especially a series of them, in a small town are almost always resolved before long. We just ask for patience while we work through this."

A reporter asked, "I have a question for the mayor. We've talked to several people who say they are going to move out of town. Are you concerned this could turn into an exodus?"

Travis Reynolds stepped over to the podium and answered, "No. There may be some people who want to get out of harm's way but we have a great little town. Most people love it here. I also want to echo what the Chief said. We do not want armed vigilante groups roaming around our town. Someone's going to get an itchy trigger finger and then we'll have a war on our hands. Just let us do our jobs."

The same reporter continued, "But Mayor, the reason people are arming themselves or moving out of town is there's a general belief that law enforcement can't save them."

Reynolds' face was getting red, "You see, there wasn't a question in there! That was a statement. No one's interested in your opinion," Reynolds drowned out the same reporter trying to follow up, "Does anybody have an actual question?"

A female reporter from Tampa spoke up, "A question for Chief Taylor. Going back to Kyle Stanton. Public information about him is sketchy, what can you tell us about him?"

Taylor didn't need any notes for this question, "He is forty-six years old and currently he's in a coma in the county hospital. Information about his early years are incomplete but they were not what you would call ideal. His mother abandoned him when he was very young, and left him with an abusive, alcoholic father. She turned up a year or two later in Miami, addicted to drugs, working as a prostitute, and was eventually found murdered in an alley. Stanton learned to survive on the streets and made his living through petty crime. As he got older he became increasingly violent and that culminated in at least two murders that we know of. Obviously he was the victim of street justice and someone seems to be seeking revenge for that but who or why has yet to be determined."

The same disrespectful YouTuber from Miami, who was at the last news conference asked loudly, "Chief, can you confirm information that is circulating around town that one of Agent Evans' priorities is to evaluate your performance as the leading law enforcement officer and determine if you need to be replaced?"

Taylor was stunned. For the first time, her mind locked up and she didn't know what to say. Fortunately Evans spoke up. "Let me answer that," his tone was terse, "First of all that's not one of the reasons why I'm here. It's never my place to weigh in on a local matter such as that. Chief Taylor is the one who contacted the bureau and requested assistance. That just sounds like a divisive rumor."

Taylor had regained her composure enough to announce, "That's all of the questions for now, we'll have another news conference tomorrow at 5:00 P.M. Thank you."

As the trio walked away they were pelted with questions until they were back inside the lobby of the police station. Reynolds continued toward the back door and bellowed, "I hate those sons of bitches!"

Taylor let out a long sigh and said to Evans, "Thank you for bailing me out. That one caught me off guard."

"I think I know where that rumor may have started. Yesterday, right here in the lobby, when I took Reynolds aside, one of the things I said to placate him was I would lend my voice to his if I thought any changes in law enforcement needed to be made. Obviously I wouldn't do that and by the way, I think you're doing a great job."

"Thanks," she managed a tired smile, "I don't doubt he's a rumor monger. I'm sure he'd use anything he could to bad mouth me."

"I think there's a good chance he suffers from roid rage as well."

Taylor nodded, "It's a really badly kept secret that he's used steroids over the years."

"I'm guessing he was a blowhard before that."

Taylor chuckled, "Yeah, he was."

Evans answered his phone after a single ring and Taylor tried not to eavesdrop while he had a brief conversation with someone. When he hung up he said, "I had an agent do some research for me. Twenty years ago, when Tommy Dalton was in Florida State Prison finishing up his last six months there, a new prisoner named Kyle Stanton arrived just starting a two year sentence for burglary."

Taylor's eyes flashed surprise. "I didn't know that."

"The prison's administration is completely new but the records show they were not held in the same housing unit. There's no documented account of them having any kind of interaction but it's possible they could have known each other in a common area like the exercise yard."

Taylor shook her head, "I just can't see the two of them working together. Stanton was the ultimate loner and Tommy hardly ever came into town. I just don't believe Tommy could do these things."

"It could be a coincidence," Evans thought for a few moments, "I have an idea. Tommy would not want to see me again. What if you took that officer that saw his truck last night, what's her name?"

"Thorson."

"Yeah, Officer Thorson. If you took her with you to ask him about it, she could get a look at him and his truck. It might clear up whether it was him she saw."

"Good idea. I'll set it up for tomorrow. By then maybe we can think of something else to ask him about."

Chapter Nine

By mid morning the next day, Friday the 17th, Chief Taylor and Officer Thorson, both in their uniforms, were driving east toward the Dalton ranch. Agent Evans stayed behind and occupied the conference room at the police station, with case files scattered all over the table. Before they left town, Taylor had called Dalton to make sure it was okay for them to pay a visit. When they arrived, the gate was already open for them. After driving the length of the private road, Taylor pulled the patrol car into the clearing and pointed at Dalton's old, red pickup truck. "Does that look like the truck you saw?"

Thorson took a long, hard look and replied, "Well, this truck does look a little older than the one I saw the night before last. I don't know, it was dark and he went by me so fast. It might or might not be the same truck. Sorry I can't be more certain."

"Hey that's alright, I appreciate your honesty," she pulled to a stop right in front of the dock and noticed Dalton climb out of the moored, white ski boat. "There's Tommy. Let's see if we can get him talking," she carried with her a manilla folder.

Dalton met them at the front of the car. "Hello Chief, I didn't expect to hear from you so soon."

"I'm sure," Taylor answered, "This is Officer Leah Thorson."

They shook hands and Thorson said, "It's good to meet you."

"Is it really?"

"Absolutely. Everyone knows you got a raw deal."

"It seems strange to hear that from a police officer."

"Our job is to enforce laws, not to write them. It's ridiculous for you to be a registered sex offender after you two got married and had children."

"I appreciate that."

"Have you looked into what it would take to be removed from the list?"

Taylor could tell Thorson had quickly turned on the charm. She thought, "You go girl."

"Yeah, you have to meet certain requirements like staying out of jail for twenty-five years, not being arrested for any other crimes, etc. So I have five years to go, then I'll have to hire an attorney willing to take my case. It wouldn't be cheap."

"Well, I wish you luck."

"Thanks," Dalton smiled and looked at Taylor, "So she's the good cop, huh?"

Taylor chuckled, "No, I wouldn't do that," she opened the folder and took out one of the two photographs and handed it to him.

Dalton held the picture and squinted in the sunlight for a long few moments. "Is this Kyle Stanton?"

She answered, "That was him two years ago."

He said, "Man, the years haven't been kind to him."

She handed him the other picture. "This was him twenty years ago."

Dalton quickly nodded, "Now this is the way I remember seeing him around town."

Taylor wanted to make sure she treaded lightly with this next question. "Can you think of a time or place where you would have had any interaction with him?"

"I actually thought about that after you left yesterday. I know I never met him in a casual setting. I had to think back to all of the construction jobs I've worked at, but I just don't think he was ever at any of them. From what I remember hearing about him, he wasn't big on working for a living."

Taylor looked him in the eyes closely to gauge his reaction to the big question, "Did you know he was in Florida State Prison at the same time you were?"

Dalton's eyes widened, "No, I sure didn't. That's why you're here."

Taylor nodded, "I'm not surprised you didn't know."

"I wasn't in there to make friends."

"No, I'm sure you weren't."

Thorson spoke up and asked a question from out of left field, "What's it like living on an island?"

Dalton smiled, "We love it out here. It's a great place for the kids to grow up. We homeschool them so we know they're safe and not threatened with bad influences."

Taylor nodded, "I can see the advantages. Do they ever interact with other children?"

"Oh yeah. There are several kids in our extended family and they visit regularly."

"That's good."

Thorson asked, "Does it have a name?"

"My family named it Abiaka Island after native Indians of the same name once lived in this area."

Taylor's phone rang and when she saw it was the station calling, a sense of dread enveloped her. She answered and after listening for a minute, shook her head and said, "Alright, I'll be there in half an hour."

Thorson asked, "What is it?"

"A white woman, apparently accidently, ran a stop sign and hit a black, female high school student. A group of her friends then attacked and beat the woman. Both are in the hospital."

"Damn."

"After the death of Darius Kelly, race relations have been very tense, and now this."

"Sorry you're going through this," Dalton said, "It's those kinds of things that make me glad we live out here."

"Hopefully we won't have to bother you anymore."

"No problem."

"Bye."

With this latest bad news, Taylor and Thorson rushed back to town, with the Chief wondering when this insanity was going to end.

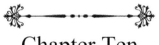

Chapter Ten

W hen Chief Taylor pulled the patrol car into the back parking lot of the police station, she saw Agent Evans and Officer Andre Turner standing at the back door talking. She said, "Just the person I wanted to talk to."

She parked the car and told Thorson, "Thank you for the help, Leah."

"Sure thing, Chief."

Taylor got out of the car and approached the two men. "Andre, do we have an officer at the hospital keeping an eye on everyone?"

"Yes, ma'am, we're rotating a couple of the reserve officers over there."

"Good. Did we arrest anyone in the assault yet?"

Turner nodded, "Marquez Johnson and Jalen Harris."

Taylor was shocked, "Those are good kids."

"I agree, but they both insisted the driver hit Raevyn, that's Jalen's girlfriend, on purpose."

"How is she?"

"She's got at least a broken leg. The ambulance took her to the hospital."

"Who hit her?"

"Dorothy Martin."

"Oh, Dorothy wouldn't do that on purpose," Taylor said with exasperation.

"I know, but the black community feels like they have a target on their back."

Taylor sighed, "It feels like we all do. How is Dorothy?"

"I was the second officer on scene. When I got there she was laying in the middle of the road, unconscious. Looked like she'd been hit in the face."

"My God, what has gotten into people."

"Jalen and Marquez have been processed and are being held until Judge Finley gets here to set bail. They both have family members camped out in the front parking lot waiting on them."

"Okay," Taylor looked at Evans, "I'll tell you about our visit with Tommy on the way to the hospital."

Evans said, "Alright."

A few minutes later when Taylor pulled into the parking lot of the small Delaney Community Hospital, she noticed how unusual it was for there to be so few parking spaces available. Once they walked through the front doors into the lobby, she understood why. While family members for both Raevyn Lewis and Dorothy Martin were milling about and going in and out of their private rooms, there were over a dozen high school students sitting in the lobby who had come to check on their friend and classmate. One of them spotted Taylor and shuffled over to her. "Sam!"

"Abbie, what are you doing here?"

"Our teachers said it was okay if we wanted to come visit Raevyn."

"Okay," Taylor could hardly blame her, "How is she?"

"Her left leg is broken in two places and she has a dislocated shoulder."

"Oh, poor girl."

"I need to ask your permission to do something. Raevyn doesn't have any insurance. I have a house full of things I'll never need or use. I'd like to have a yard sale and donate the money to Raevyn's family to help with the medical bills."

Taylor looked down into Abbie's big, green eyes and slowly shook her head in amazement. This young lady always seemed to find a way to show just how big her heart was. Taylor looked over to Evans to gauge his reaction and saw that he was grinning broadly. He told her, "Good luck trying to say no."

"A bunch of my friends say they'll help me move things," Abbie added, "They're going to see if they can find items to sell as well."

Taylor nodded, "Well, I'm not going to be a big meanie and tell you no."

Abbie hugged Taylor tightly, "Thank you, Sam!"

"You're welcome. We're going to go visit Dorothy first so you stay with your friends."

"Okay. She's in room number twelve."

"Thanks," Taylor led Evans through the lobby, past high school students who greeted her with friendliness, and others who whispered about the F.B.I. agent. Taylor knocked on door number twelve and a bald man about sixty years of age opened it. She recognized him as Dorothy's husband Joseph.

"Chief, I want charges pressed against those kids!"

"Joe, they're already in jail for assault," she pushed past him and made her way to Dorothy's bedside. She took Dorothy's outstretched hand and asked, "How are you feeling?"

"My head hurts. They say I have a concussion."

Taylor could see the sixty-one year old woman had a busted lip. "Let me see your teeth."

The woman opened her mouth revealing a chipped front tooth. "I'm sorry, Dorothy."

"They think I hit my head on the pavement."

Her husband came around the other side of the hospital bed, "Chief, I don't care if they're minors or not, they cannot get away with this! What is happening to our town?"

"Joe, everyone's on edge because of the murders."

Dorothy spoke up, "Sam, I didn't mean to hit her. The sun was bright on my windshield and I rolled too far into the intersection. I didn't see her until it was too late."

Taylor patted her hand, "I believe you."

"She's not in any trouble is she?" Joe asked.

"Well, it's ultimately up to the D.A. but I don't see any criminal intent. That would be extremely difficult to prove. They might sue, but that's what insurance is for."

"If they want to sue, we will too. We can prove they assaulted Dorothy."

"Okay, all I ask is that you keep a level head, Joe," Taylor advised.

"I will."

"We're going to pop in and check on Raevyn and I'll try and assure them it wasn't intentional and for them to keep a level head as well. Call me if you need anything."

"Thank you, Sam," Dorothy uttered.

Taylor and Evans walked across the hall and knocked on room number eleven. A couple of different voices simultaneously said, "Come in."

When they entered, Taylor recognized everyone in the room. Raevyn, her parents, an older brother, and her grandmother. "Hello everyone, this is Agent Michael Evans with the F.B.I." Several of them offered cordial greetings. Taylor went to Raevyn's side and patted her hand, "How are you feeling?"

"Not good," Raevyn answered groggily.

Her mother Sharonda said, "The pain meds have kicked in."

"What are the doctors saying?" Asked Taylor.

"She's going to be here for at least a few days but they say both her leg and shoulder should eventually heal back to normal."

"Thank God. I know some of her friends are planning to raise money for her medical bills."

"Yeah, they just talked to us. They're great kids."

"Yes, they are," Taylor agreed. "I've talked with Dorothy Martin and she feels terrible about what happened."

Raevyn's father Terrance spoke up, "We don't believe she did it on purpose. Those boys should not have hit her like that. I think they just reacted emotionally."

Taylor knew Terrance from his work with the city's parks and recreation department. He'd always been a nice guy and a good worker. She nodded, "I agree. I've known Dorothy for thirty years and she doesn't have a mean bone in her body."

Raevyn's grandmother Lecretia asked, "Chief Taylor, what's the latest on Darius Kelly?"

"We're waiting on the toxicology results to come in as well as DNA tests. Hopefully that will tell us if he was murdered."

Terrance added, "A lot of people who have never had a gun before are buying one."

Taylor nodded, "Can't blame them but we're doing everything we can to solve these cases. That's why the F.B.I. is here."

Evans jumped in, "Chief Taylor is doing a really good job considering the nature of these crimes."

Sharonda looked at Taylor, "There's a lot of people who are thankful for you."

Taylor smiled, "I appreciate that. We're going to go now but we're praying for Raevyn's complete and speedy recovery."

They all exchanged thank you's and good bye's and Taylor and Evans left the room. All of the students had left the lobby and Taylor wondered if they were making their way safely back to the high school. She turned to Evans and asked, "What do you say we grab some lunch before we meet with Deputy Chief Holt at the station."

"Sounds good."

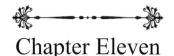

Chapter Eleven

At 1:30 P.M. Taylor and Evans walked into the conference room at the police station and Deputy Chief of Police Brandon Holt was already there with an open folder on the table in front of him. He greeted them, "Hello, Chief, Agent Evans."

"Hey, Brandon, what have you got for me?" Taylor asked, as she and Evans sat across the table from him.

He checked his notes, "We haven't completed the canvass of Jonah Sutherland's neighborhood yet but we're getting close. We have finished Darius Kelly's though. We have copies of four different security cameras and doorbell videos from the last night he was alive. Two of them show Darius walking home alone from his brother's house and it does indicate he was probably drunk. None of the videos show a strange or unidentified car in the neighborhood. All of the vehicles are either residents, someone visiting a resident, or our patrol cars."

Evans asked, "Your patrol cars were in the area that night?"

"Oh yeah," Holt answered, "Lately we've been trying to patrol every neighborhood in town at least once an hour."

"Did any of the officers report seeing him?" Taylor asked.

Holt shook his head, "No and neither did any of the neighbors, but it was late at night."

Evans asked, "Are there any indications he had a beef with any of his neighbors?"

"None. He lived alone and they're all saying he was quiet and kept to himself."

"What about the house?" Taylor asked.

"Not one unidentified fingerprint was found in the house. The family has looked over all of his possessions and they say nothing was stolen, although he didn't have much. His wallet, with thirteen dollars in it, was sitting on top of the kitchen counter with his keys and cell phone."

The lack of new information only added to Taylor's frustration. She let out a long sigh, "It's all going to come down to the DNA tests on the zip ties."

"Latest estimate is two to three months to get the results," Evans told them.

"We better get a break in these cases long before then," Taylor said.

"There's two other items," Holt added, "We got an anonymous lead from the tip line, a woman who said she didn't want to be publicly identified because she was scared. She said twenty-five or thirty years ago, that's as close as she could remember, she lived in those apartments at Maple and Gillespie. She said Kyle Stanton had a girlfriend who lived there until she got pregnant, presumably by him. Her recollection is that this girlfriend moved out to live with him somewhere in a rural area in Florida, although she either doesn't remember where or she never knew. She described which apartment it was but the property's ownership has changed so many times over the years, there doesn't appear to be any records that go that far back."

"You could try the Post Office or utility companies," Evans offered.

Holt nodded, "Yeah, we're trying to run those down but it doesn't look promising."

"We always assumed he had other children out there," Taylor said, "How many of them could know he was their father and if they did would any of them even care what happened to him?"

"There is one other thing, but I hate to bring it up. Travis approached me about organizing another no confidence vote against you. He didn't like it but I told him flat out no. There's no freaking way I want your job, especially right now. I told him I didn't think it was a good idea to change horses midstream so he stormed off and that was that."

"I appreciate you supporting me," Taylor told him.

"Once upon a time when we had one murder a decade your job looked appealing. Now I look at how grieving families are demanding answers. How the out of town press is portraying law enforcement in our town. How neighbors are turning on one another. I want no part of it."

"Can't say I blame you."

"Chief, I want you to know I'm sorry for my part in the no confidence effort against you. I was wrong. I see now how good you are at your job. And I hope you stay safe," he stood up and collected his papers, "Because there's no one else who can do what you do."

"Thank you, Brandon, that really means a lot to me," she told him earnestly.

He smiled and said, "I'll see y'all later."

"Bye."

Evans waited for him to leave the room before smiling at Taylor and saying, "That's one less problem you have."

"I'll take every small victory I can get."

Evans looked at his watch, "Press conference in a few hours."

Taylor sighed, "I've got nothing new for them."

"You might just open with a brief statement and start fielding questions."

Taylor nodded, "I think since it's Friday, I'll set the following one for Monday."

"Yeah, I think you've earned a weekend."

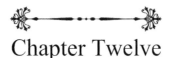

Chapter Twelve

T he 5:00 P.M. news conference began with Chief Taylor standing at the podium in front of a legion of press that looked larger than the previous day. She began, "Good afternoon ladies and gentlemen. My name is Sam Taylor, I'm the Chief of Police. To my left is Special Agent Michael Evans with the F.B.I. and to my right is Mayor Travis Reynolds. I've got a brief statement, then we'll take some of your questions. There have been a lot of inquiries about each of our open cases, so I'll detail where we are with each one so we can catch everyone up. It has been one year since Kyle Stanton was attacked and beaten into a coma. Three months after his assault, Aaron Driscoll was struck and killed while he was cycling. We have not been able to identify the car that hit him or who was driving it. Aaron was known to be at the scene of Stanton's assault but his level of participation is a matter of rumor. Three months later, Cameron Preston was gunned down while he was working on power lines just outside of town. There were no witnesses and his killer has not been found. Not one witness has contradicted Cameron's account that he came upon the scene of Stanton's assault after he was already unconscious. Six months later, his wife Olivia was murdered in their home. Her murderer has not been caught. She was never at the scene of Stanton's assault. In the past week, Darius Kelly was found hanging from a tree in his yard. We are awaiting DNA and toxicology results to make a definitive determination whether it was suicide or murder. He was also at the scene of Stanton's assault. Then the day before yesterday, Jonah Sutherland was murdered in his home. Though it was an obvious murder, we are withholding certain details to be able to weed out false confessions or to confirm a truthful one. He was at the scene of the assault as well. One last thing, the phone number posted on the front of this podium is our tip line for information on any one of these cases. The phones are manned twenty-four hours a day and we don't record or trace any of the calls. You can remain anonymous if you want to. That is where we stand right now."

An out of town male reporter on the front row asked, "Chief Taylor, with race relations in your town at a dangerous low, why didn't you address a white woman running down a black girl…"

"Hold on!" Taylor interrupted him. "No one has been run down. I didn't address it here because it was a vehicle, pedestrian accident. I know all of the people involved and I've talked to them about it. For instance the young lady's parents don't believe it was intentional so stop trying to make something out of this." Taylor couldn't believe after only one question she was already pissed off.

The same reporter wasn't finished, "But Chief, two young men who were with her thought it was intentional and even attacked the driver…"

Taylor interrupted him again, "I understand that and they were arrested. What they did was wrong. We took their statements and they've already posted bail so we'll let the judicial system play out." Taylor was surprised to see a relatively well known correspondent for a national cable news network and she pointed at him.

"Chief Taylor, we had a roundtable of law enforcement experts on our network and one of them theorized that these cases might not be connected after all. Have you considered that?"

Taylor thought, "Finally a somewhat thoughtful question," she answered, "Oh yes. As a matter of fact, when Aaron Driscoll was struck by a vehicle and killed, it was generally believed to be an accident, and the driver didn't want to come forward. Even when Cameron Preston was shot and killed, it was thought to be a random act of violence. It wasn't until his wife Olivia was murdered that it became apparent these cases could be linked. While Darius Kelly's death could still be listed as a suicide, with Jonah Sutherland's murder it's clear the link has be that four of the five people were at Stanton's assault."

A female reporter from Tampa spoke up, "Chief Taylor, with the cause of death for Mr. Sutherland still not released, what do you make of the fact that the deaths of the other four are all so different. Do you think it could be an attempt by the killer to make them seem unconnected?"

"Yes, that's possible. There's no angle we won't pursue."

Another reporter called out, "I have a question for Agent Evans. Sir, what is your experience telling you about all of this? And secondly, can we expect a profile of the suspect from the F.B.I.?"

Evans replaced Taylor in front of the microphones and began "My experience tells me to maintain an open mind. One or more of these cases may not be connected to the others. I think it is highly likely that at least some of them are connected to the assault on Kyle Stanton. I'm confident we will find out. As for a profile of the perpetrator, that is one of a number of tools that we are planning to employ."

A reporter from Tampa asked, "Chief Taylor, with the idea that solving one case could resolve all of them, which of the five are you closest to solving?"

Taylor had to give the question some thought, "That's not easy to answer. Obviously, the longer a case is open it becomes more difficult to solve. The most recent cases are still in the evidence gathering stage so I wouldn't say that any one of them is closer to being solved than another."

A male reporter asked, "Chief, we were approached by a resident here in town who said your department was investigating a registered sex offender named Thomas Dalton. Can you confirm that and also can you tell us why he's a suspect?"

Taylor wondered how that information was already publicly known. The thought of something like that being leaked from her department really irritated her and she resisted the urge to exhale a thousand miseries, "First of all, he is not a suspect. We have interviewed him just as we have numerous other people. I don't want to get into why we interviewed him but there is no evidence linking him to any of our cases."

The sarcastic YouTuber who had been at all of the news conferences yelled out a question, "Chief, considering the chaos your town is in, do you feel it's time to issue a curfew?"

Taylor tried not to let her expression show her contempt for this journalistic lightweight and obvious troublemaker but her tone was firm, "Sir, this town is not in a state of chaos and I don't see any advantage in restricting the freedom of movement of our citizens," she held her hands up attempting to cut off any additional questions. "That's all of the questions that we're going to take for now. Our

58

next scheduled news conference will be Monday at 5:00 P.M. unless there is any new information. Thank you."

Evans and Reynolds followed Taylor through the police station's front doors and once inside the mayor continued through the lobby toward the back door and bellowed, "If they're not going to ask me any questions I won't go to anymore of these!"

Taylor and Evans exchanged smiles and then she said, "What do you say we grab some barbeque to go, then pick up Abbie at her parent's house where she's getting ready for the yard sale tomorrow, and then head for home where we can have a quiet Friday night away from all the madness?"

"That does sound good."

Taylor and Evans drove to the modest, country farmhouse style home of Cameron and Olivia Preston. The couple's two cars were parked in the driveway and the overhead doors were open on the two car garage. Almost the entire floor space of the garage was cluttered with boxes of all sizes and numerous household items that Abbie had collected to sell. Taylor parked her patrol car on the street in front of the house and when she couldn't see Abbie or any of her friends, she felt a tight ball of worry suddenly develop in her stomach. They got out of the car and walked up the driveway to the garage and Taylor called out, "Abbie!" She could see through the open, inside doorway to the kitchen and when there was no answer, the ball of worry quickly began turning into a sickening feeling of dread. She hurriedly made her way around boxes and personal possessions of the Preston's and entered the kitchen with Evans right behind her. She called out louder, "Abbie!"

"Back here!" Abbie called from the back of the house.

Taylor's feeling of immense relief was quickly smothered with frustration with this seemingly oblivious girl. They found her in the master bedroom, boxing up pictures. "Abbie, are you by yourself?"

"Yeah, Ava and Lily just left."

"Abbie," Taylor exhaled frustration, "The house is wide open and there's a killer roaming around."

"I know, I had half a dozen friends here just twenty minutes ago. Everybody was in and out, I just got busy and hadn't locked up yet. I'm sorry."

Taylor walked over to her and hugged her, "You scared me. It's dangerous until we catch this person, okay?"

"Okay," her voice sounded tired.

Evans smiled to himself. Here was this childless woman with a love and protectiveness for a nearly adult girl that could almost be maternalistic. But he fully understood why Sam felt the way she did. Despite her disability, Abbie was an incredible person for many reasons and yet, considering the brutal murders of her parents, she seemed curiously unconcerned for her own safety. While Taylor hugged her, he looked at what she was wearing: a big, white, dust covered t-shirt, blue jean shorts, and a pair of yellow Converse hi top sneakers.

Taylor told her, "We have barbeque."

"Oh good, I'm starving."

"Let's lock up the house and get going."

"Okay, I'll finish up here early in the morning."

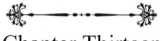

Chapter Thirteen

A few minutes after 8:00 A.M. on Monday morning, Chief Taylor and Agent Evans entered the back door of the police station. As soon as they walked into the lobby, Taylor saw a woman she'd known for many years sitting in one of the chairs. Lori Jo Keller was a recent retiree from a career as the town's librarian and a recent addition as a volunteer on the tip line. When she saw the Chief, she stood up holding a pad of lined writing paper.

"Hello, Lori Jo," Taylor could see she looked concerned about something.

"Hi, Chief Taylor, could I talk with you about something in private?"

"Sure, let's go into the conference room. Lori Jo this is F.B.I. Special Agent Michael Evans."

They shook hands and Evans followed them through the lobby and into the conference room. He shut the door behind them and sat down beside Taylor, across the table from Lori Jo.

Taylor could tell she was uncomfortable about something, "What do you have for me?"

"I was working the tip line last night," she sighed and placed the pad of paper on the table in front of her, "I wish someone else had taken the call I did."

"What is it?"

"A tip on one of the murders about someone we know."

"Who?"

"Mayor Reynolds."

"Mayor Reynolds?" Taylor didn't see that coming. She glanced at Evans but only a frown betrayed his thoughts.

"Yes. This was about 10:00 o'clock last night...I didn't get any sleep at all thinking about it. I didn't want to wake you up with this…"

"Who called in the tip?"

Lori Jo shook her head, "She said she didn't want to give her name until he was in jail. She sounded pretty scared to me. She told me she doesn't live here in town but she's been out on two dates with him. A couple of weeks ago he brought her to his house and they were drinking and he made a few attempts to get her to have sex with him. She wasn't ready for that and at first he seemed to take her rebuffs calmly but he downed a few quick drinks and then excused himself," she checked her handwritten notes before continuing. "Over the soft music she heard a weird, spring sounding door or cabinet at the other end of the house and then he came back into the room. She was about to tell him she was going to leave when he sat down on top of her. He straddled her while she was sitting on the couch so she couldn't get up. He then threw her purse across the room because it had her phone in it. He then pulled a handgun out and put it to her head. This is where she got really emotional. She said she thought he was going to shoot her right then and there because the look in his eyes was terrifying. He told her they were going to have sex or he would shoot her with the same gun he used to shoot some guy six months ago. She was too scared to say no anymore and he raped her. After it was over she promised she would never tell anyone if he let her go, and she thinks by then the alcohol had begun to wear off and he let her leave. At first she wasn't sure he was telling the truth about shooting someone until she heard about our murder cases and the second victim was a guy that was shot about six months ago. She apologized profusely about not coming forward sooner but she said she's been scared for her life."

Taylor stood up and walked over to look out of the window and uttered, "Oh my God."

Evans asked, "Lori Jo, how old did this woman sound?"

She thought for a moment, "Pretty young, twenties, maybe thirties."

"Did she have an accent of any kind?"

She shook her head, "No, I would say she's probably a local."

Evans nodded, "Did she say anything else?"

She scanned through her list of bullet points. "No, she seemed intelligent but she sounded scared. If she was lying, she was really good."

"Can we have your notes?"

"Oh sure," she tore the page from her pad and handed it to him.

"Sam, do you have anything else you want to know?" Asked Evans.

Taylor turned back toward them and said, "Lori Jo, obviously you're not to mention this to anyone."

"Oh, I know," she stood up and walked to the door, but before leaving turned around and said, "I can't see Mayor Reynolds doing that but the woman was very believable."

"Thank you, Lori Jo," Taylor told her.

"Sure," she closed the door behind her.

Taylor looked at Evans and asked, "What do you think?"

"Well, you know him a lot better than I do. My impression of him is he's an asshole and a blowhard but it hadn't occurred to me he could be involved. But, if you think about it, these are crimes committed with a great deal of rage and that certainly could apply to him."

Taylor sat down and shook her head, "I don't know if the D.A. would sign off on a warrant based solely on an anonymous tip."

"The Supreme Court has allowed the use of anonymous tips in substantiating reasonable suspicion and probable cause."

"Considering the level of pressure for a break in the case and the threat to public safety, we just might get it."

"I'll lend my voice to yours in presenting the case."

"I appreciate that," she slowly shook her head thinking about how Reynolds was going to react, "He's going to blow his stack."

Chapter Fourteen

At 10:45 that morning, three Delaney Police cars pulled up in front of a nondescript brick house in a small, middle class neighborhood. Chief Taylor and Agent Evans got out of the lead patrol car. Officers DeAndre Turner and Rebecca Daniels climbed out of the second car. Daniels was known as one of the toughest officers on the force, having fought in MMA bouts to pay her way through college. There was a joke in the department that if Turner and Daniels fought with their backs together, they could whip the rest of the force combined. Officers Leah Thorson and Miguel Ramiro got out of the third car. Ramiro was one of the bilingual officers on the force and frequently proved to be the best chess player as well.

"Everyone gather around," Taylor called out.

Turner asked, "What are we doing at the Mayor's house?"

"I just called him to meet us here, but he doesn't know why yet," she held up a folded piece of paper in her hand. "This is a warrant to search his house."

The four officers exchanged surprised and shocked expressions but it was Daniels who asked, "Why the Mayor?"

"We received a tip that the weapon used in the Cameron Preston murder could be in his house."

Thorson spoke up with an incredulous tone, "You think Mayor Reynolds killed Cameron Preston?"

"That's what we're here to find out," Taylor explained, "Now, this warrant is very specific. We are looking for one thing and one thing only. A nine millimeter handgun. If you happen to come across anything else that looks suspicious, something that could be related to one of the other cases, like a bloody knife or clothes, don't touch it. We can always get another warrant at that time. Let's wear gloves and take our time."

A few moments later, Mayor Reynolds' large, black pickup truck came screeching around the corner and pulled into his driveway.

Taylor said, "Andre, I need you to stay outside with him while we conduct the search."

"Yes, ma'am."

Reynolds got out of his truck and approached the officers. "Sam, what the hell is going on?"

"Travis, we have a warrant…"

"A warrant! For my house? Why?"

"We received a tip…"

"A tip from who?" He angrily interrupted her.

"You know I can't tell you that."

"This is fucking ridiculous!"

"It's not that we expect to find anything but we have to check out every lead. Just let us conduct the search and we'll get out of your hair."

"Well, it's not like I have a choice do I?"

Taylor shook her head and said calmly, "If you'll unlock your front door, we'll get started."

Reynolds wagged his finger at her, "When you don't find anything, I'll expect an apology!"

Taylor thought, "That'll be the day."

Reynolds turned and walked toward the front of his house with the officers in tow. Once on the small, covered front porch, he pulled his keys out and unlocked the door.

Taylor told him, "If you would, wait out here with Officer Turner."

"I don't need a fucking babysitter!" He stormed off and got back into his truck and started it up, but just sat there waiting.

"Andre, stand here and make sure he doesn't come inside until we're done."

"Yes, ma'am."

Taylor addressed the other officers, "Miguel and Leah, start in the garage and make sure you look at every little thing. Rebecca, take the kitchen, including looking inside all of the appliances. Agent Evans and I will start at the other end of the house and we'll meet somewhere in the middle."

Evans opened the door and Taylor followed him inside with the other officers close behind. He flipped the light switch, revealing a narrow foyer that opened to the right into a small dining room. Taylor followed Evans as he went directly ahead into the living room. Officer Daniels turned right and walked through the dining room into the kitchen and Thorson and Ramiro turned left and went through what was apparently the door to the garage. As soon as Taylor saw the black leather couch in the center of the room, the image of Reynolds raping a woman on it popped into her head. She shuddered and turned away, following Evans down the far hallway toward the bedrooms. He turned on the hall light and pointed to the ceiling. A cord hung down from the rectangular shape of the pull down ladder to the attic. He said, "The spring sound the caller heard."

"Of course. That hadn't occurred to me."

Evans reached up and pulled the cord down and the sound of the springs were in fact unmistakable. He unfolded the three sections of the wooden ladder and it extended to the floor. He pulled a small flashlight from his pocket and climbed up the creaking steps. With only his head above floor level, Evans panned the light around the musty attic, revealing only cobwebs and dust. Feeling like a Meerkat who's poked his head out of a hole looking for predators, he spotted a string hanging from a lightbulb, so he climbed up onto the plywood floor. He turned on the light just as Taylor ascended to the top of the ladder. The overhead light illuminated every corner of the attic. He told her, "There is literally nothing up here."

Taylor noticed something. "Look," she pointed at several footprints in the dust on the floor that led off the plywood, where insulation lay between the attic's floor joists.

Evans put on a pair of surgical gloves and carefully walked around the footprints to the edge of the plywood flooring, where the tracks ended. He pulled up the first roll of insulation and there underneath, was a black handgun. Evans recognized it as a nine millimeter Glock 19. He held up the insulation and pointed at the gun and declared, "Nine millimeter."

Taylor walked up behind him, looked down at it and said, "Oh my God."

"Does Reynolds live alone?"

She nodded, "Yeah," she took out her phone, scrolled through her contacts and hit the one she wanted, "Elena, I need you to do something as quickly as you can. Come to Mayor Reynold's house but don't tell anyone where you're going. Bring your camera and evidence collection kit and make sure you aren't being followed by the media, okay? I'll tell you all about it when you get here."

Evans replaced the insulation where he found it and they both retraced their steps to the ladder. Taylor shook her head and uttered, "I just can't believe it."

"It's going to take a ballistics match before we can take him into custody."

Taylor nodded, "I know. Technician Acevedo is an experienced ballistics expert so we should have the results by the end of the day. Of course, we'll have to send it to the State Crime Lab for confirmation."

"Let's get outta here, it's hot," Evans led the way down the ladder and once Taylor was at the bottom he asked her, "Did Reynolds and Cameron know each other?"

Taylor thought for a long few moments before answering, "I'm not aware of any interaction between the two of them. I imagine Cameron knew who Travis was, as the mayor, but I don't know about the other way around."

"Maybe Abbie would know."

"Oh, that's a good idea. I'll call her when she's at lunch and ask her."

Evans walked into the living room and observed Officer Daniels going through the kitchen cabinets. He turned to Taylor and said, "I guess it would be prudent to let them keep searching in case they find something else related to one of the cases."

"Absolutely."

"Olivia's murder weapon would be the holy grail of our cases."

"Wouldn't that be something," she shook her head, "I know he's a pompous ass but I just can't see him killing anyone."

"To that point, we need to check and make sure there's been no forced entry into his house so he can't claim later the gun was planted."

"Yes! Oh, Michael, I can't tell you enough how invaluable your knowledge and experience has been. You're a Godsend."

He smiled at her, "You're welcome. You've been so receptive and accommodating. It feels good to be appreciated."

"Oh, you are."

Just as Taylor and Evans completed the search of the living room, they heard a commotion from outside. When the Chief opened the front door, Crime Scene Technician Elena Acevedo was just stepping onto the porch while the mayor was yelling and trying to bully his way past Officer Turner. Taylor turned to Evans and asked, "Michael, will you show Elena what we need in terms of evidence gathering?"

"Sure," he led the technician into the house.

Taylor turned her attention to Reynolds, "Travis…"

"What the fuck is she doing here?"

"We found something suspicious…"

"Like what?" He yelled, his face turning beet red.

"I don't want to say until we've finished searching…"

Reynolds wagged an accusatory finger at her, "You fucking planted something in my house didn't you?"

The accusation instantly infuriated her. "Excuse me?"

"You've always wanted to get back at me for trying to get you fired!"

Turner shoved Reynolds back and vigorously shook his head at him, "Don't go there man!"

"Travis," Taylor's voice was remarkably controlled considering her anger, "My advice for you is to get an attorney."

Reynolds began to back up, huffing and puffing and his bulging eyes looked like they might pop out of the sockets. He turned and stomped to his truck, roared back out of his driveway and then raced away down the street. It was then Taylor noticed a blue sedan had pulled up behind the patrol cars parked on the side of the road. The car, an older model Hyundai, didn't look familiar but the man who got out of it did. The snarky true crime YouTuber.

"What is that jackass doing here?" Taylor exclaimed.

Turner asked, "Want me to get rid of him?"

She shook her head, "Come with me, I want to talk to him," she watched as he pulled out his phone and began filming the patrol cars and the house. She was glad he had just missed the volatile exchange with Mayor Reynolds. He trained his phone on her as she approached him and asked, "What are you doing here?"

"Police Chief Taylor of Delaney, Florida, I'm keeping my loyal viewers informed about the unfortunate string of brutal murders in your hamlet."

"How did you know to come here?"

"Whose house is this?"

"Answer my question," her voice betrayed a growing sense of impatience.

"I just employed my investigatory prowess…"

"Alright, let me see some identification."

"Okay," he turned his phone off and stuck it in the front pocket of his jeans. "I've been keeping an eye on your crime scene tech. I figured that would give me a jump on the next murder."

She motioned with her hand, "C'mon, identification."

"Am I doing something illegal?" He turned and glanced at Officer Turner as he peered into the Hyundai's windows.

"You can be arrested for refusing to identify yourself to a law enforcement officer," Taylor told him.

"Jeeze," he reached into his back pocket and took his wallet out and handed his driver's license to her. "Is this any way to treat the media?"

She read his license, "Nathan Allen Miller, twenty-four years old, and you live in Miami."

"My YouTube channel is True Crime with Nathan Miller."

"Catchy," she retorted sarcastically.

"Hey, I have over thirty thousand subscribers."

"Andre, will you run Mr. Miller's license?"

"Sure thing," he took the I.D. from her and walked to his patrol car.

"I'm clean," Miller held his hands out as if open body language would reinforce his innocence, "I'm a member of the media for God's sake."

Taylor sized him up. Slightly above average height, a little on the pudgy side with a mop of unkempt sandy hair and a very unremarkable face. "You've been an ass during the news conferences."

He chuckled, "That's my shtick. My on air persona. I'm the edgy, sarcastic, intrepid crime reporter."

Taylor rolled her eyes, resisting the urge to ask him if he still lived at home with his parents. "Can you provide an alibi for the times our murders occurred?"

His mouth dropped open, "You're kidding me right?"

"Where were you when the last murder was committed?" She made a point of not telling him exactly when that was.

"Uh," his voice suddenly became a little unsteady, "That was last Thursday right?"

"You tell me."

"I dunno, the days have kind of run together since I've been here. I've just been freelancing everyday, getting video of the town and the crime scenes. Talking with townspeople and getting their theories. My viewers eat that stuff up. If you'll tell me when the murder occured I might be able to run down where I was at the time."

Taylor didn't think for one minute this young man was a killer but she couldn't resist exacting a little revenge for the impudence he'd exhibited during the press conferences. "What a clever way to fly under the radar of law enforcement. Reporting on the crimes you were actually committing yourself."

"Yeah, it really would," he laughed until he saw Taylor's eyebrows go up and realized what he'd said. Suddenly serious he corrected himself, "I mean, no. That wouldn't be funny at all. I wouldn't do that."

"Where are you staying?" Asked Taylor.

"The Ocean Breeze Motor Inn."

Taylor nodded, "Our finest temporary lodging."

Miller added, "Yeah, the complimentary breakfast is a honey bun from a QT."

Taylor tried but failed to suppress a grin. She was struck by how hard it was to believe that the guy who had been such a jerk during the news conferences would ever say something that would make her smile. She knew though, that she needed to get him away from the Mayor's house. The last thing they needed was for this story to get out before they were ready for the inevitable media onslaught. She told him, "Mr. Miller, would you be willing to go down to the police station and give us an account of where you were Wednesday night and Thursday morning?"

An incredulous look dawned on his face, "You can't be serious."

"You don't have to but a refusal to be cooperative would certainly be looked upon as suspicious."

Miller exhaled, his mind clearly racing about what to do. He asked, "You just need a statement about where I was?"

"Yes," Taylor told him, "And if you have any corroborating pictures, videos, or media posts that would eliminate you, that would help."

"Yeah, I guess so," he sounded somewhat reluctant.

"Just think, you'll be able to tell your viewers you were questioned and released."

"Yeah, that's true. I'd be right in the thick of things," he was obviously thinking about the potential publicity so he nodded with new found enthusiasm, "Okay, I'll do it."

Turner returned and handed Miller's driver's license back to him and stated, "He's clean."

Taylor asked him, "Andre, will you follow Mr. Miller to the station, he's going to give us a statement as to his whereabouts during the last murder?"

"Yes, ma'am."

As Miller started to get into his car, he stopped as if something had just occurred to him, and asked her, "Could I get an interview with you?"

"I'll think about it," she couldn't resist one last dig at him, "We have to clear you of murder first."

Miller suddenly looked a little ill. He answered with a whisper, "Right."

Taylor watched as Miller pulled away with Turner following him in his patrol car. She glanced at her watch and realized Abbie would already be at lunch. She pulled her phone out and hit the contact button for her.

Abbie answered after the first ring, "Hi, Sam!"

"Hey, what are you doing?"

"Standing outside of the school with my friends smoking pot."

"What?" Taylor yelled.

Abbie giggled, "I'm kidding!"

She could hear Abbie's friends laughing in the background. "Girl, you almost gave me a heart attack!"

"I'm sorry," but she was still giggling.

"I have to ask you something."

"Okay."

"Did your parents know Mayor Reynolds or interact with him?"

"Um," she thought for a few long moments, "I don't think they knew each other. The mayor did speak at the school a couple of times and mom was there but I don't recall them ever talking."

"Okay, if you think of anything different let me know, alright?"

"Why did you want to know?"

"I'll tell you later, okay?"

"Oh, I wanted to tell you! Raevyn's mom came to the school during homeroom and Principal Jones let her make an announcement over the intercom about us raising $3600 for Raevyn's medical bills. She actually credited me with getting it started and my class broke out into applause and I couldn't help it but it made me cry."

"Awwww, everyone knows you're such a good kid!"

"My friends are making fun of me cause I cried."

"It's because they like you so much," Taylor was so proud of her. "Did her mom say when Raevyn is getting released?"

"She was stopping by here on her way to pick her up at the hospital. We're going over to her house after school and sign her cast."

"Alright, you stay with your friends at all times, okay?"

"I will."

"I'll see you at dinner time."

"Okay, Sam."

"Bye."

"Bye."

Taylor hung up, her heart buoyed just by talking to Abbie. Such a sweet, happy soul in what seemed like an increasingly cruel, sinister world. She turned and gazed at Reynold's ordinary looking house. A place she had never been in before today but had driven by hundreds if not thousands of times over the years on the force. She had a hard time picturing him shooting Cameron Preston, a good man by any measure. A man he apparently didn't even know. It wasn't as hard to believe he could rape a woman but it didn't seem feasible that he was responsible for all of the crimes. She knew in her gut that even if they had a good case against him in one of the murders, they were dealing with a much darker evil.

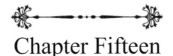

Chapter Fifteen

L ater that day, at 5:00 P.M. Taylor and Evans walked out of the police station and took their places behind the microphone-filled podium. Of all of the news conferences so far, this one Taylor dreaded the most. The throng of media was at least as big as the last one on Friday. She began, "Good afternoon ladies and gentlemen. My name is Samantha Taylor, I'm the Police Chief here in Delaney and this is F.B.I. Special Agent Michael Evans. I'm leading off with a statement and then we'll take some questions. We are totally committed to following every lead no matter where that takes us. No one is above the law and that includes being the subject of a murder investigation. Without going into too much detail, we received an anonymous tip that the weapon used in the Cameron Preston murder could be found at a residence here in Delaney. This morning, we executed a search warrant at that residence and found a handgun that matched the type used in the killing. A ballistics test was conducted this afternoon and the weapon was a perfect match to the one that killed Cameron. The gun has been sent to the State Crime Lab for confirmation of our findings. A warrant was then issued for the suspect, Travis Reynolds, our mayor," Taylor let that information sink in as some of the media and townspeople gasped or whispered among themselves. Several of the reporters started to ask questions but Taylor held her hands up. "Let me finish. Mr. Reynolds came to the police station of his own volition and turned himself in. He proclaimed his innocence but refused to be interviewed. That is his right. Bond was set at $500,000 and he is attempting to raise the money to get out of jail. The search of his residence, office, and vehicle did not produce evidence linking him to any of our other open cases. I think it would be easier if you would raise your hands and let me call on you rather than all of you screaming questions at the same time," she pointed at a female reporter from Tampa on the first row.

"Chief Taylor, two questions. One, you said it was an anonymous tip, is that enough justification for a search warrant and two, is he a suspect in any of the other cases?"

"The District Attorney's office made a determination that there was a sufficient legal basis to issue the search warrant. We are still in the evidence gathering stage of the investigation so we are trying to find any possible links to the other cases. So far there is none," she chose another reporter.

"Chief, how is it possible that the mayor of your town could be involved in this murder without raising any red flags and also what can you tell us about the anonymous tipster?"

"Let me take the second part first. We would like the anonymous tipster to contact us again, like they said they would. That person's knowledge is crucial to the investigation. As for red flags, there weren't any. I've known Travis for years and this comes as a complete shock to me," she gestured to a male reporter from Gainesville.

"Yeah, Chief, you say it's a shock but it's widely known that you were the arresting officer in his DUI years ago and there's been a running feud between the two of you including his attempt to remove you from office. Is there any concern that your relationship with him might complicate the case against him?"

Taylor took a deep breath and made sure the aggravating question didn't register on her face. "No, it doesn't have anything to do with it. It's no secret how he felt about me but I always approached interactions with him cordially and professionally," she decided on the next media member.

"This is a question for Agent Evans. Have you ever seen a case like this, with a town's mayor accused of murder?"

Evans took Taylor's place at the podium. "I have never heard of a sitting mayor charged with murder before but there have been instances where former mayors were charged and convicted of murder. Most politicians are investigated for crimes that are committed in office such as bribery, kickbacks, etc. So, no, this is extremely rare."

Another reporter jumped the gun. "Chief Taylor, can you detail the relationship between Mr. Reynolds and Cameron Preston and what the motive might be?"

"Right now we have not established that they even knew each other so the motive is unknown at this time," she scanned the sea of faces and raised hands and saw a familiar one. Nathan Miller. She couldn't resist calling on him. She was sure he'd learned his lesson.

"Chief Taylor, is it possible Mayor Reynolds committed the murder, and maybe others, to discredit you or the police department?"

She thought, "What a troublemaking little twerp." She was mad at herself for giving him another chance. She answered evenly, "I think it would be irresponsible to speculate as to motive. We are just going to follow the evidence and see where that takes us," she noticed a correspondent from a national cable news network and pointed at him.

"Chief Taylor, since we're on the subject of motive, do you know if Mayor Reynolds knew Kyle Stanton or any of the victims?"

"We have not been able to establish whether Travis knew Kyle Stanton or any of the victims beyond just being an acquaintance. It's one of the many avenue's we're exploring," even though it wasn't a bad question, she'd already had enough. "We are at the very beginning of this investigation so there's nothing more I can tell you at this time. Again, we'd like for the anonymous caller to contact us and we'll have another news conference tomorrow at 5:00 P.M. Thank you."

As she and Evans made their way toward the police station, one question was shouted above the din of others being hurled at them. It said, "If the mayor is released will you feel safe?" She was glad she didn't have to answer that question publicly because she couldn't truthfully respond to it with a yes.

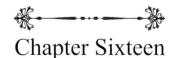

Chapter Sixteen

The next day, Tuesday, at 9:30 A.M. Taylor and Evans were hunkered down in the conference room of the police station. There were five stacks of files arranged on the top of the table, each one representing one of their cases. Aaron Driscoll, Cameron Preston, Olivia Preston, Darius Kelly, and Jonah Sutherland. A corresponding number of empty bankers boxes littered the floor around the conference table. They were both going through every file on Cameron's case when there was a knock at the door and Deputy Chief of Police Brandon Holt poked his head in and said, "Travis has made bail and his attorney is here to pick him up. Did you want to see him for anything?"

Taylor shook her head, "I'm probably the last person he wants to see."

"Okay, just checking," he left them alone.

Taylor noticed Evans staring out of the windows, seemingly lost in thought so she asked him, "What are you thinking about?"

"Oh, something that's been rattling around in my brain since we served the search warrant on Travis' house. The way he reacted to the search warrant and Technician Acevedo's arrival at his house was quite believable. Most innocent people react angrily when they're falsely accused and he was fighting mad."

"Travis is always mad."

Evans nodded knowingly, "Yeah, I know, it's just- my experience tells me he could be telling the truth."

Taylor couldn't believe what she was hearing, "We found no evidence of forced entry and Travis said he has the only set of keys to his house…"

He interrupted her, "There were no fingerprints found on the gun."

If Taylor didn't know better she would swear he was trying to irritate her. "So, he wiped it down."

"It was a black market gun, not one that he legally bought."

"Just the kind of weapon he would use to commit a murder."

"And hide it in his attic?"

"So, he's not a criminal mastermind."

"We still can't come up with a logical motive."

She looked at him with a mixture of annoyance and dismay, asking him, "Are you going to be a member of his defense team?"

He laughed out loud, "Oh no. I'm just pointing out what we're up against. Any defense attorney worth his salt will pounce on these things."

"Well, hopefully we'll get a DNA hit on the gun."

"That's going to take several months…"

There was a knock at the door and Jessica Bradley, the on duty 911 operator stepped inside and said, "Chief Taylor, sorry to interrupt but, I've got a guy on the non-emergency line who can't find his girlfriend."

"Why is he calling in a missing person on that line?" Taylor asked with a hint of exasperation.

"I asked him that," Bradley answered, "He said it's because she's kinda famous and he didn't think she would want the kind of publicity a 911 call would bring."

"What's her name?"

"Skylar Pittman but I've never heard of her."

"Oh Lord, Sexy Skylar."

Evans asked, "Who's that?"

"That's her porn name," Taylor explained, "She does these webcam videos where people, usually men, pay for her to do sexual things on camera."

"Oh," Evans tried not to smile since she might be missing.

Taylor told Bradley, "I'll talk to him in here, Jessica."

"Okay, thanks," before Bradley left the room she said, "I've got all of his contact numbers and information if you need it,"

"Thank you," Taylor reached over and picked up the landline phone and punched in the correct button for the non-emergency line. "This is Police Chief Taylor, who am I talking to?"

"Blake Archer, I'm Skylar's boyfriend, well, the closest thing she has to a boyfriend."

The name didn't sound familiar to Taylor. "You say she's missing?"

"Yeah, here's the deal. I live in Tampa and she lives here. Um, do you know what she does for a living?"

"Yes."

"Okay, I usually come here on the weekends because I work during the week but she'll occasionally come to visit me. Anyway, I was here until Sunday afternoon and then I drove home. I texted with her yesterday but then she didn't answer late last night, which she'll do every once and awhile. But when she wouldn't answer her phone again this morning, I just took off from work and drove here as fast as I could to check on her. She's not in her house, her car isn't here, and she's still not answering her phone."

"What kind of car does she drive?"

"A black Land Rover Sport SUV."

"Oh yeah, I've seen it."

"I'm just getting a really bad feeling ya know?"

"Where are you now?"

"At her house."

"Remind me where she lives."

"The Beechnut Tree Trailer Park."

The words hit Taylor like a ton of bricks. Suddenly feeling sick to her stomach, she didn't know what to say next.

Archer asked, "Are you there?"

"Yeah," Taylor tried to think straight, "Can you come to the police station and give us a report?"

"Sure, I'm on my way."

"I'll talk to you when you get here."

"Okay."

Evans watched her hang up the phone and observed, "You don't look so good all of a sudden."

"This girl is missing from the Beechnut Tree Mobile Home Park."

"Oh no," Evans said worriedly, "The site of Kyle Stanton's assault."

Taylor picked up the phone again and punched the button for dispatch. "Jessica, what is Skylar's phone number?" She wrote the number down on a legal pad, "Okay, do me a favor. She owns a black Land Rover Sport SUV. Get the license plate number and broadcast an APB for it. Then run a report on her and the boyfriend's criminal records and bring them to me. Thanks," she hit the button for the front desk, "Christina, there should be a guy by the name of

78

Blake Archer walking in the door in the next few minutes. Let me know when he does. Thank you."

Evans watched as Taylor stood up and walked over to gaze out of the windows and he told her, "Despite the shock, you handled that pretty well."

"She's only been missing since last night or this morning. It definitely wasn't Travis this time."

"No," Evans shook his head, "It's usually the boyfriend in cases like this but considering the connection to the same trailer park, it can't be a coincidence."

She turned and looked at Evans, "Unless he's counting on that to throw suspicion off of him."

"Man, that would be ballsy."

"Yeah it would," she took out her phone as she walked back to the table and looked down at the phone number she was given for Skylar. "I'm going to call in a favor with a friend of mine with the state police," she hit a contact on her phone and waited after a couple of rings for a man to answer. "Hey Cory, how are you? I'm okay, hey I need a favor. Can you trace a cell phone for me? I've got a missing person. The number is 863-555-3323. Thank you. Bye."

A few minutes later, Evans and Taylor were standing in the lobby holding the criminal records of their two principals. He read from the report, "Blake Archer, twenty-six years old from Tampa. One count of possession of marijuana and another count of public indecency. Skylar Pittman, twenty-two years old from Delaney. Two separate instances of public indecency. One of them was from here in Delaney two years ago. She was caught undressed and masturbating in a public park."

"I remember it all too well. It was real early on a Sunday morning when we got a call from a man walking his dog who spotted her filming herself on the playground, naked as a jaybird," she noticed Evans seemed to be having trouble holding back a grin so she asked him, "Do you think that's funny?"

"No, of course not," he was trying hard to keep his lips from turning up into a smile.

"Once the complaints started coming in from the public, it cost the city $1200 to have the playground power washed."

Evans was grateful to be let off the hook when the front door swung open and a man who could only be Blake Archer, entered the lobby. He was of average height and had a medium build with black, unkempt hair and about a week's worth of scruffy whiskers. He wore a slightly wrinkled t-shirt, blue jeans, and black tennis shoes.

Taylor spoke up, "Blake?"

"Yes, ma'am."

"I'm Chief Taylor and this is F.B.I. Special Agent Michael Evans."

"F.B.I.?" Archer suddenly looked panicked.

"He's here assisting us with our murder cases," Taylor explained.

"You don't think that has anything to do with Skylar?" Asked Archer.

"We have no reason to but let's talk," Taylor motioned toward interrogation room number one.

"Oh God," Archer uttered before he followed them into the room and sat down in the single chair on the other side of the table.

Evans closed the door behind them and sat down next to Taylor. She began, "How long have you known Skylar?"

"Four years."

"And you've dated since then?"

"Off and on. I was one of her first customers when she started doing videos. I had never paid into any of those before but she was different. Just eighteen years old and beautiful. I was just captivated by her so I reached out to her on social media and we started talking. Next thing you know we agreed to meet and we just hit it off. We were instantly sexual and she wanted me to film her doing things. Then it progressed to the point where I was in some of the videos with her."

"Why is the relationship off and on?" Asked Taylor.

Archer looked up at the ceiling and exhaled, "She's a very sexual person, as you can imagine. She insisted on variety in her videos, whether that was locations, acts, or partners. You know, to keep interest up for her videos. It's a very competitive field. I didn't mind other girls but it bothered me when she introduced a new boy toy, as she called them."

Evans jumped in, "So you were jealous?"

"Hell yes! Who wouldn't be? But lately she's gotten better about it. More girls, more toys, more everything else, except guys."

"So Sunday afternoon was the last time you saw her?" Taylor asked.

"Yes, I left about 4:00, that put me home about 5:45."

"But you said you texted her after that."

"Yeah," he pulled his phone out and scrolled to the thread of texts between the two of them, "Here," he showed Taylor where he told her he had arrived home at 5:37 and she responded with a 'Cool, love you, M.O.'

"M.O.?" Taylor asked.

Archer snorted, "Yeah, they're initials for a nickname she gave me. Massive One."

Taylor turned to gauge Evans' reaction and noticed that he already had a huge grin on his face.

Archer scrolled down and showed her, "Here at 9:30 last night I asked her what she was doing, no answer and then at 11:00 I said I was going to bed. Again no answer. At 6:30 this morning I sent her this text, 'Hey!' When she didn't answer I started calling her. I left a couple of voicemails but no call back. By 7:30 I was in panic mode so I called in sick to my job and hauled ass down here."

"What do you do for a living?" Asked Evans.

"I drive a truck delivering cars to various dealerships around the Tampa area."

"So you get here and she's not home?" Taylor asked.

"Yeah, I called her every fifteen or twenty minutes on the way here. When I got to her house, I was actually glad her car wasn't there. I thought maybe she was out doing something and her phone crapped out. I looked through her house to make sure…"

Evans interjected, "You have a key to her house?"

"Yeah, I did a walk through just to make sure there wasn't anything wrong in there and then I called you guys."

"Does she have any family?"

Archer shook his head, "No. She was raised by her grandmother, in fact she inherited the double-wide she's living in when her granny died. She never knew her father and has only a vague recollection of her mother before she ran off."

"Any close friends?" Taylor asked.

"Not really. Just a few fuck buddies, excuse my language."

"Do you know how she communicates with them?"

"Social media."

"Do you think you could put us in contact with them?"

81

"Yeah, I know where she keeps a hard copy of all the passwords to her social media accounts."

"Do you know who she has her cell phone service with?"

"Uh," he seemed to be thinking hard, "I think she got new service a year ago but I don't remember if she ever told me with who."

"Now this is really important. About a year ago there was a mob that assaulted a man in the trailer park."

Archer had a puzzled look on his face before asking, "What does that have to do with anything?"

"Have you seen any of our news conferences?"

He shook his head, "I don't watch the news."

"Well, what do you know about the assault?" Taylor wondered how anyone could be so uninformed about the latest news on the killings.

"Oh, I remember it like it was yesterday. I had just taken a shower and was in the bedroom dressing when Skylar ran in and said there was a fight outside. We both ran out there and saw some big guy laying in the middle of the road surrounded by twenty or thirty people. This guy was bloody as Hell and not moving at all. He looked dead to me. I asked a dude out there what happened and he said the guy had murdered some girls and people had attacked him for it. We never saw anyone hit him or anything. A minute or two later a cop car comes racing in there, lights and siren blaring. Cop jumps out of the car screaming for everybody to get away from him but people were still crowding around trying to get a better look so she pulls her gun out and starts pointing it at them! People started freaking out and yelling at her. I told Skylar, we need to get the Hell out of there. We went back inside and watched from the windows."

"What happened then?"

"Well, once the cop started waving her gun around people scattered like cockroaches. Looked like she tried to help the dude but there wasn't much that could be done. Couple minutes later the ambulance got there and took him away. The police fanned out and talked to a lot of the residents who were out there, including us but we told the truth, we didn't see anybody hit him. He was already down for the count when we went out there."

Evans asked, "What have you heard from the neighbors since then?"

Archer shrugged, "Rumors and gossip. People will say he did this and she did that but I haven't heard anyone admit to anything. But then again, we don't interact with the neighbors that much. Skylar is basically an outcast there because of what she does. There's mostly families who live there and well, damn, I've tried talking her into moving to Tampa but she likes living here. Plus, I think she likes having a house that's paid for. What does this have to do with anything?"

Taylor and Evans exchanged glances but it was the chief who answered him, "There seems to be a connection between what happened to that guy and our murders."

Archer shook his head, as if trying to process what she'd just told him, "How?"

Evans jumped in, "How much do you know about our murder cases?"

"There's been four, right?"

"Five," Evans corrected him.

"I only know of four. The last one, the black guy that was hanged, the teacher, who Skylar said she had in school, and her husband."

"Olivia Preston was Skylar's teacher?" Asked Evans.

"That's what she said. Fourth or fifth grade I think. That's about all I know. Like I said, I don't watch the news."

It didn't surprise Taylor one bit that one of Skylar's middle school teachers was Olivia Preston. It was the inevitable interaction of people in a small town. "What did she say about her?"

"She was really upset about it. Said she was a sweet lady, and probably her all time favorite teacher."

Taylor was sure a lot of people felt the same way about her dear old friend. "Will you let us in Skylar's house to see if we can find a clue where she went?"

Archer suddenly looked a little uncomfortable, "I don't think she would like that."

"Why?" Evans asked.

"She's not big on cops."

"Blake, if she's in trouble, we need all the help we can get," Taylor coaxed him with an empathetic tone.

Archer sighed, "Okay, but there's some things in there you might not want to see."

"That's okay," Taylor assured him, "The only thing we want is to find her safe."

"What about pot?"

"We don't care about that," she made certain her tone was emphatic.

"Okay, let's go."

"Did you park in the front?"

"Yeah."

"Okay, we're parked in the back. We'll be in a patrol car so when we come around we'll follow you to the house."

"Okay."

"What are you driving?"

"A red pickup."

Evans couldn't hide his surprise. "You drive a red pickup truck?"

"Yeah why?"

"What year?"

"2003, but it runs great."

Taylor tried to sound as though she wasn't suddenly suspicious, "Okay, we'll meet you out front in just a minute."

"Alright."

Taylor and Evans waited until Archer left the room before they exchanged knowing glances.

"Just when I was beginning to believe everything he said," Taylor told him.

"I did too," Evans agreed, "But I hate coincidences."

"I'll have Officer Thorson drive by over there and see if that could be the truck she saw."

"Good idea," Evans followed Taylor out of the room and toward the back door.

Chapter Seventeen

F ive minutes later, Taylor followed Blake Archer in his red
pickup truck into the Beechnut Tree Mobile Home Park. After
first a right hand turn and then a left, Archer pulled into the
gravel driveway of a dark blue, double-wide home and Taylor
parked behind him. All three got out of the vehicles and Archer told
them, "This is it."

Taylor and Evans followed him up onto the large, covered porch
and Archer unlocked the door.

"You can come inside," Taylor told him, "But don't touch
anything."

"I understand."

Evans led the way into a large living room decorated with what he
thought might be furniture from Skylar's grandmother. Sofa and
loveseat with a matching floral design and light brown furniture
arranged in front of a very new looking 65 inch TV. A kitchen with a
lot of dishes piled up in the sink and a dining area with a table and
chairs.

Archer pointed down the hallway past the kitchen and said,
"Utility room is the first door, then the master bedroom, and the
other two bedrooms are on the other end of the house."

Taylor walked that way and glanced into the utility room to make
sure it was empty, then followed Evans into the master bedroom. He
turned on the overhead light and saw the unmade bed was queen
sized, and the furniture was dark brown, heavy, and old. There on
the nightstand with the lamp and clock radio, was a glass bong and a
baggie of marijuana. The blinds on the windows were covered by
thick blue curtains. There was an armoire and a matching dresser
that had a large mirror anchored on it. Skylar had apparently kept her
grandmother's bedroom furniture as well.

While Taylor went into the master bathroom, Evans looked into
the large walk-in closet and saw that Skylar had a lot of clothes and
shoes, costumes and hats. He turned to Archer, standing in the

bedroom doorway and asked, "Can you go through her clothes and see what she might be wearing or if she packed?"

"I'll try."

Taylor and Evans left the bedroom and Archer headed for the walk-in closet. Evans walked across the living room toward the other bedrooms and Taylor turned right into the kitchen. There on the countertop was a tall stack of mail. Taylor sifted through the bills and advertisements that had obviously been collected over many days until she came across the hard copy of Skylar's cell phone bill. She hung onto it and continued looking through the kitchen and the living room until Evans called for her. She walked that way and the first door she came to opened to a guest bedroom that once again was almost certainly furnished by Skylar's grandmother. The second door was to the guest bathroom. When she stepped into the last room, Evans stood just inside watching her expression of astonishment. All four walls were covered with dark red draperies. The queen sized, four poster bed had only a white sheet covering it, but there were chains with leather cuffs attached to each of the corner posts. There was no other furniture in the room but there were all manner of adult toys scattered across the beige, carpeted floor. Up against the wall to the right was a tripod, obviously for a phone or camera. Evans carefully stepped over and around the sex paraphernalia to look into the closet. It was jammed packed with an impressive variety of BDSM equipment, the most conspicuous of which was a wooden stockade. Taylor followed behind him and looked inside and said, "My God."

"I guess you've never seen any of her videos?" Evans asked.

"No," Taylor shook her head. "I've heard all about them but I always prefered to remember her the way I would see her around town when she was growing up. A cute, blonde haired, friendly little girl. I just never wanted to see her like this."

Suddenly Archer was at the bedroom door. "Sorry to interrupt but, Skylar has a four piece luggage set and they're all in her closet. Her pink tennis shoes are gone so she's probably wearing pink shorts and a t-shirt. Her purse and phone are not here either."

They heard a knock at the front door so the three of them headed that way and Archer opened it. Officer Leah Thorson was standing there in her uniform. Taylor said, "Just the person I needed to talk to, excuse me gentlemen," she stepped out onto the porch and closed the door behind her. She pointed at Archer's red pickup truck, "Do you think that could be the truck you saw?"

Thorson's dark eyes squinted as the sun glinted off the truck, "I was just looking it over. Don't be mad at me but I'm not sure."

"Oh, I'm not, Leah."

"It might be but it might not. I thought the truck I saw originally was Tommy Dalton's but when I got a good look at it on his ranch, I thought it looked too old. This one might be closer to what I saw but it was really dark. Damn, I wish I had turned around and got the tag number at least."

Taylor waved her off, "Eh, you couldn't have known."

"What's going on here?"

Taylor's phone rang, "Hang on just a moment, Leah," she answered and listened intently for a minute. She ended the conversation with, "Thank you, Cory, I owe you one," she opened the door and saw Evans and Archer standing in the living room talking. "Michael, you and I need to run an errand. Blake, if you would, stay here in case Skylar comes back. If she does call us immediately."

"Okay."

"We'll keep you informed as soon as we learn anything."

"Thank you."

Evans could tell Taylor's demeanor had changed. Perhaps it was an increase in the level of her anxiety or concern and he wondered if Archer had picked up on it as well. He followed her and Thorson out to the patrol cars before asking, "So, what's up?"

"My friend at the state police traced Skylar's phone to the southwest part of town."

Thorson asked, "Why are we looking for Skylar Pittman?"

"Her boyfriend reported her missing," explained Taylor.

Evans looked at Thorson and said, "I see you know of Skylar."

"Oh yeah, she's probably our most infamous resident."

"He says it's been pinging near the area of 23rd street and Da Costa since last night," Taylor informed them. "The old industrial part of town."

"23rd and Da Costa," Thorson repeated thoughtfully, "The only thing that's out there is the old Valiant Trucking Company location."

Taylor knew she was right and her stomach tightened into a knot, "Leah, follow us over there but don't report your position over the radio."

"Alright."

They got back into their patrol cars and Taylor led the way.

Evans couldn't help but notice how fast Taylor was driving and asked, "Why is a trucking company significant?"

"They've been out of business for years. It's a huge property, twenty-some acres. For the longest time we were chasing kids out of there. All kinds of shenanigans were going on until an investor bought the property at auction and put a tall, chain link fence around it."

Evans now knew why she was so worried all of a sudden. "In other words, there's no reason for Skylar's phone to be out there since last night."

"No good reason," Taylor felt an overwhelming sense of dread, "Oh Michael, I'm getting a really bad feeling about this."

Evans felt so bad for Taylor. He didn't know what he could say to alleviate her very understandable concern but he would try. "Well, maybe her phone is out there but she isn't. I admit it doesn't look good though."

Four minutes later the patrol cars pulled up to the front gate of the property. It was padlocked and the eight foot tall chain link fence, topped with razor wire, ran a block in either direction before running down the lengths of the sides of the property. The three of them got out of the cars and Taylor asked, "Leah, do you have bolt cutters?"

"No, I sure don't."

"Look," Evans walked up to the gate and grabbed the lock and pulled it off. "It was dummy locked."

"That's weird," Taylor wasn't sure who would've done that or why but it didn't make her feel any better. As Evans pushed the gate open, Taylor said, "Leah, let's drive in opposite directions. We're looking for Skylar's black, Land Rover Sport SUV."

"Okay."

"If you find it, don't go into any of the buildings alone, wait for us."

"Alright."

They got back into their patrol cars with Thorson going left and Taylor driving to the right. Grass was growing up through the cracks in the driveways and parking lots and the large buildings that were constructed with slabs of concrete were now a dirty, off-white color. Taylor steered the car to the far corner, driving slow enough that they wouldn't miss anything. She turned left and went along the backside of the buildings. About two hundred yards down there was a driveway to the left that extended between buildings and Taylor turned that way rather than continue along the outside perimeter. After they passed between the first two buildings, Evans pointed and said loudly, "There!"

A black SUV was parked right in front of a steel door that was situated in the middle of two dozen roll up dock doors. As Taylor turned and headed that way she grabbed her phone and hit the button for Thorson. "Leah, we found her car. Come around to the west side, the last right hand turn, go between the buildings and you'll see us down on the right. We'll wait on you."

As Taylor pulled in behind the SUV, Evans said, "It's hers alright, plate number matches up."

"I feel sick," Taylor uttered. She and Evans grabbed their flashlights and got out of the car.   They shielded their eyes to look into the locked SUV's windows but the vehicle was empty.

Evans took out a surgical glove and put it on his left hand. He walked up the three metal steps and pulled on the doorknob. It opened. With Taylor ascending the steps behind him, Evans leaned through the doorway and yelled into the dark, cavernous warehouse. "Skylar!"

His echo was the only answer. Just then, Thorson's patrol car roared across the parking lot toward them and pulled to a stop alongside the chief's car. She jumped out with a flashlight in her hand. Evans stepped inside and directed his light around on the inside wall looking for a light switch. He found it and flipped it to the on position. Nothing happened. He said, "I guess it's flashlights only."

"Let's stick together," Taylor advised.

"Definitely," agreed Thorson.

They panned their beams of light in all directions only to reveal a huge, empty warehouse. Evans trained his light on a doorway at the far end and said, "Let's try going through there." He led the way and they walked to the door and again with his gloved hand, Evans turned the knob. The door opened and their three beams of light illuminated a long hallway with numerous open doorways along the length of it. He shouted, "Skylar!" This time not even an echo answered him. He stepped into the hallway and walked to the first doorway on the right. The room was empty with the exception of papers and trash. They made their way down the length of the corridor, looking into each office, but there was no sign of Skylar. They retraced their steps to the midway point of the hallway where a staircase went up to the second floor. Evans led the way with Thorson bringing up the rear. On the second floor the hallway to the right mirrored the first floor's layout. To the left, the corridor ended with double doors that were open, with large windows on the far wall of the room that appeared to overlook the warehouse. Evans went that way. He paused in the doorway and panned his light around the room. He froze when the light illuminated an old wooden desk against the wall with what looked like an unclothed mannequin lying on top of it. Evans quickly walked that way but knew as he approached that it was not a mannequin. It was Skylar Pittman and he could tell she was no longer alive.

Taylor walked up behind him, her voice trembling, "Oh, God!"

Evans looked at her and said sympathetically, "I'm sorry, Sam."

Thorson stood motionless fifteen feet back, apparently not wanting to get any closer.

Taylor turned away and pulled her phone out. She took deep breaths trying to calm herself but she was clearly struggling to maintain her composure. She hit the contact button for Jessica Bradley, the on duty 911 operator. She answered, "Yes, Chief."

"Jessica...we've got another body."

"Oh no."

"Yeah...what officers are on duty right now?"

"Turner, Thorson, Daniels, and Ramiro."

"Are any of them in the office?"

"Daniels is."

"Okay, have her bring Elena to the old Valiant Trucking Company site. We're in a warehouse without electricity so tell her she's going to need battery powered lighting. Then, call the other officers on their cell phones and tell them to come here. Don't use the radio, I want to secure the scene before the media gets wind of this."

Bradley exhaled, "Okay."

"Call Raymond and tell him where we are."

"Okay."

"Then call in a couple of the auxiliary officers to cover the normal patrols."

"I'll get right on it, Chief."

"Thanks, Jessica."

While Taylor was making the phone call, Evans examined the scene more closely. On the floor, beside the desk, Skylar's clothes and purse were arranged neatly: A white t-shirt, pink shorts, white underwear, and a pair of pink tennis shoes with white, ankle socks stuffed into them. He had steeled himself to the possibility of finding her body but he was not prepared for how young and small she was. The desk was about five feet long but neither her head or feet would've extended over the ends if she was stretched out. She was lying on her back with her arms basically at her sides with her hands appearing to clutch invisible tennis balls. Her cell phone was lying on the desk only a couple of inches from her right hand as if she'd dropped it there. Her legs were spread apart, the knees bent at forty five degree angles. He felt a little guilty for looking at the purple vibrator that was still lodged in her vagina. He directed his light on her head and could clearly see one end of a woman's necktie wrapped around her neck and the other end secured to a metal conduit that ran from the floor to the ceiling. Her shoulder-length blonde hair spilled across the desktop on either side of her head. Her eyes were wide open but they were clouded over and staring into infinity. Her mouth was open as if she had been in the middle of a conversation when she died. He exhaled a long sigh and shook his head. No matter how many bodies he'd seen in his career, it never got any easier. In fact, as he got older, each one seemed to bother him increasingly more.

As Taylor walked back toward Evans, Thorson spoke up, "Chief, is it okay if I step outside?"

Taylor looked at the officer who didn't appear as though she felt very well and told her, "Oh sure, Leah. I'll be there in a minute."

"Look at this," Evans trained his light on each of Skylar's wrists and ankles. Just barely visible on the pale skin were marks that looked like they were made from restraints of some kind.

"Someone had her tied up," surmised Taylor.

"Well, considering what she did for a living, it's possible they're old bruises."

"What do you mean?"

"I know we're a long way from anything definitive but this could be the result of autoerotic asphyxia."

Taylor was shocked. She had not even considered that. She was certain this was the latest murder in the series. "You mean, she might have accidentally killed herself?"

Evans nodded, "Possibly, look at this," he directed his light on the necktie, "The knot attached to the pipe is very tight. The one around her neck is looser. One pull on the top of the knot should have untied it but it wasn't. She could've passed out and the weight of her head basically strangled her."

"Oh my God."

"But," he hated to bring it up but he had to, "I don't believe in coincidences."

"Kyle Stanton."

"Yeah," he nodded, "Each one of our cases taken individually, could be categorized as a suicide, an accident, or a one off murder. But taken together, the odds that they're not connected are astronomical."

"What the Hell has happened to the world?"

"I think someone is going to a lot of trouble to make our cases seem like something they're not. I think this poor girl, like all of our victims, was methodically and brutally murdered in revenge for being at Kyle Stanton's assault."

"How crazy is that."

"I would say more evil than crazy because the perpetrator seems to be operating at a high level of organization. Checking her phone could be crucial to learn if she videotaped herself or if she met someone here. We also need to get her phone records as soon as possible."

Taylor illuminated Skylar's face and said sadly, "The little girl whose grandmother would take her to and from school everyday... I never could have imagined in a million years she would end up like this. Not in my town."

"I'm going to try again to get additional help from the bureau. I don't give a damn how busy they are, they can't be worse off than we are."

Taylor turned away and said, "Thank you, Michael. Would you mind waiting here? I need to get some fresh air."

"No problem," he felt so bad for her but he tried to sound reassuring, "And Sam, we are going to figure this out."

"Yeah," she answered sorrowfully before walking away. It had been a long time, if ever that she had felt this depressed. She felt as dark and empty as the building they were in. As soon as Taylor stepped outside she was grateful to be bathed in sunlight. Thorson was leaning back against the front fender of her car just as another police cruiser headed their way across the parking lot. Taylor walked out to greet the officer who was driving the patrol car.

It was Miguel Ramiro who asked, "Chief, what's going on?"

"We've got another body."

"Fuck! Who is it?"

"Skylar Pittman."

"Oh man, I know who that is. Damn."

"Miguel, I need you to guard the front gate. Daniels is bringing Elena here and Raymond should be showing up soon so let them in and tell them where we are. Other than those two, only allow our officers to go in or out. When Andre gets here, have him man the gate with you."

"Yes, ma'am."

As he drove away, Taylor turned to Thorson and said, "Leah, I want you to check the fence all the way around the property. Make sure there's no holes in it and check the padlocks on all the gates to make sure none of them are dummy locked."

"Okay, I'm on my way."

As Taylor watched her drive away, she dreaded her next move. She would have to inform Blake Archer of Skylar's death. She didn't think he had anything to do with it but she just wasn't sure. She wasn't sure about very much at all right at the moment. Six unexplained deaths and the only arrest in one of them was the town's mayor. She thought back over the years when she would see Skylar around town. She would wave at her and the little girl would always wave back. To see how she ended up was heartbreaking. Because she was in a position of leadership, Taylor never wanted to let anyone see her cry but she was alone, and she couldn't help it. She slowly began to sob.

Chapter Eighteen

With the Skylar Pittman crime scene secured, Taylor and Evans began driving back to the Beechnut Tree Mobile Home Park with Officer Rebecca Daniels following in her patrol car. Enroute, Taylor called Deputy Chief of Police, Brandon Holt.

He answered on the first ring, "Hey, Chief."

"Brandon, we have another murder."

"Oh God! Who is it?"

"Skylar Pittman."

"Oh my God! I know her!"

"I know, we all did. Listen, I need you to come into work early. Meet us at Skylar's house in the Beechnut Tree Mobile Home Park and help secure her house for evidence."

"Okay, yeah. Uh, Chief...there's something I need to tell you."

"What?"

He sighed, "I was one of Skylar's customers."

"Oh, dammit Brandon!"

"I know. I'm not proud of it but...she asked me to come over to her house a couple of times over the years but I always told her I couldn't because of my position on the force. It just seemed like the online thing was harmless...until now."

"I appreciate you telling me."

"I'm sure you were going to find out soon enough anyway. I think you'll be surprised how many customers she had and not just people here in town. What happened to her?"

"We're not sure yet. How soon can you be over here?"

"Give me ten."

"Okay, thanks," she hung up and could tell Evans was curious. She told him simply, "Brandon was a customer of Skylar."

Evans exhaled an aggravated groan, "We can't give him access inside Skylar's house."

"I know," she concurred, "I'll have him help secure the outside perimeter."

Taylor parked on the street in front of Skylar's house and Officer Daniels pulled in behind her. They got out of the cars and Taylor approached her officer. "Rebecca, I need you to make sure no one enters Skylar's house. Brandon should be here in a few minutes and that goes for him as well."

"Yes, ma'am."

Taylor knew Daniels, with her athletic frame, braided hair, and no nonsense attitude would make sure her order would be carried out. The three of them walked toward the house, Taylor dreading every step of the way. Daniels stood as a sentry at the bottom of the stairs as Evans knocked on the door.

Archer opened the door almost immediately and held up a sheet of paper. "Chief Taylor, I have the masterlist for all of Skylar's social media accounts."

Taylor took the paper and said, "Thanks, Blake. Let's sit down."

Archer took a few steps backward into the house and worriedly asked, "What's wrong?" He was clearly picking up on their solemn demeanor. He slowly shook his head as he watched Taylor begin to tear up, "No...no...no. Don't tell me."

Taylor nodded her head, trying hard but unsuccessfully not to become emotional.

"No! Skylar can't be dead!" Archer turned and almost staggered to the couch and sat down as if he were in a daze and slowly began to cry.

Evans said sympathetically, "We're sorry, Blake."

"I can't believe it," his voice breaking and tears now running down his cheeks, "What happened to her?"

"We're not sure yet," answered Evans.

"You said this might have something to do with that guy that was beat up?"

"It looks like it."

"What the fuck? We didn't do anything! Why Skylar?"

"Other than just being there, we don't know," answered Evans. "But that also means you could be in danger as well."

"I sleep with a shotgun by my bed."

That made Evans think of something. "Did Skylar have a gun?"

"Oh no," Archer replied, "She hated guns. When she came to my house I had to keep my shotgun out of sight. Now she does have mace in her purse."

"Has she ever had to use it?"

"No, I don't think so."

"I know you're hurting but these are important questions."

"Okay," Archer had composed himself fairly well.

"Would Skylar ever go into a dark, abandoned building…?"

"No," he answered emphatically, not even letting Evans finish the question. "She was afraid of the dark."

"Not even to film herself in a provocative way?"

Archer shook his head, "No way. She would push the envelope in a public place or go out into the country if I was with her but alone, in the dark, no way."

That just reaffirmed Evan's hypothesis that Skylar's body was staged.

Taylor's phone chirped. It was a text from Officer Daniels outside. When she read it, Taylor blurted out, "You've got to be kidding me!"

"What is it?" Evans asked her as she jumped up and went to the front windows and pulled one of the blinds down to look outside.

"The fucking media!"

"Already?" Evans couldn't believe how fast they'd found out about Skylar.

Taylor remembered what Nathan Miller had told her about following the crime scene technician. She suspected something similar had occurred here. "I think they're stalking us, trying to follow Elena or observing where our patrol cars congregate. As if on cue her phone rang. It was Officer Andre Turner at Skylar's crime scene. She answered, "Let me guess, the media."

"That's why I'm calling. I've got two TV news crews and several print guys asking questions."

"It's just you and Miguel there at the front gate right?"

"Yes, ma'am."

"Do you need any more help?"

"No, we got it covered."

"Okay, let me know when Elena is finished there, I'm going to need her over here at Skylar's house."

"Will do."

"Bye," as Taylor looked out of the window at the gathering of media members, Evans' phone rang and she listened to his side of the conversation.

"Agent Evans," he answered and listened for a few moments and said, "Excellent. Yes sir, I've met her several times. I'm familiar with her big case. Thank you, sir. It's very much appreciated here. Alright, goodbye," he looked at Taylor and said, "Good news. I guess earlier when I called the Associate Deputy Director and used colorful language, that got his attention so we're getting another agent and she's a good one. Do you remember last year, the missing girls in Webber, Iowa?"

"Oh yeah, I remember it well. It was in the news for months."

"She's the one who actually found the girls. She and her partner."

"Oh, that is good news," Taylor was grateful for additional help. She asked, "When will she get here?"

"Agent Emma Riley will be driving in from Tampa this evening."

"Riley, that's right. I remember the name," Taylor walked back over to the sofa where Archer sat staring forlornly at the floor. "Blake, do you feel up to writing out a report on your whereabouts last night and this morning before you head for home?"

He nodded, "Yeah, I'd like to get it over with. I have a lot to do. I guess I have a funeral to plan."

She genuinely felt terrible for him, his red truck notwithstanding. They would check to see if there was any connection between him and the other victims but she truly believed his grief over the loss of Skylar was real. "If you want I can have someone who's knowledgeable about funerals and estates contact you to offer ideas and options."

"Sure," he stood up and asked, "Can I just write it out on a pad of paper?"

"That'll be fine."

He walked over and pulled a pen and paper out of a kitchen drawer and then sat down at the dining table and began to write.

Evans looked out through the blinds and said, "I guess they didn't want to wait for the news conference."

Taylor groaned, "The news conference. You know things are going badly when I dread each one more than the one before."

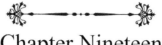

Chapter Nineteen

At 5:00 P.M. that afternoon, Chief Taylor and Agent Evans stood before a horde of media bigger than any they'd had to date. Taylor began, "Good afternoon everyone. My name is Samantha Taylor, I'm the Chief of Police here in Delaney and this is Special Agent Michael Evans with the F.B.I. I'm going to open with a statement and then we'll take some questions. Since there are so many of you, I want you to raise your hand if you have a question and I'll call on some of you. Obviously we cannot answer everyone's questions so for those of you who are looking for answers not provided here, continue to call our information officer. Again, the phone number for our tip line is on the front of this podium and a reminder, we don't record or trace calls so you can remain anonymous. One last related item. We would like the caller who phoned in the tip about Travis Reynolds to call us back. Now to the most pressing issue," Taylor took a deep breath, reminding herself not to become emotional. "Our community has suffered another loss. Today, we located the body of twenty-two year old Skylar Pittman. Skylar was born and raised in Delaney, and spent her whole life here. The circumstances about her death are still undetermined, so we're unable to attribute it to the series of murders and unexplained deaths but once again there is the unmistakable pattern. Skylar lived in the Beechnut Tree Mobile Home Park where the assault on Kyle Stanton occurred. She came upon the scene after it happened as so many others did. So let's start with some questions. Literally dozens of hands went up with a few unsolicited questions being yelled out but Taylor ignored those and pointed to a female reporter on the front row.

"Chief Taylor, Skylar Pittman was obviously in the adult entertainment industry. Is there any thought that may have played a role in her murder?"

"Okay, first of all, her death has not been ruled a homicide yet. Could that happen? Yes. It hasn't yet though. As with all of our cases, the only connection seems to be the Kyle Stanton attack so there is nothing to indicate her job had anything to do with it," she motioned to a male reporter on the second row.

"Chief Taylor, I know you say her occupation doesn't have anything to do with it but people are speculating that someone could be taking advantage of the other murders to include her in those to steer suspicion away from themselves."

"In all of our cases we look at that. Each one is investigated individually. Case in point is Travis Reynolds. He is charged in only one of the cases and while the investigation continues we are searching for connections to other crimes."

She acknowledged another media member in a sea of hands.

"Chief, speaking of Mayor Reynolds. He met briefly with a few reporters when he was released from jail and he angrily denied the charges against him. He said when he's exonerated, he's going to sue the city and he was particularly furious with you. He seemed to indicate that he thought you had planted evidence in his house. How would you respond to that?"

Taylor tried to keep her face from flushing because the question really pissed her off. "I'll only address the last part of the question. I have never planted evidence. That is not something that I would ever do. It would be unconscionable to imprison an innocent person and allow the guilty party to get off scot free to continue a reign of murder."

Taylor gestured toward another reporter.

"Chief, going back to Skylar's occupation, we've heard that she had an older boyfriend that participated in her videos and some people are saying they're suspicious of him. Any information about him?"

"I'm not going to publicly identify him but we have talked to him and he's been very cooperative with the investigation. We are going to confirm everything he's told us but we don't believe he had anything to do with Skylar's death."

She pointed to another correspondent.

"Yes, you mentioned the only connection to these cases is that the victims were at the scene of that assault. If that is the case it would seem to make it easier to protect people who were there, right?"

Taylor had to think about the question to make sure she answered it correctly. "One of the six cases was never on the scene. As far as we have been able to determine, some of the other five came upon the scene after it happened. We understand dozens of people were out there but nowhere near that many are willing to admit it. There are hundreds of people who live in the Beechnut Tree Mobile Home Park and while we've increased patrols and tried to educate everyone, we can't be everywhere all of the time. Everyone just needs to know, if you were at that scene a year ago, you need to take extra precautions. And once again, we are willing to help advise you on your security needs." Taylor called on a reporter farther toward the back.

"I have a question for Agent Evans. Sir, what assistance is the F.B.I. giving to Delaney PD?"

Evans stepped to the microphones and replied, "We are strictly in an advisory role in these cases but we offer the highest level of behavioral science, forensics, and laboratory analysis, if needed. We understand the Florida State Crime Lab is top notch, however. I am pleased to announce that an additional agent is arriving this evening," he pointed at a female reporter.

"A question for Chief Taylor. Now that Tropical Storm Walter has turned into a hurricane in the Atlantic, if it hits Florida in the next five or six days as it's expected to, according to the modeling forecasts, how would that impact your investigation?"

Taylor wasn't about to admit that she hadn't heard about a potential new hurricane. "Well, Floridians are quite familiar with hurricanes so we would just batten down the hatches and wait it out. We are far enough inland to be safe from the storm surge so we would just have to deal with the wind and rain, and the possibility of secondary tornadoes. Nothing is going to stop these investigations however. Now, ladies and gentlemen, that's all of the new information we have for you right now. We will make a determination tomorrow when to have the next news conference. As soon as we have anything new to report we will schedule one. Thank you."

Taylor didn't feel bad for cutting it short one bit. She really had no more information she wanted to impart and emotionally she had dealt with enough questions, especially when they turned weather related. Taylor and Evans made their way toward the police station amid a barrage of additional questions that went unanswered.

As soon as they entered the main doors, Christina, the young lady manning the front desk told them, "There's an F.B.I. agent waiting in the conference room."

Evans said, "Excellent," and headed that way with Taylor following behind. As soon as Evans walked through the open doorway he saw twenty-four year old Special Agent Emma Riley standing at the windows overlooking the parking lot that was filled with media. With a big smile he said, "Agent Riley, I presume?"

She turned around and said, "I know you!"

They shook hands and he said, "It's good to see you, Emma."

"It's good to see you again, Michael," she smiled. The agent wearing business casual clothes said, "Looks like you have a media circus out there."

"You have no idea. Let me introduce you to Delaney Police Chief Samantha Taylor."

Taylor was so shocked by Riley's looks that she was sure it registered on her face. With blond hair and blue eyes, the attractive agent didn't look old enough to be in the F.B.I. and when they shook hands, Taylor was a head taller than Riley. "Good to meet you. Call me Sam."

"Nice to meet you too. Call me Emma," Riley said.

Evans asked, "Can I get you something to drink?"

"Oh no, I'm fine."

"Have a seat."

As she sat down Riley looked at the stacks of papers and folders on the table and asked, "Are these your case files?"

"They sure are," Evans answered, "Now we have to add another one today."

"That must be why I was diverted here from Tampa."

"It is," Evans explained. "I've only been here a week and we've had three additional deaths."

"Oh no."

"That's on top of three prior to my arrival."

"I've seen some of the media coverage. Are all of them murders?"

"It looks like it. Someone is killing these people in different ways and trying to make some of them look like an accident or a suicide," Taylor and Evans exchanged looks and he asked her, "Do you want to give her an overview?"

"Sure, so this all started with a career criminal named Kyle Stanton. He grew up here, raised by an alcoholic, abusive father. He was always in trouble and he escalated from being a petty criminal and bully to being a murderer. Once DNA proved that a year ago, we started looking for him but a mob of townspeople found him first. He was beaten into a coma, and he's still in one to this day. No one was charged with his assault because everyone on the scene claimed to have arrived after he was already beaten to a bloody pulp. The only videos taken at the scene, that people have submitted to us, were filmed after the initial assault took place. A few months later, one of the guys we know was at the scene of the assault was hit and killed on his bicycle. There were no witnesses and we could never track down the vehicle or the driver. It was assumed to be an accidental hit and run and the guilty party didn't want to come forward and admit to it. A few months later, another man who was just an observer at the Stanton attack, was shot to death just outside of town. Again, no witnesses and no suspects until just recently. I'll come back to that. Six months later, his wife was stabbed to death in her home and she was found by her disabled daughter. She was a lifelong friend of mine and since there was no other family, I took in her only child. A couple of weeks later, another person at the assault scene was found hanging from a tree. He was black and it may or may not have been a suicide. A couple of days later another person who had been at the scene was found bludgeoned to death in his home. And now today, we found a woman deceased who apparently was just a spectator at the Stanton assault. Last week, following up on a tip, we found the gun that was used to kill our second victim in the house of our Mayor."

"Wow," Riley looked at Evans. "Now I know why you requested help."

Jessica Bradley, the 911 operator appeared in the doorway, "Chief, I'm sorry to interrupt but I just took a call on the non emergency number from Asia Martin, you know she's a checker at the grocery store. She heard about Skylar Pittman and she said some guy was harassing her at the store last night."

Taylor and Evans exchanged looks before he asked Riley, "Ready to jump in it?"

"Sure."

Taylor stood up, "Thanks, Jessica, we'll go talk to her."

Evans asked the chief, "How bout I ride with Emma and we follow you over there?"

"Sounds good," Taylor answered before leading the way toward the back door.

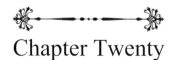

Chapter Twenty

Taylor parked two rows away from the front of the Publix Grocery Store and Riley pulled her white, rental sedan alongside her. They got out of the cars and Taylor led the way toward the supermarket. When the automatic doors opened they were enveloped in cold air conditioning. As soon as they walked in, Asia Martin saw the chief and held up her index finger to signal 'give me a minute.' The light above her checkout line changed from green to red and once she finished checking out the last customer, Martin made her way over to them.

Taylor greeted the black woman in her late twenties, "Hello, Asia."

"Hi, Chief Taylor."

"These are F.B.I. agents Evans and Riley."

"Whoa," Martin's eyes widened.

"Is there somewhere we could talk in private?"

"Yeah, the breakroom should be empty right now. This way," she led them down an aisle to the back of the store, through double swinging doors then turned left into a four hundred square foot room that was lined with vending machines. It was in fact empty of employees. Asia sat at the first table and the others followed suit.

Taylor asked her, "So Skylar Pittman was in here last night?"

Yeah," answered Martin, "You know, a lot of people looked down on her for what she did for a living but she was always nice to me."

"I know, me too."

"Anyway she came in about 7:00 o'clock…"

"Sorry to interrupt but was she alone?"

"Yeah, she was."

"Do you remember what she was wearing?"

"Uh, a white t-shirt," she thought for a moment, "Oh, and matching pink shorts and tennis shoes. I remember because they looked really cute on her."

"You said a guy was harassing her?"

"Yeah, so this guy came in before her. I'm observant and I noticed him because he didn't look familiar to me. Between customers I looked around and saw him over in the fruit and vegetable section talking with Skylar. It wasn't unusual for someone to have a conversation with her but it caught my eye because he was a stranger. Within a matter of minutes, Skylar was in my line and this guy was right behind her and it seemed like he was doing most of the talking. Before they got right in front of me, I heard him say something about sharing some kind of advertising together but she said nah, she wasn't interested. Then when I actually rang her up, he asked her if he could take her to dinner, that he would pay for it and she could go anywhere she wanted. She kept shaking her head and said no several times. I asked her if everything was alright and she said yes, but she seemed annoyed by him. So when she grabs her bags and starts walking out he follows her. He didn't even have any groceries. I think the last thing I heard was him asking her to go get a drink. It's like he wouldn't take no for an answer."

"Did you see them go out into the parking lot?"

"No, they both walked outside and went to the right out of view. Damn, I wished I had followed them but we were busy. That poor girl, I just had a bad feeling about that guy."

Evans spoke up, "Would you recognize him if you saw him again?"

"Oh yeah."

"Can you describe him?"

"White, I'd say probably...mid twenties. Blonde, kinda sandy colored hair, chubby..."

That caught Taylor's attention. "Sandy hair and chubby?"

"Yeah, his hair was kinda messy and his clothes looked rumpled."

Taylor pulled her phone out and went to YouTube and typed in True Crime with Nathan Miller. She showed Martin his picture.

"That's him!" She blurted out.

Taylor and Evans shook their heads knowingly at each other. Riley didn't know who this guy was but she got a sense he had just risen to the top of the suspect list.

Evans asked Martin, "I saw a lot of security cameras out there. Do you think we could get a copy of the videotape from last night?"

"I imagine so. Let me talk to Gilbert, he's the manager," she got up and quickly walked out of the room.

Riley spoke up, "I guess you've dealt with this guy before."

Taylor snorted, "You could say that. His name is Nathan Miller. He has one of those true crime channels on YouTube. He considers himself an amateur sleuth. He's been asking obnoxious questions during our news conferences and he even followed our crime scene technician to the mayor's house when we went there executing a search warrant."

"I've got to admit, I thought he was a dufus," Evans said.

Taylor nodded, "What do you say we get this security video, then go find Miller and have a chat with him?"

Evans smiled and looked first to Riley and then back to Taylor and said, "I volunteer to be the bad cop."

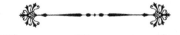

Chapter Twenty-One

Having viewed the security video from the grocery store to confirm it was in fact Nathan Miller with Skylar, Taylor secured a hard copy of it. It sat on the front seat of Taylor's patrol car as she pulled into the parking lot of the Ocean Breeze Motor Inn. Riley parked next to her and the three of them got out of the cars. Taylor walked into the well lit office and a tall, skinny, middle aged man stood behind the front desk. He didn't look familiar to Taylor so she said, "I'm Chief of Police Samantha Taylor. I need to ask for the room number for one of your guests."

"Yes, ma'am, what's their name?"

"Nathan Miller."

"Oh, yeah, he's in room number twenty three," he pointed directly out of the side windows, "Next to the last one. Uh, just so you know he was checking out in the morning."

She gave him a stern look, "Do not call him and tell him we're coming."

He held his hands up in a don't shoot posture, "Oh no, ma'am, I would not interfere."

"Thank you," she walked out of the office and pointed in the direction of Miller's room and told Evans and Riley, "This way."

They walked purposefully across the courtyard and at the door with the number twenty three on it, Taylor knocked loudly. After a moment, Miller pulled the curtains aside and looked at Taylor. He frowned and then went away. Although she expected him to open the door any second, he didn't. She knocked again and loudly yelled, "Nathan open up!"

After a couple of minutes he opened the door wearing a t-shirt and pajama bottoms. His eyes were red and watery and he asked, "This is about Skylar isn't it?"

Evans moved past Taylor and stepped into the room and asked, "Mind if we come in?"

"You're already in."

Even before Evans had pushed past Miller, he could smell the strong odor of marijuana. "Enjoying a little evening refer, huh?"

Taylor began reading Miller his Miranda rights "You have the right to remain silent…"

"Whoa, whoa, whoa, I'm under arrest?"

"You're being detained for questioning," Taylor told him, "I have to read your rights to you. Anything you say can and will be used against you in a court of law. You have the right to an attorney. If you cannot afford an attorney, one will be appointed for you. Do you understand your rights?"

"Yeah."

Evans noticed an open suitcase on the dresser, the bed was unmade, and half a dozen empty beer cans were on the nightstand. He continued walking into the bathroom and saw the green, leafy remnants of marijuana in the toilet bowl. He walked back into the room and said, "Trying to get rid of evidence, huh?"

Standing in the doorway, Taylor could smell the marijuana as well. She told him, "Nathan, put on some clothes so we can go to the station and talk."

Miller noticed Riley standing behind Taylor and asked, "Who are you?"

"F.B.I." Riley answered.

Miller looked surprised, "You're an F.B.I. agent?"

"Nathan!" Taylor said forcefully, getting his attention. "This is serious. Change clothes."

"Alright," he turned and walked to his suitcase and began pulling out a change of clothes. He took them into the bathroom as Evans made a visual check of the bedroom.

Riley's initial impression of Miller was in line with Evans'. He seemed like a dufus but she knew from experience you couldn't assume he wasn't capable of horrible violence.

Five minutes later, Miller was sitting in the back of Taylor's patrol car heading for the police station with Evans and Riley following behind. She didn't know if it was because he was high or in fear of incriminating himself, but the normally loquacious Miller was silent the whole way there.

At the station, per prior arrangement, Evans led Miller into interrogation room number one while Taylor went to her office and called her friend Cory at the State Police for another favor. She had him run a trace on Miller's phone for the last twenty four hours. If they could pinpoint his phone last night near the location where Skylar's body was found, she felt confident they had the right person. At least in this case.

With Riley watching the live video feed, Taylor and Evans walked into the interrogation room and sat down across the table from him. Taylor began, "Okay Nathan, do you know why you're here?"

Miller looked up at the ceiling with eyes that were a little less red than they were earlier. "I'm sure it has to do with Skylar Pittman."

"Why do you say that?"

"Because I talked to her at the grocery store and then she turned up dead."

"It's more than that," she kept an even, almost understanding tone because she knew Evans was going to go at him hard. "You are the last person we can verify who was with her before she died."

Miller sighed wearily, "Oh, man."

"First things first. Do you know Skylar?"

"No."

"Are you a paying customer of hers?"

"No. I don't pay for porn."

"But you knew who she was?"

"Oh yeah. I've seen her videos that have been downloaded on porn sites but they were always free. There's so much free porn out there you don't have to pay for it."

"So walk us through your visit to the store last night."

"I went to buy beer and food and out of the blue, there she was in the produce section. I recognized her right away. I didn't even know she lived in Delaney. I went up and introduced myself, you know, tried to be friendly. She was a little standoffish but I figured she gets hit on all the time. I explained we had a lot in common, you know, both of us making a living on the internet. I asked her if we could collaborate or if I could get an interview with her but she said no. This is where I pushed it a little too far. I asked her if she wanted to go get something to eat or drink but she declined. I made the mistake of following her to her car. She wasn't interested but I just...I dunno...I tried too hard. Guess I was just lonely and she was so hot. I mean she was always one of my favorites and here she was in the flesh. She looked even better in person. Anyway, she told me to leave her alone or she'd call the cops and she drove off."

"Then what did you do?"

"Walked to my car and headed for the motel, but stopped on the way to buy beer. Didn't really feel like shopping anymore."

"What did you do last night?"

"Same thing I did all day today. Smoke and drink. I only went out once at lunch for a burger."

"Why did you skip today's news conference?"

"I heard what happened to Skylar. I was bummed, plus I knew I would be a suspect because of the store thing."

Evans sensed an opening, "So you gave notice that you were checking out tomorrow morning and running back to Miami."

"Not running," Miller shook his head, "Just been here long enough."

"Why?"

He shrugged his shoulders, "There just hasn't been a whole lot of anything new to report and now with Skylar's death...I'm just depressed."

"Could you be depressed because you know you might be charged with murder?"

"Hell no! I did not kill her!"

"Listen to me. If you accidentally killed her, this is the time to tell us because if you don't, it could make you look like a cold blooded killer."

"I did not kill her," Miller stated emphatically.

Evans bore down, "Right now we're tracing your phone to see if it puts you at the crime scene. If it does, you've had it."

"I was not there."

Taylor spoke up, "Where is there? Where is the crime scene?"

"I heard on the news it was at a warehouse on the south side of town. I was not there."

Evans picked up the thread again, "This is very important. Have you ever touched Skylar?"

"No, I didn't touch her."

"Because if you did, but you claim you didn't, and we find your DNA on her or her clothes, you're toast."

"I didn't, I'm sure."

Taylor asked, "How about her car? Are your fingerprints or DNA going to show up on it?"

Miller paused as if thinking for a moment then answered unconvincingly, "No."

"Are you sure?"

"Yeah."

Taylor got the distinct impression he wasn't sure or he was lying but she pivoted to a different line of attack, "When we check her phone records and social media accounts, is there going to be any connection to you?"

"No."

Taylor's phone began to ring so she said, "Excuse me," and she went into the hall and shut the door behind her. "Hello, Cory."

"Hey, Sam, I have something for you. The phone you asked about was not in the vicinity of the victim's phone after that early evening meeting, as far as we can tell. But, last night at 7:57, it was powered off. Not just turned off but powered off. It may have even had the battery removed. It didn't get powered back up again until 9:13 this morning."

Now Taylor was very suspicious. "Thank you, Cory, you've been a huge help."

"Anything for you."

"Thanks, bye."

"Bye."

Taylor hung up and thought for a moment. She walked into the conference room where Riley was watching Evans ask Miller questions on closed circuit TV. She told her, "I have an idea."

"Okay."

"I just found out, Miller's phone was powered off between 7:57 last night and 9:13 this morning. Skylar left the grocery store about 7:10. She didn't respond to her boyfriend's text at 9:30, so she could have been murdered between that time. Which falls into the period when his phone was off. I know you don't know much about the case but you're closer to his age, and he likes girls so maybe he might say something to you he wouldn't to us."

"I'm willing to try."

"Thanks. I'll tell Michael I need to show him something and you can go in. We'll watch."

Riley stood up and said, "Okay," then followed Taylor to the interrogation room.

Taylor opened the door and said, "Michael, I need to show you something." Taylor was glad she detected more than a slight look of concern on Miller's face. Evans stood up and walked out and Riley went into the room and closed the door behind her.

Riley noticed Miller's body language as she sat down across the table from him. He straightened his back and lifted his chin, unconsciously signaling he was strong and had no fear of her. She introduced herself, "I'm Special Agent Emma Riley with the F.B.I."

"Why does that name sound familiar? As a matter of fact, you look familiar."

"I was involved in a big case a year ago. Do you remember the missing girls of Webber, Iowa?"

"Oh yeah! That is you! You're the one who found them, right?"

"My partner Andy figured it out."

"I did a lot of shows about your case. Yeah, that was a real mystery. I have a true crime channel on YouTube. Man, I would love to interview you. That would give me a huge ratings boost. Your partner was shot and killed right?"

"Yeah," she answered sadly. Even a year later the pain of that day was palpable for Riley. Whenever someone brought it up, which was often, it all came flooding back to her. She had hoped over time to come to terms with the loss of Andy and the horror of it all, but by now she knew it was going to haunt her for the rest of her life.

"Man, I wish I could've traveled there to do some shows."

Riley wanted very much to change the subject to Miller's case. "Listen, I only arrived here this afternoon, so I don't know much but these guys think they have you dead to rights."

"What do you mean?" He asked worriedly.

She leaned forward and lowered her voice as if confiding in him, "They already know you turned your phone off during the time the murder was committed. That makes you look really guilty. Couple that with the fact that you were the last person to be seen with her alive, and you were harassing her on top of that. They could say Skylar rejected you and you forced her to have sex and then killed her to cover it up."

His expression of worry morphed into one of fear and his eyes began to fill with tears, "But...I didn't..."

"I mean, at this point, your attorney is almost in the position of having to prove you didn't do it."

"Attorney? I... I don't have an attorney."

"Can you afford one?"

"I have $1500 in the bank and rent on my apartment is due in a week and a half."

Riley sighed and said, "That's not good. Public defenders mean well and they try hard but they don't fare very well against these powerful district attorneys with all of their resources."

"Oh my God! What am I going to do?"

Riley watched a tear roll down Miller's face and dangle at the corner of his mouth. She knew this man was genuinely afraid. She asked him, "One of the first questions a prosecutor is going to ask is, why did you power your phone off?"

"I'll tell you the truth. When Skylar shot me down, I was totally bummed out. Here was a girl, a beautiful girl that has sex with all kinds of people but she wouldn't even give me the time of day. Now I admit, I've had trouble getting girls in the past but here was a porn star...and she's rejecting me like I'm garbage. Well, that's the way I felt, like garbage. All I wanted to do was just go to my motel room and get as high and drunk as I could. I usually do an end of the day video but I just wasn't up for it. I knew I would probably be getting calls from my mom and my IT guy but I didn't want to talk to anyone, so I just powered it down."

"But why power it off instead of ignoring it or switching it to vibrate?"

"I didn't even want to know when it went off. I just wanted to be completely detached from everyone and everything."

Riley thought she would try one last approach, "Look, you seem like a nice guy. I would not feel good about you spending the rest of your life in prison. She was a porn star, maybe sex between the two of you became just a little too rough and it was an accident. The punishment would be far less."

Miller shook his head vigorously, "No, that didn't happen. I realize that would be better and if that's what had happened, I would tell you."

Riley nodded and said, "Okay. Sit tight and let me go check and see what they want to do."

"Thank you."

Riley got up and walked out of the room and Taylor and Evans met her in the hallway.

Taylor said, "Emma, that was awesome!"

Riley smiled and said, "Thanks."

"Good job," Evans told her, "What do you think?"

"I believe him," Riley replied simply, "I could be wrong but I think he's too much of a dufus to have pulled it off."

Evans groaned, "I don't believe him. It's all a little too coincidental for me. He's a true crime buff. I think he thinks he's smarter than he really is. He does have the dufus act down pat, I'll give him that."

"I don't know," Taylor sighed, "I've gone back and forth on this guy. It looks bad for him but he came across believable."

"Regardless, I don't think we have enough to hold him," Evans said.

"Agreed, let's kick him loose," Taylor heard someone in the breakroom so she walked that way and saw Officer Daniels making a protein shake. "Rebecca, will you run an interviewee over to the Ocean Breeze Motor Inn?"

"Sure, no problem."

"Thank you," Taylor walked back to the interrogation room and opened the door. "Okay, Nathan, we are going to release you and continue the investigation. You're free to go back to Miami if you want, just know we'll be in touch. Officer Daniels will give you a ride back to the motel."

"Oh God! Thank you!" He stood up and walked out of the room. When he passed by Taylor he stopped and said, "Chief, Taylor, I really didn't do anything to Skylar except pester her."

Taylor wasn't in the mood to hear anymore from him. "Good bye, Nathan." She watched as he followed Officer Daniels through the lobby and down the hallway toward the back door.

Riley asked Evans, "What hotel are you staying in?"

"I'm staying with Chief Taylor."

"Oh," Riley wasn't expecting that.

Taylor told her, "I have one more spare bedroom, please stay with us."

"Oh, I can't do that."

"You would probably have to drive over an hour to find a decent hotel room. I was going to pick up some fajitas for dinner and I'd like you to meet Abbie."

"Your daughter?"

114

She laughed, "Practically. She's the one I took in when her parents were murdered."

"That is so good of you," Riley was genuinely impressed with Taylor.

"Her mom was a lifelong friend of mine. It was the least I could do."

Evans told her, "Abbie is amazing. Wait till you meet her."

"I am pretty tired," Riley admitted.

"That settles it," Taylor declared, "Michael if you'll go with her and direct her to my house, I'll stop and pick up the fajitas."

"Okay," he said.

Taylor asked her, "Chicken or beef?"

"Chicken."

"Okay, see you in a few minutes."

With the sky turning into a beautiful yellow and orange palette in the minutes before sunset, Riley pulled into Taylor's driveway and turned off the ignition. Evans shifted the conversation about the local cases to one which he knew Riley was most known for. "I hope we have time at some point so you can tell me about your case with Andy O'Neil."

"Did you know Andy?"

"I only met him once, at a conference, but we sat together and had a chance to talk for a while. I was impressed with his intelligence but I didn't think he fit his reputation."

Riley smiled, "You mean about him being rebellious and sarcastic?"

Evans laughed, "Among other things."

Riley nodded knowingly, "He was all of those things and more. I learned so much from him in only one week, I didn't even realize it at the time."

"I know you've probably been asked this a hundred times but how did he figure out where those girls were being held?"

Riley slowly shook her head and said, "I tried to attribute it to every logical method imaginable but I couldn't. It seemed almost supernatural. So I thought back to some of the things that Andy told me to help me answer that question. He said he truly believed that he was put on this Earth to chase bad guys. Like when he single handedly caught Steven Richter, the serial killer. He had a sixth sense about evil people that he attributed to God."

"Wow, I wasn't expecting that."

"Neither did I," she admitted, "But he believed it so I thought, who am I to dispute it? It has actually strengthened my bond with God."

Evans smiled at her, "That's really inspiring. You know in our line of work, we don't see evidence of God very often."

Riley nodded, "I know."

"How do you think Andy would approach our cases here in Delaney?"

Riley laughed, "So many times I've tried channeling Andy on my cases but it doesn't work. I never knew what off the wall thing he was going to try next. Not all of them worked but it didn't deter him. He would just come up with something else, consequences be damned."

Chief Taylor pulled in behind them and Riley remarked, "I'm impressed with Sam."

"Oh, she's a great person and a very good Chief of Police. I feel terrible for her because she's had an impossible situation thrust upon her."

Riley and Evans got out of the car and she pulled a suitcase out of the backseat. Taylor led the way toward the house carrying two white plastic bags filled with Mexican food. The porch light came on and the door opened. Abbie stood just inside the foyer with her hand on the door. Taylor looked forward to introducing the new agent to her. "Abbie, this is F.B.I. Special Agent Emma Riley."

"Wow! You're too young and pretty to be an F.B.I. agent," Abbie effused.

Riley laughed, "Well, thank you."

"What about me?" Evans asked.

"You're pretty too, Michael," Abbie said playfully.

He laughed, "That's more like it."

Abbie looked at Riley and said, "I think I might be taller than you!"

"Don't be fooled," advised Evans, "Emma is a black belt in karate."

"Oh, that is so cool!"

He continued, "She actually takes vacations to enter karate tournaments."

"Have you met Officer Daniels yet?" Abbie asked her.

116

"I don't think so," answered Riley.

Taylor explained, "She's the one who gave Nathan Miller a ride back to the motel."

"Oh, the one with the braids," Riley acknowledged.

"She used to be an MMA fighter," Abbie told her.

"Yeah, she looks tough. I hope I don't have to find out."

Taylor held up the bags of food, "Who's hungry?"

"I'm starving!" Abbie declared with ample exaggeration.

"You're always starving," Taylor told her as she made her way toward the dining room table with the mini caravan of hungry bellies trailing behind her.

Chapter Twenty-Two

The next morning, Wednesday, at 7:15, Taylor heard someone in the kitchen while she was putting on her uniform after taking a shower. When she walked out there she was surprised to see Abbie in the middle of cooking, something she had never seen before. She asked, "What are you doing?"

"Pancakes for everybody."

"Awwww, you are such a good kid."

"I just wanted to be hospitable."

"Well, you are," she sat down at the table in the nook just as Evans walked into the room.

"What's going on here?" He asked.

"Pancakes," Abbie told him.

"I didn't know you knew how to cook."

"Pancakes are my specialty," she said as she poured more batter on the griddle.

"Look at this," Taylor pointed at the two pitchers in the middle of the table, "Coffee and orange juice."

As Evans sat down he said, "It's like being at IHOP."

Next to come into the room was Riley who said, "Something smells good."

Taylor joked, "I'm going to remember that you can cook, Abbie."

"Coffee or orange juice, Emma?" Asked Evans.

Riley answered, "Coffee," as she took a seat.

Once there were stacks of pancakes on their four plates, the butter and syrup was distributed around the table. Abbie joined them and they all began to eat.

"These are good, Abbie," Riley said.

Taylor asked Abbie, "When did you decide to do this?"

"Last night when I got to know Emma."

"Oh sure," Evans said playfully, "Emma shows up and you roll out the red carpet for her."

"I started reading about your case in Iowa last year and I was riveted by it. I read for over an hour and a half so I was up way too late. I can't believe those girls were around my age."

"That's right, they were," Riley said.

"Including the girl who abducted them, their classmate."

Riley nodded, "It's hard to believe but yes."

"They could never be sure of a motive because she's dead. I mean, obviously, you know that. What do you think her motive was?"

"She was around your age, what do you think?"

Abbie thought for a few moments in between bites and answered, "I think she abducted the first one because she had a crush on her but then got rejected. The other two were pretty girls who looked a lot like the first one, so I think to her it may have felt like she was abducting her crush all over again. She probably got a rush from it, especially considering she was bullied by other students who ridiculed her for her looks."

Riley's blue eyes were big with surprise, "Abbie, that is very good. That's right along the lines of what I think."

"You may have a career with the F.B.I. in a few years," Evans told her.

Taylor was amazed, "You surmised that from what you read on the internet about it?"

Abbie nodded, "I have an interest in psychology."

Taylor said, "Maybe you could be a psychologist and have your paintings in an art gallery at the same time."

Recalling the paintings that Abbie had shown her the night before Riley told her, "I'd like to buy one from you before you become famous."

"I'll give you one."

"Oh no, only if I buy one."

Taylor winked playfully at Abbie and said, "You have a lot to learn about business, kid."

They finished breakfast and all pitched in to clean the kitchen before they parted ways to start their day. Abbie went off to school where she was happy and loved. The other three went off to work in a desperate battle of wits against a faceless evil.

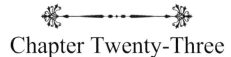

Chapter Twenty-Three

T hey arrived at the police station a few minutes after 8:00 o'clock with Taylor leading the way through the back door. She waved to Christina, the young woman manning the front desk in the lobby, on their way to the conference room. Riley was eager to immerse herself in the files to bring herself up to speed on the cases. As soon as they were settled in, Riley began reading documents on the first victim, Aaron Driscoll, when there was a knock at the door. It was 911 operator Jessica Bradley. She said, "Morning, Chief Taylor."

"Good morning, Jessica."

"Doris Stein just called to say Travis didn't show up for an 8:00 o'clock meeting with the city council to discuss his possible termination. She says he's not answering his phone either."

Taylor felt the all too familiar ball of dread tighten in her gut but she tried not to let it show. "Send the closest unit to his house to do a welfare check on him."

"Okay, Chief."

Taylor had an additional thought, "Jessica. Send two units if they're not busy and call them on their phones, not the radio."

"Okay."

Taylor looked at Evans and his uneasy expression mirrored hers. It wasn't like Reynolds to be late for anything and this wasn't just a random appointment. She knew the opportunity to speak before the city council to plead for his job was not something he would intentionally miss. Her imagination suddenly went wild thinking about whether he had committed suicide, went on the lam, or God forbide he was murdered.

Evans told Riley, "Travis Reynolds is the town's mayor and he's been charged with the murder of our second victim after the weapon used was found in his house. He was released on bail yesterday morning."

"And he's missing?" Asked Riley.

"Possibly," he answered.

Riley thought for a moment, "How was the weapon found?"

"An anonymous tip," he explained.

"Hmmmm. The weapon matched up?"

"Perfectly," Evans looked at Taylor and he could tell her mind was somewhere else but he could hardly blame her. After everything that had happened, it was hard not to go to a worse case scenario.

Riley asked, "Any other evidence against him?"

Evans shook his head, "No."

"Does he have a connection to any of the other cases?"

"Not yet."

Riley started reading again but found it difficult to concentrate while Taylor and Evans sat quietly waiting for news from the responding officers. A few minutes later Jessica was back at the door, "Chief, I've got Turner and Daniels at the house and they say Travis' truck isn't there and there's no answer at the door. Officer Daniels says Travis has a fishing boat that he keeps parked beside his garage and it's gone too."

Taylor tried to make sense of that information. It didn't seem reasonable that he would go on the run with his small fishing boat. If he was murdered no one would steal that old motor boat. Then again, why would he go fishing on the day he was released on bail for a murder charge? None of it made any sense. "Jessica, have both of them standby, we're on the way there."

"Okay."

Taylor pulled her phone out and called Brandon Holt, the closest friend Travis had in the police department. He answered, "Hello, Chief."

"How soon can you meet me at Travis' house?"

"Why, what's wrong?"

"He didn't show up for his meeting with the city council and he's not answering his phone."

"Oh, shit," he sounded really worried. "Is his truck there?"

"No."

"If his truck's not there he's not there."

"We've got to gain entry into his house to make sure he's not lying in there incapacitated and someone didn't steal his truck. I want you there when we go in."

"Give me five minutes.

"Thanks."

Evans and Riley were already heading for the door.

Four minutes later, Taylor's patrol car screeched to a halt in front of Reynolds' house, followed by Riley's rental sedan. Daniels and Turner's patrol cars were already parked on the street and the officers were standing beside them talking. Taylor got out of her car and approached them. "Have you checked the doors?"

"Yes, ma'am, they're all locked," Turner said. "The windows appear to be locked as well."

Taylor introduced her officers to Riley while they waited on Holt to arrive. "Andre, Rebecca, this is F.B.I. Special Agent Emma Riley. Emma, this is officers Turner and Daniels."

They exchanged greetings and a moment later, Brandon Holt's green and white pickup truck came around the corner and pulled in behind the other vehicles. He jumped out and approached the group and asked, "Still no word from him?"

"No," Taylor answered.

"His phone goes right to voicemail," Holt explained. "That never happens."

"I don't suppose you have a key to his house?" Taylor asked him.

"No."

Taylor turned to Turner, "Andre, I want you to kick the front door in."

"Yes, ma'am," he answered simply, as if she asked him to do that everyday.

The five of them followed the football player sized officer toward the house and Taylor introduced her second in command to Riley. They shook hands as they walked and Turner barely paused on the porch before one powerful kick, close to the doorknob, splintered the door frame and the door flew inward. He hollered into the dark house, "Travis!" There was no answer.

"Just a reminder, don't touch anything, let's just make sure he's not inside the house," advised Taylor.

They searched every room and closet, the garage and the attic, but there was nowhere to hide. Travis was not there. The house was neat, so there was no indication of a struggle. Nor did it appear as though he'd packed anything. Holt observed Reynold's collection of body building supplements on the kitchen counter. Whey protein powder and creatine, amino acids and testosterone boosters. He told Taylor, "He wouldn't go anywhere without these."

Taylor felt it was time to mention the absent boat to him. "Travis's fishing boat is missing too."

Holt frowned and thought for a moment, "Travis never goes fishing during the week unless he's on vacation."

"So would you also agree it's unlikely he would go fishing on the day he's released from jail for murder?"

Holt didn't know what was going on but he had to agree. He sighed, "Yeah."

As the others crowded around in the kitchen, Taylor asked him, "Where would he go?"

"If he was going for a short trip, he'd probably go out to the pond on Walter Schreiber's farm. They're friends and Travis can go out there anytime he wants. He's taken me a couple of times. There's a back way that he would go without having to go through the front gate. He has a key to the padlock at a side entrance."

Without hesitation Taylor told him, "Lead the way."

"Okay."

Turner spoke up, "Chief, I fixed the front door enough that it doesn't look broken. We can lock it and it won't open unless you kick it again. It wouldn't take much of a kick though."

"Thank you, Andre. We'll get it repaired later. Let's go."

The five vehicle caravan, led by Holt's pickup truck, headed northwest out of town. Twenty minutes later, he turned onto a private road that ran directly north. After traveling two miles, Holt turned left onto a dirt road that wound its way through moss covered trees and low lying swampy areas. Four hundred and fifty feet later, Holt pulled his truck to a stop in front of a gate in a chain link fence. Everyone got out of their cars and walked that way. Through the fence, about a hundred yards away, they could see Reynold's large, black pickup truck parked close to a large pond.

"Dammit it's padlocked!" Holt said frustratingly.

Evans went up to it for a closer look and pulled it off the hasp. He turned and looked at Taylor, "Dummy locked."

"Just like the one at the Valiant Trucking Company." It was just another reason for her belly to start aching more.

As Holt pushed open the gate, Taylor said, "Let's just walk it."

Evans asked Holt, "How big is this pond?"

"Uh… about twenty four acres."

"Do you know how deep it is?"

"I think Travis said eight to ten feet."

When the six of them were about halfway along the well worn ribbon of dirt that cut through the tall grass leading to Reynold's truck, Holt pointed and yelled, "Look!"

There roughly in the middle of the pond was a small motor boat that didn't appear to have anyone in it.

As they picked up the pace, Holt declared, "That is Travis' boat."

Near Reynold's truck was a short, concrete boat ramp but there were no other watercraft there or on the water.

Evans shielded his eyes up against the driver's side window and looked into the truck and declared, "It's empty."

"Brandon, do you know Walter Schreiber?" Asked Taylor.

"I met him one of the times Travis brought me out here. He was here fishing with his grandson."

"I need you to go get him and bring one of his boats so we can tow Travis' in."

"Okay," he replied. "I'm going to get my truck cause he lives about a mile up this back road."

Taylor turned to Turner and Daniels and said, "Rebecca, Andre, I need you to go back to where the private road turns off the highway. No one gets through unless it's for official business or it's someone who lives here."

"Okay."

"Yes, ma'am."

Taylor pulled out her phone and looked at Evans and Riley and said, "I've got to call the county sheriff's department and have them bring their dive team out here."

Chapter Twenty-Four

An hour and a half later, they were all back in Delaney, having turned over the scene of Reynold's disappearance to the county sheriff, who had jurisdiction. Turner and Daniels were back on patrol, Holt went home to change into his uniform, and Taylor, Evans, and Riley were back in the police station's conference room.

Taylor's mind was racing with all of the information she had absorbed during the morning. They had towed Reynold's boat back to shore and were careful not to disturb the contents to preserve the evidence for the sheriff's department. Travis' phone, wallet, and keys were in a ziplock bag on one of the benches in the boat. Holt had told them that was normal for Travis to do. There was a tackle box and a fishing pole that was lying in the boat with the line in the water and a dead fish on the hook. Most telling, there was a twelve pack of beer, nine of which were open. Eight were empty and lay crushed on the bottom of the boat and one was partially full and lying on its side.

Evans watched Taylor nervously walk back and forth. "Sam, you're pacing again."

"I know, I'm sorry. I'm just really anxious."

"Relax, it could be hours before we know anything."

Riley asked her, "Sam, you know him better than we do. What do you think?"

"Brandon told me Travis was a decent swimmer even if he was muscle bound."

"I've never tried swimming after drinking nine beers," Evans posited.

Taylor asked him, "So you think he drowned?"

"Well, if it's staged it's set up perfectly. I mean, after he drank all of those beers he stood up to pee and fell into the water and the boat drifted away and he was so drunk he drowned."

"Aren't you the one who says you don't believe in coincidences?"

Evans grinned, "There does seem to be a lot of that going around."

"Do you think he would go fishing having just gotten out of jail on a murder charge?" Riley asked.

Taylor sat down and shook her head, "At first I was very skeptical. But maybe he wanted to just get away, be outside since he was in jail for awhile. You know, do something that he likes doing, like fishing and getting hammered," the intercom buzzed and Taylor said, "Yes?"

It was Christina at the front desk. "Chief Taylor, Officer Martinez would like to speak with you."

"Send him in," Taylor then told Evans and Riley, "He's a reserve officer for us, computer expert, and our social media detective."

The clean cut, thirty something year old man appeared in the doorway. "Hello, Chief."

"Hey, Anthony, what's up?

"I've been going through Skylar Pittman's social media, business, and financial accounts and I came across something I think you'll want to know. I'm familiar with all of the murder cases so when I saw the name, a major red flag went up."

"Who?"

"Tommy Dalton."

Taylor shot a glance at Evans whose eyebrows were already raised. She asked, "What about him?"

"On her main business website, where people pay her to do things, he shows up as having been a customer of her's for years. The way it's set up, the more extreme things you want to see, the more money you pay. From what I've seen, he seems to be in the most extreme category for activity. For example, he's paid for her to dress up like a little girl and he was particularly interested in something called breath play. Having the boyfriend choke her, simulate her being hanged, and even putting a clear plastic bag over her head while she's having sex. I know that correlates to how she died."

Taylor let out a long sigh and then answered wearily, "Yeah."

Martinez continued, "Curiously, there's been no activity for several months and he closed his account within hours of the time her body was found."

Taylor wondered if she was getting a stomach ulcer as much as it hurt.

Martinez added, "Business must have been good, she has over twenty thousand dollars in her checking account."

Taylor nodded, "How far along in the process are you?"

"Oh, maybe a third of the way."

"Okay, If you come across any other name that relates to one of our cases let me know, Anthony."

"I sure will. Bye."

"Backstory," Riley requested.

Evans knew he'd be doing Taylor a favor if he explained the history to Riley. "Our fifth victim was a man named Jonah Sutherland, a mechanic here in town. Late on the night we believe he was murdered, one of the officers on patrol thought they saw Tommy Dalton driving his old, red pickup truck near where the murder occured. It was on the highway leading out of town in the direction where Dalton lives. So we paid him a visit and suffice it to say he didn't care for my direct approach to questioning. I ended up sitting alone in the car while Sam finished up the talk with him. Later on, we found out he did time in the same prison with Kyle Stanton, although no proof exists that they knew each other. Sam and the officer who saw him in his truck that night paid him a visit the following day but she was unable to confirm it was him or the truck. He denied being in town that night. When Dalton was twenty-four he dated a sixteen year old girl and long story short, was ultimately convicted of statutory rape, thus the prison sentence. The girl always loved and supported him and they got married as soon as he was released from prison. They live on an island on a ranch his family owns. Has a couple of kids ages...?"

"Nine and seven," Taylor answered for him.

"Which seems a little scary at the moment. Although he was somewhat defensive with me, I didn't get the feeling that he was lying about anything. Sam got along with him a lot better though. So, are you going to call him?"

"I have an idea," Taylor said thoughtfully, "He seemed to like Officer Thorson. I bet he would like Emma."

Riley almost winced, "I don't like the sound of that."

"Your knowledge of behavioural science might come in handy with this guy," Evans suggested.

"Sure, whatever you need."

"We have to check on those kids," Taylor pulled her phone out, "I'm going to call him to make sure he's receptive," she dialed the saved contact number she had for him and listened to it ring four times before voicemail answered. Taylor tried sounding as though nothing was wrong. "Hello, Tommy, this is Police Chief Taylor, it's Wednesday and I'd like to have another visit with you. Call me back, thank you."

Evans said, "You're going out there aren't you?"

"Yep."

Riley stood up, "I'm ready."

As the two women began to walk out of the room, Evans, feeling a little left out, said, "Don't worry, I'll hold down the fort."

Fifteen minutes later, about halfway to the Dalton ranch, Taylor was driving her patrol car with Riley in the passenger seat. Taylor was detailing all of the information about Dalton that she could remember when her phone rang. It was the coroner and she knew why he was calling. She answered, "Hello, Raymond."

"Hello, Chief. I've completed the autopsy on Skylar Pittman and issued the death certificate."

"What's your determination?"

"Homicide caused by manual strangulation."

"That's what I was expecting."

"I estimate the time of death to be between 9:00 P.M. and midnight."

"Okay, what were the injuries?"

"There was bruising around the neck that was somewhat puzzling. The marks were two and a half, to three times wider than the width of the tie wrapped around her neck. That would seem to indicate that the killer either had trouble strangling her or they were torturing her."

Taylor had a sickening feeling which was the case. "Any others?

"Well, the bruising around her wrists and ankles were both new and old. The old ones were just barely perceptible. The new ones around the wrists were probably made with either handcuffs or steel cables of some kind. The ones around the ankles were almost certainly made by rope. The contusions and abrasions indicate she struggled very hard against the restraints."

Taylor hated the image of that popping into her head. She quickly asked, "Anything else of note?"

"Just that the toxicology will take a few weeks."

"Okay, I appreciate your good work, Raymond."

"You're welcome, Chief."

"Bye," she hung up and told Riley, "Our last victim, Skylar Pittman, homicide by strangulation."

"I know that's not the result you wanted."

"No it's not," she sighed. "I watched that young girl grow up. And even though she wasn't a model citizen, she didn't deserve to die like that. None of the victims did."

"This Tommy Dalton, do you think he's capable of murder?"

"No," she shook her head, "But I have a hard time envisioning anyone in our town committing these murders. It's inexplicable."

Ten minutes later they arrived at the big, steel gate to the Dalton ranch. Taylor pulled up to the intercom mounted on a short, metal pole and pressed the button. A few moments later, a female voice said, "Hello?"

"Is this Vanessa?"

"Yes."

"This is Sam Taylor, Chief of Police in Delaney. I wonder if I could talk to you and Tommy."

"He's working on a project at his father's ranch."

"Okay, can we talk with you a bit?"

There was a long pause before she answered, "I'm watching my kids right now."

"That's okay, it's very important."

After another long pause she said, "I'll meet you at the dock."

The gate began to open and Taylor said, "Thank you."

Once the gate was all the way open, Taylor drove through and continued along the sandy, gravel driveway until it deadened at the parking area in front of the dock. The old, red pickup truck was parked there but the white SUV was not. A few minutes later, they could see across the one hundred and fifty yards of water at the pier on the island as Vanessa Dalton bundled her two kids into the white ski boat. As the boat headed their way, Taylor and Riley got out of the patrol car, and walked to the edge of the water. With evident skill, Vanessa Dalton cut the engine and steered the boat to a gentle bump against the rubber tires mounted alongside the dock. She tied a rope to one of the posts and climbed up onto the wooden platform.

The two kids stayed seated in the boat, each occupied by an electronic tablet.

Taylor held her hand out and said, "Vanessa, I don't believe we've met. I'm Sam Taylor and this is F.B.I. Special Agent Emma Riley."

While Vanessa shook Taylor's hand she looked at Riley, "F.B.I.?"

"Yes, the F.B.I. is assisting Delaney Police with the string of murders," Riley answered, then shook the brunette's hand, who appeared to the agent to be in her late thirties.

"Does this have anything to do with Skylar Pittman?"

"As a matter of fact it does," Taylor replied. "How do you know of her?"

Vanessa turned around and glanced to check on her kids before answering, "This is really embarrassing."

Taylor waved her off, "We've heard it all before."

"Well, we saw the story on the news about her. The latest death in Delaney, it's just horrible."

"Yes it is," agreed Taylor.

"Tommy told me she was one of his favorite porn interests. As soon as he heard the news, he deleted his account with her."

Taylor asked, "Did he know her?"

"No, but he knew she was from Delaney. I think that was one of the allures."

Riley asked, "Does he have a problem with pornography?"

Vanessa suddenly looked uncomfortable, "He would be so mad if he knew I was talking to you about this."

"It's okay," Taylor told her, "We won't mention this to him."

She nodded, "He used to. A lot of it was my fault, though. After having two kids, I suffered from postpartum depression. What we didn't know was there can be a ripple effect, causing emotional strain on the father. As you can see, we live an isolated existence out here so without much of a support system we started drinking too much to mask the pain. Whenever his parents would watch the kids for us, we were even worse towards each other. Sex was rare and even when we did, it was...abusive. We finally went to the doctor and got medication that helped. We stopped drinking and recommitted to putting the kids' welfare first. Up until recently it was the happiest that we'd ever been."

"What do you mean?" Asked Taylor.

"He's been going through a tough time lately," she explained. "I think it might be a mid-life crisis."

"How so?"

She thought for a few moments, "He's been questioning his life's decisions. Roaming around the ranch at all hours of the night. I mean, he's always been a night owl but he's been spending more time away from the island than he used to. Could be cabin fever also. I get it too sometimes."

"When you say lately, how long has that been?"

"Two or three weeks, I guess."

Riley asked, "What does he do in the middle of the night?"

"Well, for one thing, he's always had an interest in astronomy so he bought a really powerful telescope about six months ago. He says there's too many lights on the island so he likes to go out on the ranch to get a clearer view. As much as he loves the kids, I think he likes his alone time also."

"Does he take his phone with him when he goes out?" Taylor asked.

"Yeah, but I try not to bug him if I can help it."

Taylor was ready to get to the crux of the matter, "Did he go out the night before last? Say, between 9:00 and midnight?"

"Night before last...was Monday," she thought for a moment. "Yes. Why do you ask?"

When Taylor and Riley exchanged glances, it seemed to dawn on Vanessa, "Does that have anything to do with Skylar Pittman?"

"That's what we're checking up on," answered Taylor.

"Are you saying that you think Tommy may have had something to do with it?" Vanessa asked with an incredulous tone.

"Let me tell you why we're here. During the investigation into Skylar's death we learned that Tommy had an account with her for several years that included scenes in which he paid to see her choked or suffocated and that's how she died."

"Oh my God!" She turned around to make sure her kids weren't paying any attention. They weren't. "That poor girl. Listen, Tommy would never murder anyone."

"Let's take this one step at a time," Taylor said, "Did you know about his breath play predilection?"

"Yes, but it was a few years ago when we were both going through the dark period as we call it. We tried a lot of weird, kinky things trying to find happiness where there was none."

"He paid to have her dress like a little girl," Taylor let the statement stand on its own to see how she would respond.

"I'm not surprised. I think once you check there will be a lot of things he requested from her. It was probably curiosity and maybe a desire for something new or exciting. I remember he used to say she was one of his favorites."

"That's why we wanted to check on your kids as well."

Vanessa's expression transformed into one of dismay, "You think Tommy would do something to his children?"

"We're not saying that. We're just making sure because of Skylar's death, Tommy's request for breath play, and wanting her to dress up like a little girl."

"Oh my God. He would never harm the kids," she turned to check on them in the boat again. "He loves them more than life itself."

Riley asked, "Would you mind if we met them?"

"Not at all, c'mon," she led the way down the length of the dock to the boat and got her kids attention, "Hey guys someone wants to meet you."

The young boy looked up at Taylor and stated, "You're police."

"That's right, what's your name?"

"Aiden, I'm seven."

"Seven huh," Taylor looked at the young girl, "What's your name?"

"Charlotte, I'm nine."

"What are you reading?"

"American history," Charlotte answered. "I'm learning about the presidents."

"How about you?" Taylor asked Aiden.

"Stupid math."

That got a laugh out of everyone. Riley asked, "What's it like to live on an island?"

"It's fun," Aiden responded.

"My friends are jealous," Charlotte told her.

"Do you see your friends a lot?"

"Yeah, they either come here or we go to their house. They think it's more fun here."

132

"I bet so," Riley said, "Where's your dad?"

Charlotte answered, "He's working."

"What kind of work does he do?"

"He builds things and fixes things."

Aiden added proudly, "He can fix anything!"

"He built my dollhouse," Charlotte said.

"And my treehouse," added Aiden.

"Wow, that's awesome! What will you do when he gets home?"

Aiden said effusively, "It's funny movie night!"

"That sounds like fun," Riley excitedly told them, "Are you going to have popcorn?"

"Yeah, I like mine with butter," Charlotte explained.

Riley laughed, "Me too."

Even though it was a very brief meeting, Taylor thought the kids seemed happy and normal so she casually started to walk off and Vanessa took the cue to say, "Okay guys, finish up your school work so we can get the chores out of the way before daddy comes home."

They walked back to the front of the dock and Taylor said, "Great kids."

"We're proud of them, and very protective," Vanessa said. "You can see they're just fine."

"With all of the violent deaths, we just want to make sure especially when it comes to kids."

"I can understand that, but I'm positive Tommy would never harm his kids or kill anyone."

"You have cameras at the entrances to your ranch. If he left would you know?"

"Yes. Although I guess he could use the old gate on the north side. It's been locked for years and it's so overgrown it would be hard to get through there but it doesn't have a camera."

Taylor pressed the issue, "Does he have a vehicle to get into town without you knowing?"

Vanessa looked down and thought for a long few moments, "He's restoring an old Mustang in a barn here on the ranch. It runs so yes, it's possible, but it's not street legal and he hates going to town anyway. Bottom line, he wouldn't do that without telling me."

Taylor thought they'd gotten about as much out of Vanessa as they were going to, "Okay, we appreciate your time. Our visit can be a secret if you want."

"No. We don't keep things from each other."

"Okay," Taylor produced a card from her pocket and handed it to Vanessa, "If you need anything or just want to talk, give me a call, anytime."

"Thank you for being so nice."

"You too."

"Bye."

"Bye."

Taylor and Riley got back into the patrol car and began to pull away just as Vanessa pushed the boat away from the dock to begin heading back to the island. Taylor asked, "I'm curious with your background what you thought of her."

"Seemed like a nice lady. Surprisingly open and honest, considering the subject matter."

"That's what I thought, but there's a few things that bother me. One, she said he bought that telescope six months ago. That's about when Cameron Preston was shot, our second victim. Two, she said he might be having a mid-life crisis the last two or three weeks. That's during the time when the last four murders have occured, assuming Darius Kelly wasn't a suicide. Three, he was out roaming around Monday night, when Skylar was murdered."

"You said earlier you didn't think he was capable of murder. Do you still feel that way?"

Taylor slowly shook her head, "I didn't think so before now but...I hate to say it but I think he's at the top of the list."

"Looks like he had the means, opportunity, and motive."

Taylor nodded, "I believe Vanessa was telling the truth."

"Agreed, but history is replete with wives who didn't know their husbands were going out killing people."

"My God, what has happened to my town?"

"Just remember, it's not your fault."

"Thank you," Taylor answered, appreciative of Riley's efforts to help her feel better. As she drove out of the ranch's driveway onto the two-lane blacktop back to town, she took her phone out and punched in Cory's number at the State Police. Once again she would have him run a trace on a cell phone. This time, to see if Tommy Dalton left his ranch with it on Monday night.

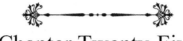

Chapter Twenty-Five

Before lunch from a popular deli was brought in and readily consumed, Taylor and Riley briefed Evans on what they learned during their visit to the Dalton ranch. Afterward, they were reading through the case files and discussing the details in the conference room with each other. A few minutes before 1:00 P.M. the intercom buzzed on the landline. Taylor answered, "Yes."

It was Christina at the front desk, "Chief, Sheriff Anderson is on line one for you."

"Thank you."

Evans said, "I wonder if they found him."

Taylor picked up the receiver and hit line one, "Hello, Mark."

"Hello, Sam, are you sitting down?"

"Yeah," she answered warily. "Did you find him?"

"Not yet, the search is about thirty-five to forty percent complete."

"What's wrong then?"

"We've been going through Travis' phone and found something you need to know."

"Okay," Taylor had no idea what was coming next.

"There's a message thread going back several months to a number that comes back to a trac phone. We tried to trace the purchase but it was too long ago. It's apparent Travis had an ongoing sexual relationship with what is obviously a woman. Anyway, yesterday he sent her a message that said, 'going fishing.' The response was three hearts. The troubling part was the conversation that took place before that where he blamed you for planting evidence that got him arrested and might ultimately send him to prison. She agreed and said that you ruined his life. Travis then responds by saying he was going to get back at you by ruining your life."

"Oh no," Taylor couldn't believe what she was hearing.

"There are literally hundreds of messages between the two of them. We're still going back through them and it's not only clear that the two of them were very sexual together but it was a wild and intense relationship. It seems as though they met at his gym. It also appears that she knows you."

The words hit Taylor like a brick. "Why?"

Anderson sighed, "They call you names and even reference how bad a job you're doing because of the murders."

"Good Lord."

"Sorry to have to tell you all of this."

"Do you have a name?"

"They never refer to each other by name and I can only assume that's intentional since she's using a burner phone. He only refers to her as baby or slut. She uses names like babe, master, and daddy. But, in his contacts she is listed as broodmare."

"That sounds familiar. Is it a name?"

"I had to look it up. It's a female horse used for breeding."

"What the Hell?"

"One of my deputies is a big horse guy. He says a broodmare is the female equivalent to a stud."

"Nice," she was suddenly aware of a pounding headache.

"As soon as I get back to the office, I'll get a printout of the texts and email them to you."

"I appreciate it."

"Hopefully we'll pull Travis' body out of the pond in the next few hours and you won't have to worry about him anymore."

"Yeah," Taylor felt guilty that the choice was either Travis being dead, or alive but coming after her. "Thank you, Mark."

"I'll call you as soon as we finish here."

"Okay, bye."

"Bye."

Taylor hung up the phone and Evans said, "You don't look so well."

"I've got to take something for a headache," she stood up and walked out of the room. She went into the breakroom, opened the first aid kit and grabbed a packet of ibuprofen. She washed it down with a cup of water from the watercooler. She stood there running through her mind everything the sheriff had just told her. Coming on the heels of the revelations about Tommy Dalton, it all seemed so surreal. It made her even more grateful for the help Evans and Riley were providing. She started to head back to the conference room but

Christina stopped her, "Chief, there's a Detective Hernandez with the Miami Police Department on line three."

"Okay, thanks Christina."

She went back into the conference room and picked up the phone, "This is Chief Taylor."

"Chief Taylor, this is Detective Paul Hernandez with Miami PD."

"Yes, sir."

"We have issued an arrest warrant for a man we believe may be in your town."

"Oh, what's his name?"

"Nathan Allen Miller, he's twenty-four..."

"I know who he is."

"Oh good, so he is there?"

"Well, he was going to check out of a local motel today...if you'll hang on a minute I can check and see."

"Sure, thanks."

She put him on hold, took out her phone and looked up the motel's number. She dialed it and a man's voice said, "Ocean Breeze Motor Inn."

"This is Chief of Police Sam Taylor, I need to know if Nathan Miller checked out today."

"No, ma'am, he changed his mind. He's paid up through tomorrow morning at the least."

"Is he there now?"

"Uh, nope, his car is gone."

"Okay, don't mention that I called, understand?"

"Oh, yes, ma'am."

She hung up and picked up the landline and said, "He's still here so we should be able to run him down for you."

"Oh good, because we need to get him off the street."

"Why's that?"

"Solicitation of sex with a minor."

"Oh no, I can't believe it."

"Last week, the parents of a sixteen year old girl caught her boarding a bus in Tampa. She was running away to be with Nathan Miller who she only knew online. The parents searched her social media accounts and could clearly see he was manipulating her. He promised her this great life if she ditched her overly restrictive parents and came to live with him here in Miami. Tampa PD immediately called us and we've confirmed everything the parents have reported. Miller was definitely grooming her and his communication with her was overtly sexual in nature."

"I'm surprised but I guess I shouldn't be."

"Yeah, if you pick him up, don't fall for his simpleton act."

"What do you mean?"

"We have a detective on our staff who dealt with Miller a few years ago in another case and he said this guy can come across as a real dork because of his looks but he's actually very smart and quite possibly a dangerous psychopath."

Taylor was stunned. She managed to ask, "Why a dangerous psychopath?"

"For one thing, he has a juvenile record for peeping into the windows of young girls in his neighborhood. Then a few years ago, when Miller still lived with his parents, neighborhood pets began turning up butchered. I don't recall the exact number. He was never caught at it but when he moved out, the killings stopped."

"Oh my God."

"When his arrest warrant was issued, we gained access to his bank account and saw that he had made numerous purchases in Delaney over the past week. I know you've had murders there so we wanted you to know, we wouldn't put it past Miller to be involved in something like that."

"Damnit," as shocked as Taylor was, she remembered something Miller had told Riley about not having enough money for an attorney. She asked, "Do you know how much money is in his account?"

"Yeah, I have it right here. $32,736.24. He has a true crime channel on YouTube that apparently makes good money."

Miller had been lying. It was all an act. She couldn't believe it. She managed to say, "Yeah."

"If you pick him up, let us know. We'll come get him."

"We'll start looking immediately."

"Thank you, Chief."

"You're welcome," she hung up and looked at Evans first and then Riley, who were both regarding her with great expectation. She hit the intercom button for the dispatch office and 911 operator Jessica Bradley picked up. "Jessica, put out an APB for Nathan Allen Miller. Have them initiate a felony stop on him. We have

138

information on him and his car in the computer. He currently has a room at the Ocean Breeze Motor Inn so maybe we can catch him there. Also, call in a couple of the reserve officers to aid in the search, I'll okay the overtime."

"Sure will, Chief."

Taylor hung up and looked at Evans and Riley and said, "You are not going to believe those last two calls."

Evans asked, "What about Nathan Miller?"

Taylor leaned back in her chair and sighed, "You were right about him."

"How so?"

"Tampa PD has a warrant out for him for solicitation of sex with a minor. He was grooming a sixteen year old girl. Her parents caught her boarding a bus to go meet him. He also has a juvenile record for peeping into young girls' windows. And they think he may be a dangerous psychopath, having killed numerous neighborhood pets a few years ago."

"Damn," Riley said, "He had me fooled."

"They say it's an act. A dufus, a simpleton, all an act."

"How did you have him pegged correctly and I didn't see it?" Riley asked Evans.

"I read a study once. They determined that men could spot male psychopaths easier than women and vice versa. Maybe it's as simple as that."

Riley added, "I'm sure your experience had a lot to do with it."

"Remember when he said he was going to have trouble even making his rent?" Taylor asked Riley, "He has over thirty thousand dollars in the bank."

"What about the other call?" Asked Evans.

"They're still searching the pond. No body yet. On Travis' phone though, they found hundreds of text messages to an untraceable tracfone. Whoever it belongs to is someone who he's had a sexual relationship with for months. Someone who's familiar with me and apparently uses his gym. Yesterday, after telling this person he was going fishing, he said he was going to get back at me by ruining my life."

"If they don't find his body, that could be a problem," Evans admitted.

"I guess it's a good thing we're with you almost all of the time," Riley posited. "I have an idea though."

"Okay," Taylor was open to almost anything at this point.

"We all agree this goes back to the assault on Kyle Stanton. Since we have reluctant witnesses in the public, why don't we bring in the first responding officers and have an informal talk with them about what they saw?"

"We have written statements from each of them," Evans told her.

"I know, I just read them, but it's been a year. Maybe thinking back after all of this time they may remember something important."

"Hey, it's worth a try," Taylor admitted. She picked up the phone and pushed the button for dispatch. "Jessica, is Leah busy right now?"

"She's looking for Nathan Miller."

"We can spare her for a few minutes. Have her stop by here and see me."

"Sure will."

Seven minutes later, Officer Leah Thorson knocked on the conference room door.

"Hey, Leah," Taylor greeted her. "You've met Agent Evans but this is F.B.I. Special Agent Emma Riley."

The two women shook hands and Evans pulled out a chair for her.

Taylor began, "Leah, we're just going back over the events of a year ago when Kyle Stanton was assaulted. I know we have your statement and we talked to you at the time but we're going to ask you, Rebecca, and Brandon to recount what happened that day in the hopes that maybe you'll think of something new."

"Oh sure."

"Start wherever you'd like."

"It was about 1:00 in the afternoon that day. I was on patrol and a call came in about a fight at the Beechnut Tree Mobile Home Park. I was only a couple of minutes away so I signaled I was enroute. By the time I got there, additional calls were coming in requesting an ambulance so I knew someone was hurt. When I pulled onto the main street that runs through the park, there were literally dozens of people clogging the road. I hit the siren and laid on my horn but I could only get within a hundred feet of the scene. I jumped out of the car and started running toward what appeared from a distance to be a brawl. The closer I got, the more people were in my way. Around the immediate scene, people were five or six deep and they wouldn't move out of the way. People were literally trying to physically block me from getting through, for what reason I didn't know, so I started yelling and shoving people aside. When I finally got to the center of the mass of people, there was a man lying in the middle of the road, bloody from head to toe. People were so crowded around him they could've kicked him if they wanted to and I'm sure some did. I was yelling at them to give him some air but people were screaming at me that it was Kyle Stanton, he was a murderer, he was trying to rape a little girl, but for some reason they were hostile towards me. When they started crowding me, I debated using pepper spray but in such close quarters and with so many people I was afraid it would affect me as well. I straddled the man and finally pulled my service weapon out and actually had to point it at these people to get them to back off. Before they started moving away much at all, I heard another unit with the siren blaring. A minute later, Rebecca, Officer Daniels that is, arrived and made her way to me and that's when I started first aid on the man. He wasn't breathing and I couldn't get a pulse so I started CPR. I could hear Rebecca arguing and fighting with people just as I had. What seemed like a long time but was probably only about two or three minutes, Brandon showed up and helped Rebecca disperse the crowd. I kept working on him for another couple of minutes until the paramedics arrived. They were getting a faint pulse so they loaded him up and took off for the hospital. I was physically and emotionally exhausted and my hands and uniform were covered in blood."

Taylor smiled at her proudly, "And you volunteered to keep working that day."

Evans was impressed with the bravery of this petite woman, who clearly risked her life by running into an angry mob to save a career criminal from being beaten to death. He asked her, "Did you know who the victim was?"

"Not until some of the people began yelling his name. You couldn't tell it was him by looking at him."

"But, you knew who he was?"

"Oh yes. He was wanted for murder."

Riley asked, "Did you ever have any interaction with him before that?"

141

"Once. I assisted another officer who was arresting him for a DUI but that's it. I'd seen him around town for years so I knew who he was."

Evans asked her, "How many people on our list of murder victims did you see out there?"

"Uh, I did not see Olivia Preston but everyone else was out there. Aaron Driscoll, Darius Kelly, and Jonah Sutherland were right in the middle of it all. In fact, I'm sure all three of them were among the people I was in a shoving match with. Skylar and her boyfriend were a ways back and Cameron Preston was even farther away just observing."

"Leah, you provided us with a list of names of other people that were out there, can you think of any others now?" Taylor asked.

She shook her head, "No, that's as thorough a list as I can come up with."

Evans asked, "Can you think of anyone who was out there who might want revenge?"

Thorson thought for a moment and said, "You know, I've thought about that. There were a lot of people out there and not all of them would have approved of what they saw. We never could establish who Stanton was there to see, if anyone, but whoever it was they could be the ones exacting revenge."

There was a pause with everyone looking at each other so Evans took the cue and stood up and extended his hand, "Leah, I must say, what you did was very brave."

She stood up and smiled and while shaking his hand said, "I just did what was right."

"Thank you, Leah," Taylor said.

"Bye."

"Bye."

After Thorson had left, Christina came to the door. "Chief, we are inundated with requests from the media about when the next news conference will be."

Taylor was in no mood for a press conference, especially when they may not have an answer about Travis before the end of the day. "Christina, issue a press release that the next news conference will be tomorrow afternoon at 5:00 P.M."

"Okay, thanks," she sounded relieved.

Taylor rang dispatch, "Jessica, Leah is going back out, can you route Rebecca by here as soon as you can?"

"I sure will."

"Thank you."

Twelve minutes later the 5'10" Officer Rebecca Daniels, with broad shoulders and short, braided hair, arrived at the station and came to the conference room. Taylor greeted her, "Hello, Rebecca."

"Hello."

"You've met Agent Evans, and Agent Riley."

They shook hands and exchanged greetings before Daniels took a seat.

Taylor began, "Rebecca, we are revisiting the events that happened when Kyle Stanton was assaulted."

"Okay."

"I know we have your original statement but if you would tell us what happened, the agents may have some questions."

"Alright. Just after lunch, I believe around 1:00 P.M. a fight in progress was called in from the Beechtree Mobile Home Park. Not an unheard of occurrence for that location. We'd had a lot of problems coming out of there but in the three or four minutes it took me to get there, different kinds of calls were coming in. A gang fight and an all out brawl, a knife fight and a request for an ambulance, so I knew it was bad. When I pulled onto the property, it was swarming with people. My initial feeling was there were more people out there than actually lived there. Officer Thorson's vehicle was already there so I parked behind her. I got out and ran towards what looked like the center of the action. I had to push and shove my way to the inner circle of people and it was only then that I first saw Officer Thorson. At first I didn't know what in the Hell was going on because Thorson had her gun out and was pointing it at people who were yelling and cussing at her. Then I noticed the big, bloody guy lying on the ground at her feet. While people started pushing me and screaming at me, I heard Thorson yelling for them to get back and give him some air and I knew then that this was an out of control mob. As soon as I got there, Thorson kneeled down and started CPR on the victim so I knew it didn't look good. All of a sudden someone grabs my uniform by the left sleeve and starts to yank me away so I just hauled off and popped him. Hit him on the left side of the head and ear, and it turned out to be Aaron Driscoll. He let go. Now I'm really amped up. I started aggressively pushing and shoving people back, yelling for them to leave, threatening to arrest them. I really considered pulling my weapon out like Thorson did, but I was afraid I'd have to use it. A minute or two later, Deputy Chief Holt shows up and he jumps in there and helps me push back the perimeter ten or twelve feet. With his help and more sirens coming, I think that's when the crowd began to disperse. Officer Thorson continued CPR until the MICU arrived. When they left with the victim, Holt had to help Thorson to her car because she was just physically spent and a bloody mess. She was a trooper though, especially considering how small she is and how irate that crowd was. I mean they were enraged, it was chaos. It came close to turning really bad."

Evans knew what he wanted to ask first, "Did you know Aaron Driscoll before or after this happened?"

"No, I didn't know him but I knew who he was. I'd see him cycling just about everywhere around town."

"What was his reaction to being hit?"

Daniels laughed, "It's funny now but it wasn't then. He was actually pointing at me and whining that I hit him. I was a little too busy to respond but I thought, yeah, if you grab me again, I'll pop you again."

Evans fought the urge to laugh. He had no doubt Daniels was a former MMA fighter. "Did you encounter any of the other people out there that have been murdered?"

"Oh yeah. Darius Kelly and Jonah Sutherland would not obey my commands to back off or leave. I kept pushing them back and they kept coming forward. I was yelling at both of them that I would arrest them while they were hollering about Stanton being a rapist and a killer. As for the others, I only saw Skylar Pittman and her boyfriend."

"So, no Cameron Preston?"

She shook her head, "I don't remember seeing him out there."

Riley jumped in, "Did you know Kyle Stanton?"

"I didn't know him personally but I knew all about him and I'd see him around town every so often. I had one official encounter with him. A few years ago there was a bar on Main Street that's no longer there. We get a call of a fight in progress at that location. Officer Turner and I responded and there was a guy lying in the parking lot dazed and beaten in the face. The man claimed he didn't remember what happened but I didn't believe him. There were windows in the bar that overlooked the parking lot so I went inside to see what I could find out. No one admitted to seeing anything but I noticed blood on the shirt of Kyle Stanton. I asked him to step outside and he gets an attitude with me by saying, 'what are you going to do, arrest me little lady?' I said, 'If you give me a reason, that's exactly what I'll do.' Long story short, he did come outside but he wasn't wanted for anything and the victim couldn't or wouldn't press charges so we cut him loose. It shows just how much people were afraid of him."

Taylor asked, "Rebecca, the list of people that you provided who you saw out there that day, can you think of any more?"

Daniels sighed, "I don't think so, especially after this long. There were a lot more people out there that I either didn't know or was just too busy to recognize."

"Can you think of anyone who was out there or not that would want to get revenge for Stanton's assault?"

"I've given that a lot of thought and no, I don't."

With the line of questions having drawn to an end, Evans thought he would mention something for fun. "I understand you were an MMA fighter."

Daniels smiled, "Yeah, I fought through college. It did wonders for my self esteem, toughness, and physical fitness. It gave me the confidence to be a police officer."

"That is impressive," Evans told her. "Agent Riley is a second degree black belt in karate."

"Oh man, I have great respect for karate masters. It's a great discipline. I can tell you would be underestimated."

Riley smiled, "Yeah, I am. I'll take whatever advantage I can get."

Taylor spoke up, "Rebecca, thanks for the good information. We'll let you get back on patrol."

"No problem, hope I helped."

"You did."

"Bye."

Once Daniels had left the room Riley said, "Their stories are remarkably consistent."

"They sure are," Evans agreed. "Two down, one to go,"

Taylor phoned the dispatch office once again. "Jessica, Brandon is on patrol right?"

"Yes, he's the back up to the team staking out the Ocean Breeze Motor Inn."

"Okay, have Rebecca take his place, and have Brandon come in here."

"Yes, ma'am."

A few minutes later Christina buzzed the conference room.

Taylor answered, "Yes."

"Chief, County Emergency Management Director Edward Peterson is on line two for you."

"Oh, I know what this is about," she picked up the phone, "Hello, Ed."

"Hi, Sam, how are you?"

"Up to my ass in alligators."

He laughed. "I've heard about it. I hate to throw you another one but I wanted to give you an update on Hurricane Walter. It's definitely going to hit Florida, as you probably already know, the only question is whether it will be a cat 3 or 4."

"Great," she responded sardonically.

"The National Weather Service has moved up the time for landfall from Saturday morning to Friday night."

"You're just full of good news today, Ed."

He laughed, "I know, I just wanted to keep you informed, I know you're busy."

"I appreciate that."

"When it hits, just let me know what you need and I'll direct state and federal resources your way."

"Thanks, Ed."

"Take care."

"Bye."

Taylor hung up the phone and announced to no one in particular, "Hurricane Walter will make landfall Friday night."

Evans felt so bad for Taylor he thought she could use some levity, "If we get a plague of locusts you'll really have a problem."

Riley laughed because it sounded like something that Andy would say. Taylor looked at the grin on Evans' face and she too laughed. Not that it was particularly funny but that Evans thought it was. A few minutes later Deputy Chief of Police Brandon Holt was at the door.

"Hey, Brandon, have a seat. You know everyone here."

146

"Am I in trouble?" He asked as he sat down.

Taylor smiled at him, "Not at all. What we're doing is re-interviewing the first responders to Kyle Stanton's attack."

"Oh, okay."

"So just tell it as you remember it and we may have some questions."

"Okay, uh, my understanding is I got there about two minutes after Rebecca arrived. I pulled in behind the two patrol cars already parked there because there were so many people in the street I didn't think I could get any closer. I jumped out and started running toward what looked like a fight between one of our officers and people in the crowd. I had to dodge and weave to get close and by the time I got on scene I had to literally push people out of the way. When I got there, I could see it wasn't really a fight so much as Rebecca pushing and shoving people to back away from Kyle Stanton all bloody on the ground and Leah performing CPR on him. I immediately started helping Rebecca, forcing the crowd back, telling them to go home. They were yelling at us, we were yelling at them, it was unbelievable. I've never seen a crowd that ginned up. I mean they were hostile. My granddad was a sheriff's deputy, and he used to tell me about the olden days when mobs of people would exact justice on their own. You know, those local cops were few and far between in those small towns, and a lot of the time they wouldn't or couldn't stop it. It was almost to that degree here."

"Can you remember people who were out there?" Evans asked.

"Most of the people in the crowd lived there. On our murder list there was Aaron Driscoll on the front row hollering about how Rebecca had punched him in the face. I didn't believe it because if Rebecca punched you in the face that would leave a mark. When I first approached the mobile home park, I saw Cameron Preston's work truck parked on the side of the road. I did see him later a couple of doors down talking to some people. He seemed like a bystander to me. Darius Kelly was right on the front row refusing to back off. I pushed him back two or three times and I know Rebecca pushed him several times. He was agitated as hell. Jonah Sutherland was another one right in the middle of everything, pointing at Stanton and yelling about some girl."

"What girl was he referring to?"

"I don't know, it was so loud and chaotic. Some people we're hollering about Stanton having a girlfriend that lived there. Others were screaming that he was trying to find a young girl to molest. Most of the people there already knew he was wanted for murder. I think it was just a hodgepodge of reasons to attack this guy. I saw Skylar out there with her boyfriend about thirty or forty feet away. She was filming the whole scene with her phone. We finally got the crowd pushed back eight to ten feet. A couple of minutes after I got there, the paramedics showed up and took over working on Stanton. I had to help Leah to her feet. I felt terrible for her because she was really emotionally, physically spent, and covered in Stanton's blood. Andre and Miguel, that is Officers Turner and Ramiro had arrived but the crowd had thinned out by then. There were still a lot of people milling about but they were no longer aggressive at least. I walked Leah to her car and made sure she was okay to drive home to clean up and put a new uniform on. Looking back, I feel bad because even though she said she was okay, it had to be traumatic. I mean it was a bad scene. These people were willing to try and go through the police to get to this guy, and he was already bloody and unmoving on the ground! I just think years of Stanton's bullying and intimidation caught up to him. Once they had him outnumbered, on the run, and injured it was like a self perpetuating thing."

"Did you have any run-ins with him?"

"Oh sure. I arrested him a couple of times and he would make it difficult every time I encountered him. He was a big guy, 6'6", maybe 300 lbs. He knew when to stop pushing it with the police but the average person out there, he was a menace. Woe betide if you were going to testify against him. My impression of him was that he was miserable and he wanted everyone he came into contact with to be miserable too."

"How well did you know our murder victims?" Asked Evans.

"I wasn't friends with any of them but I'd see Aaron Driscoll riding his bike all the time. I'd see Cameron Preston working on the power lines. I knew Olivia Preston a little bit more. I'd see her at school functions and sporting events. I didn't know Darius Kelly but I'd see him walking around. I knew Jonah Sutherland fairly well. He worked on my truck up at the shop. Of course I knew Skylar better than the others but I wouldn't say we were friends."

"Can you think of anyone who was out there or not who would want revenge for what happened to him?" Taylor asked.

"I have wracked my brain thinking about that. I have a theory but that's all it is. I think Stanton knew somebody out there, maybe that girlfriend some of those people were talking about. Even though we never could narrow down who it was. I think someone saw what happened to him by Aaron Driscoll, Darius Kelly, and Jonah Sutherland, as well as others and they are getting revenge by taking them out one at a time. Cameron Preston and Skylar don't make any sense for just being there, and of course Olivia Preston wasn't there at all. So my theory only makes sense to a degree."

When there were apparently no other questions Taylor said, "Okay, Brandon, we appreciate you coming in and detailing everything for us. We'll let you get back out on patrol."

"No problem," he stood up, "Bye, y'all."

For the next couple of hours they discussed the similarities between the responders' recollections of the event and their written statements at the time, as well as carefully viewing the seven videos made after the assault had taken place, submitted by some of the residents there. Their interactions regarding the cases continued as Riley became increasingly knowledgeable about each one. At 4:25, the call they'd been waiting for came in.

"Hello, Mark," Taylor held her breath, waiting for the sheriff to tell her about the search.

"Hey, Sam. I don't know what you wanted to hear but Travis Reynolds' body is not in that pond."

Taylor shook her head so Evans could see the answer, "I had a feeling you were going to say that."

"He should've known we were going to drag the pond and he wouldn't be in there. Maybe he just wanted a head start on his next move. I don't have to tell you to be careful, Sam."

"I have two F.B.I. agents that are with me almost all the time, including at home."

"Oh, excellent! You should be safe then."

"I am. Thank your team for me."

"I will. Holler if you need anything, Sam."

"Okay, thanks Mark."

Evans watched her hang up the phone, "So no body, huh?"

"Nope."

Evans looked at Riley, knowing she'd seen pictures and video of Reynolds, and said, "We're going to have to keep a lookout for this guy. He's such a hothead there's no telling what he might do."

Riley nodded and looked at Taylor, "Any idea what he might be planning?"

Taylor shook her head, "I thought I knew the man. Either I don't or he's gone mad."

Evans could tell that Taylor didn't feel very well so he suggested, "What do you say we pack up some files, grab some food to go, and head home early?"

Taylor flashed him a tired smile, "Yeah, good idea."

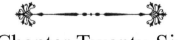

Chapter Twenty-Six

The agents followed Taylor on her way home including when she stopped at a local restaurant that served American cuisine. She picked up a to go order of burgers and chicken sandwiches, fries and onion rings for all of them and Abbie. As she drove home she ran through her mind what she was going to tell Abbie about Reynolds' disappearance and his threats. Abbie already knew that he was charged with the murder of her father and had bonded out, and much to Taylor's surprise had seemed remarkably unaffected by it all. As she pulled into her driveway, Taylor saw Abbie walking with her distinctive gait toward home through the front yard of a house three doors away. Taylor growled in frustration, feeling like she wanted to scold Abbie for walking around the neighborhood alone. Her sudden anger was tempered by remembering everything the poor girl had been through recently. She was going to have to sit down and explain to her the new, dangerous dynamic with Reynolds on the loose. It was not a conversation she was looking forward to. She climbed out of the car with the bags of food as Riley pulled in behind her. As Taylor stood there with an impatient stance, watching Abbie walk with obvious difficulty toward her, the frustration just melted away. She thought the world of this kid and she knew there was no way she could stay mad at her.

When she was close, Abbie said, "Oh, I'm glad you have food, I'm starving!"

In the best angry parent voice she could muster, Taylor said, "I should send you to your bedroom without any dinner!"

"I know, but Mrs. Kesselring's Pomeranian got out of her backyard and I just had to help look for him. I called my friends and we found him two streets over."

Taylor shook her head. She was trying so hard to be mad at her, but there was Abbie helping an eighty-one year old widow who lived alone, find her lost dog. "C'mon inside we need to talk."

When Riley and Evans pulled in behind Taylor, they too saw Abbie struggling to walk home in the uneven grass. Riley wanted confirmation of what she thought she knew. "Abbie does know Reynolds is out on bond, right?"

"Yeah." Evans was perplexed how someone as smart as Abbie could be so clueless about the danger of her being alone. Especially considering her parents were murdered separately and brutally, possibly by the man who was now roaming free somewhere. He was sure Taylor would give her a stern talking to. They both climbed out and followed Taylor and Abbie inside the house.

Taylor pulled a dining room chair out for Abbie and she sat down. While Evans and Riley seated themselves, Taylor said, "Abbie, we need to have an important talk."

"I know, I'm sorry but I called my friends…"

Taylor waved her off, "No, there's more to it than that."

"Allow me," Riley interjected, "Abbie, what do you think about Mayor Reynolds being accused of killing your father?"

"I don't know," she answered quietly. "It's hard to believe."

"Why?"

"He had no reason to. I mean, how could anyone kill my dad?"

Riley's heart ached for this wonderful, young girl. She knew all too well the intense anguish and sorrow a murder can produce.

Taylor jumped right to the point, "Abbie, Mayor Reynolds has disappeared. He tried to make it look like he drowned but they searched for him, and he's not there. He's hiding out there somewhere and here's the worst part. He blames me for everything that's happened to him and he said he was going to get back at me by ruining my life," she let that sink in before continuing, "One of the ways he could ruin my life is by doing something to you."

Abbie suddenly looked downcast as if the seriousness of it all finally dawned on her. "So you don't want me to be alone anymore?"

"That would be hard to do. We just have to be really careful until he's caught. You know how big and strong he is."

"Okay, I understand," she said earnestly.

Taylor exchanged smiles with Evans and Riley, believing she had finally convinced her of the danger. She reached over and started to open one of the white, plastic bags and asked Abbie, "Burger or chicken sandwich?"

"Burger."

"Fries or onion rings?"

"Both."

"You have to pick one."

Riley stepped up to the plate, "I'll share some of my fries if you'll share your onion rings."

"Deal."

Taylor smiled but before she could dispense the food her phone rang. It was Cory at the State Police. In all of the confusion of the day, she had forgotten about him. She said, "I'll take this outside," on her way out of the front door she answered, "Hello, Cory."

"Hey, Sam, I'm sorry it took so long to get back with you. It's a madhouse here."

"I know the feeling."

"I've got something interesting for you. The phone you gave me to trace did not leave that ranch Monday night. However, I used the services of one of our phone geeks to access that number's text messages. Unofficially, of course. At 10:35, his wife I guess, sent him a text that read, 'going to bed, love you.' He never responded. So I did a little more checking. We went back over the previous three nights and on two of them, she sent similar messages between 10:30 and 11:15 and he replied both times."

Taylor was quiet while she tried to understand the importance of what she'd just heard.

"Are you there?" Cory asked.

"Yeah, it's just...I wasn't expecting that."

"I don't know what else you have on him but while this doesn't mean he did it, he at least had the opportunity. It's suspicious."

"Yes it certainly is," Taylor agreed.

"If there's anything else you need don't hesitate to call."

"Thank you, Cory. You're a lifesaver."

"You're welcome, bye."

"Bye." Taylor stood there on her porch trying to process the enormity of the day's events. Travis disappears and apparently fakes his own death. His menacing threats against her. Tommy Dalton's lustful obsession with Skylar. Meeting Vanessa Dalton and her two cute kids. Finding out the dufus Nathan Miller was actually a psychopath. Hearing her officers recount what happened that awful day a year ago when Kyle Stanton was beaten into a coma by a mob of enraged townspeople. And now, learning that Tommy Dalton may have snuck away from his ranch Monday night when the object of his obsession was murdered. And all the while Travis Reynolds and Nathan Miller were out there somewhere, doing who knows what. She looked around her quiet neighborhood at the familiar houses with their well kept lawns. On this warm, muggy evening with barely a perceptible breeze, she knew that was going to change. In forty- eight hours a hurricane was going to come roaring through the area. Taylor had never believed in premonitions before but the approaching storm seemed foreboding. As bad as things had been up until now, she knew in her heart, the worst was yet to come.

Chapter Twenty-Seven

The next morning was Thursday, and Taylor, Evans, Riley, and Abbie were seated at the table eating an assortment of breakfast foods. Cereal and fruit, toast and muffins, when Taylor's phone rang at 7:15. It was the station calling and Taylor immediately thought they had probably picked up Nathan Miller overnight. She answered, "Chief, Taylor."

"Chief, Taylor, it's Jessica."

Taylor immediately detected worry in the voice of the 911 operator. "What's wrong?"

"Well, Officer Ramiro has a dentist appointment this morning so Brandon was supposed to fill in for him but he's late. I mean, it's only fifteen minutes but it's not like him. I've left two voicemails…"

"Okay, is the rest of the first shift working?"

"Yes."

"Call two of them on their phones, don't use the radios. Have them go to his house and see if his truck is there. If it is there have them wake him up, he probably overslept."

"Okay, Chief."

Taylor hung up, but the tight ball of worry was back in her stomach. In all of her years on the force, she couldn't recall a time when Brandon didn't show up for work.

Both Evans and Riley resisted the urge to ask who may have overslept because Abbie was listening intensely.

Taylor looked at Abbie and asked, "I know Mrs. Davis normally gives you a ride to school but we need to drop you off so we can get to work. How soon can you be ready?"

Abbie didn't even ask why, "I just have to brush my teeth."

"Okay, I'll call her and let her know that we're taking you."

Seven minutes later Taylor dropped Abbie off at the high school, with Evans and Riley right behind her in the rental car. As soon as Abbie was out of the car, Taylor called Jessica on the non-emergency line and asked her, "Have you heard anything yet?"

"Officers Turner and Daniels are at his house. They say Brandon's truck is there and they're trying to wake him up."

"Okay, stay on the line with me. I'm at the high school so I'm about six minutes away. I'm heading over there just in case something's wrong."

"Alright."

Taylor drove fast and Riley did well just to keep up with her. Three minutes later, Jessica put her on hold and answered the other line and Taylor literally held her breath. When Jessica came back, her voice was clearly more worried and nervous. "They say he's not answering and all the doors and windows are locked."

"Okay, have them wait on us, we'll be there in just a few minutes."

"Alright, Chief."

"Jessica, don't tell a soul."

"Yes, ma'am."

Three minutes later they arrived at the edge of town where the lots were large and the older houses were set back from the road eighty to a hundred feet. Holt's gray, single story, Old Craftsman style bungalow with a veranda was about a hundred yards from the nearest neighbor. As Taylor pulled into the driveway, she could see Holt's green and white pickup truck parked in front of a detached two car garage. Andre Turner and Rebecca Daniels' patrol cars were parked beside the house and the officers were nervously pacing about. Taylor parked behind them and Riley pulled in beside her. They got out of the cars and an agitated Turner approached Taylor, "Something ain't right here."

"I know Andre, I need you to kick the door in."

Turner turned around and quickly headed for the house without saying a word. Taylor noticed the worry in Daniels' eyes as they followed Turner up onto the porch.

Evans touched Taylor on the elbow and said, "Sam, why don't you wait out here."

"No, no. This is my Deputy Chief of Police we're talking about."

Evans was getting a really bad feeling about Holt not answering his door so he thought briefly about asking her again but he knew she was adamant.

It took two powerful kicks for the door to fly inward. Taylor told Turner, "Andre, you and Rebecca stay out here. No one else gets in."

"Yes, ma'am."

Taylor stepped into the foyer with Evans and Riley right behind her and yelled, "Brandon!"

There was no answer. Taylor looked into the living room and noticed two lamps were on despite there being plenty of natural light. On the coffee table were two separate clusters of beer cans. One had four and the other had three as if two people had been drinking. Taylor hoped and prayed Brandon was passed out drunk in his bed. She turned left and walked down the hallway toward the bedrooms. The only light visible was coming from the last room on the right and it was the unmistakable flicker of light from a ceiling fan. Through the open doorway, the first thing she saw was a dresser up against the wall on the left hand side and then the bed. She saw a bare foot and then a leg, and suddenly she stopped dead in her tracks. Taylor's brain simply couldn't comprehend what she was seeing.

Evans stepped around her and looked into the room. Even decades of experience was inadequate preparation for what he was seeing. The first thing that popped into his mind were the crime scene photos of a victim of Jack the Ripper. He turned around and looked at Taylor's already ashen face. He took her by the shoulders and said, "Sam, there's no need to go in there. We need to preserve the crime scene."

She slowly looked at him as if she were in a state of shock and uttered, "What in God's name is happening?"

All he could do was shake his head. There were just no words. He turned to Riley who had taken a step past him to look into the room and when she turned back to him, her blue eyes were filled with horror. He asked her, "Emma, will you take Sam outside?"

Her answer was a mere nod of her head.

He watched as Riley put her hand on Taylor's back and walked with her down the hall and made a right turn to walk out of the front door. He stood there for a full minute, steeling himself against what he was about to see up close. He turned and walked into the doorway. He reminded himself not to touch anything and he had no doubt everything he was seeing would be committed to memory. Holt was lying naked, face up, and spreadeagled on a full-sized bed. Lengths of strong but common hemp rope tied his wrists to the steel headboard and his ankles to the matching footboard. But it was the condition of his body that was so shocking and obscene. There was dried blood from head to toe from what looked like innumerable cuts, many of them so small they could only mean one thing. Torture. His penis had been cut off and lay to the left of the body. His scrotum had been removed and lay to the right of him. His eyes were open as if staring at the spinning ceiling fan and there was about a four inch length of duct tape covering his mouth. The nearest house was so far away that Evans reasoned the killer wasn't worried about Holt being heard by anyone else as much as they didn't want to hear his screams themselves.

When Taylor and Riley walked outside, Turner and Daniels could tell from their expressions that Brandon Holt was dead. Turner yelled loudly, "Dammit!"

Daniels stood there teary eyed, slowly shaking her head, "We're being hunted down one by one."

Taylor and Riley sat down on the steps and watched as Turner stomped around the yard in a distraught state. Riley asked her, "Do you want me to call it in?"

Taylor shook her head and sighed heavily, "No. It's my job and I'm going to see it through."

Riley watched as Taylor pulled her phone out and called the station. She really liked Sam and felt so bad for her but the chief had already proved to her to be mentally tough and very dedicated.

When the 911 operator picked up the non-emergency line, Taylor said, "Jessica, it's me."

"Oh no!" She could hear it in Taylor's voice.

"Yeah," she didn't even want to say the words. "I need you to call Raymond and Elena and get them out here ASAP."

"Oh God!"

"Then call the reserve officers and get them out here for crowd control. Tell everyone to keep this quiet. When the media finds out about this it's going to be a circus."

"Okay, I will," she replied tearfully.

"I'm sorry, Jessica, I know you liked Brandon."

"I can't believe it."

"I can't either," she hung up and in a helpless tone admitted, "I don't know what to do."

Riley knew how she felt and tried to console her as much as she could. "There's not much that you can do right now. Just know it's not your fault."

Taylor appreciated Riley's reassuring words and comforting tone, knowing she spoke from the depths of her own dark, painful experience.

Finally, Evans came out of the house and closed the door behind him. He announced, "I've cleared the house."

Taylor was so grateful for Evans. She wasn't sure she was thinking clearly enough to exercise proper police procedure and she certainly didn't want to assign that horrible duty to one of her officers who were already grieving. Turner and Daniels had both gravitated toward her perhaps protectively. Normally strong and tough warriors, they now stood like fragile pillars of sorrow.

Twelve long minutes later, Taylor watched as the first car to arrive was a reserve officer for crowd control that was inevitably going to be needed. Soon to be followed by other officers, the coroner, the crime scene technician, the media, and a curious public, all while a young man in the prime of his life lay butchered in his own house. It was just overwhelming. She watched as a cardinal landed on the railing only a few feet away and appeared to be looking at them. She instantly remembered the old folklore saying that when a cardinal appears, it's a visitor from heaven. She could no longer hold it in and she suddenly burst into tears.

Chapter Twenty-Eight

B y mid-morning, Taylor, Evans, and Riley were back in the very somber police station coordinating a suddenly frenetic schedule. Foremost was calling Holt's parents in Georgia and informing them of the death of their son, offering heartfelt condolences, and promising the utmost effort for justice. Issuing a properly worded press release about the death of the town's Deputy Chief of Police and to reiterate the next news conference would be at 5:00 P.M. that afternoon. Making contact with every employee of the department and offering grief counseling. Updating the work schedule to cover Holt's shifts and bringing in additional staff to help answer phones that had begun to ring off the hook.

In the conference room, a few minutes after 11:00, Taylor's phone rang from an unfamiliar number. She answered, "Chief Taylor."

"Chief Taylor, this is Vanessa Dalton."

"Oh, hey Vanessa."

"I just saw the news and I wanted to tell you how sorry I am about your deputy."

"Thank you, it is a very tough time right now."

"Even though I've been gone a long time, my heart aches for my hometown."

"Thank you," she seemed like such a nice lady, Taylor thought she would ask, "How are things at home?"

"Oh, I don't want to bother you with that now."

That piqued Taylor's curiosity. "That's okay, I'd like to know."

"Well, Tommy and I had a big fight when he came home yesterday. I told him about your visit and he blew up. He was mad because he thought that you brought another F.B.I. agent to interview me and the kids when he wasn't here. I think that's what made him the maddest is he thought a federal agent was interrogating his children. I tried to explain it to him but he's very protective of the kids. He was so mad at me for allowing it, he slept in a bunk in one of the barns."

"Has he ever done that before?"

"No, that's just how mad he was. He said some pretty ugly things, including about you, but he didn't mean it. He came back home this morning very apologetic. I could tell he didn't sleep well, in fact he went back to bed and he's still sleeping."

Even over her grief, Taylor's radar was going off. "What did he say about me?"

"He only said you were going to be sorry for what you did. Now, when he came home this morning, I'd just heard about your deputy so I told him about it and he was shocked. When I asked him what he meant by saying you were going to be sorry, he told me he'd intended to use his father's attorney to file some kind of lawsuit, but after sleeping on it he told me he didn't mean it. That he was just mad."

As much as Taylor would like to pay Tommy another visit, she knew that it almost certainly would be counterproductive from an investigative perspective and it would also put additional stress on this woman's marriage and family. She quickly made up her mind how she would approach it. "Okay, I hope you and I will keep in touch. If anything changes feel free to call me anytime and I have your number now if I need something."

"I sure will Chief Taylor, and again, I'm sorry for your deputy."

"Thank you, Vanessa, bye."

Evans and Riley were both looking at Taylor expectantly when she explained, "Tommy and Vanessa got into an argument about our visit out there yesterday. He spent the night in a barn."

"A barn?" Evans found that hard to believe.

"Yeah, after telling her that I was going to be sorry for interrogating his wife and kids."

Evans thought about it for a moment, "Well, a non-specific threat made during an argument, recited by a third party...no warrant's going to be issued for that."

"Once again though," Riley added, "He had the opportunity."

Taylor shook her head, "I can't see Tommy killing Brandon just to get back at me for talking to his wife and kids. That's crazy."

"What happened to Brandon was crazy," Riley added.

"Let's think about this," Taylor said. "Brandon was definitely heterosexual. The way he was tied naked to the bed, the beers, it all seems to indicate a female."

161

"Unless he was forced to at gunpoint," speculated Riley.

"Oh, no," Taylor shook her head, "Brandon was the type to say, you can shoot me but you're not tying me down. He would know that would be a worse way to go."

Evans asked, "And you say that he didn't have a girlfriend?"

"Not for a while now," answered Taylor.

"We can just throw Tommy into the suspect hopper along with Travis and Nathan Miller," said Evans.

"That reminds me," Taylor took her phone out and dialed the number for the Ocean Breeze Motor Inn. When a man answered Taylor said, "This is Chief of Police Taylor, has Nathan Miller come back to his room?"

"No, ma'am. I just came back from his room because his checkout time was 11:00, but his room is empty. Guess he took his stuff."

"Okay, thank you," she hung up and informed them, "Nathan Miller is long gone."

"I can't believe we haven't picked him up yet," Evans said.

"Guess that proves he's not the dufus he portrayed himself to be," Taylor ventured.

"I've been thinking," Evans began, "What if you had your friend at the state police trace the locations of that burner phone linked to Travis say, over the last few days or couple of weeks. It might reveal where that person is or if they were anywhere near our crime scenes."

Taylor liked the idea, "It's certainly worth a shot." While she dialed and waited for Cory to answer, she thought ahead to the news conference at 5:00 that afternoon. She knew it was going to be the most emotionally difficult one yet. The last thing she wanted to do was break down on TV. She made a mental note to have Evans and Riley prep her before she went out there and faced what could only be a throng of media that was voracious for information.

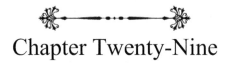

Chapter Twenty-Nine

A t 5:00 P.M. Riley agreed to join Taylor and Evans at the news conference as much for moral support as an attempt to demonstrate that additional help from the F.B.I. had arrived. The multitude of media members and townspeople had grown to the point where they overflowed from the parking lot onto the sidewalk and even forced the closure of an adjacent street. There were more people in attendance than could ever hope to have one of their questions heard. Taylor knew this was a big moment in her career and she was determined to be a leader and the presence of Evans and Riley gave her an extra boost of confidence. She began, "Good afternoon ladies and gentlemen, I'm Delaney Chief of Police Samantha Taylor. To my right is F.B.I. Special Agent Michael Evans and to my left is F.B.I. Special Agent Emma Riley. I'm going to start off with a statement and then we'll take some questions. Our community, our police department, and me personally, have a very heavy heart today because we've lost one of our own. Deputy Chief of Police Brandon Holt was found deceased in his home this morning. The manner of death is a closely guarded secret at this time for investigative purposes but he was the victim of a homicide. He was a dear friend to many, a great police officer, and a beloved member of our community. His family has been notified and obviously funeral arrangements have not been scheduled yet. Just to reiterate, the phone number on the front of this podium is our tip line and we ask if you have any information on any of our active cases, please call in. Now I know a lot has been made of the connection between our victims and the assault on Kyle Stanton a year ago. Just to set the record straight, Brandon was the third officer to arrive on the scene and he helped prevent any further damage to Stanton so the motive of the killer, assuming it's just one, is still unknown. The other major topic is the disappearance of Travis Reynolds. Up until yesterday, he was the mayor of Delaney. The city council terminated his employment at a meeting yesterday that Reynolds failed to attend. The day before yesterday, the day he was released from jail on bond, he took his fishing boat out on an area pond. We found the boat empty yesterday, with the exception of his personal effects. The pond was searched but his body was not there. It is our determination that he is on the run and we expect his bail to be revoked. One other related item. We believe that Reynolds has had a secret relationship with a female that we have not been able to identify. If anyone knows who that person is, please call our tip line. You can remain anonymous. We'll take some questions but since there's so many people assembled here, raise your hand and let me call on you. Dozens of hands flew up in the sea of people and numerous reporters called out questions but Taylor ignored them and pointed to a female media member on the front row.

"Chief Taylor, what alerted you to Brandon Holt's murder and are there any suspects?"

"Brandon was late for work this morning so we conducted a welfare check and found his body. As for suspects, we do have several that we are looking at but we're in the evidence gathering stage right now."

A reporter asked, "Chief Taylor, I know you're keeping Brandon Holt's manner of death a secret, but is there anything in his case that would tie it to the others such as some kind of signature?"

Taylor hesitated to give what little information they had or even to admit just how sparse the evidence was. She decided to try something different. To give the killer something to think about. She said, "We believe we are dealing with one killer or perhaps a killer with an accomplice. I don't want to discuss something as important as a signature but I can tell you there's been an effort to make these killings seem unrelated or accidental and that alone could be considered a signature."

A correspondent with a cable news network asked, "Chief Taylor, how is it possible that the killer could get so close to the Deputy Chief of Police without him suspecting anything? And considering that seems to be the case, if the police aren't safe, how safe can anyone be?"

The question irked Taylor but she would try and answer it to the best of her ability. "If we knew the answer to your first question, it would probably lead directly to the killer. As for the second part, I think it's obvious now that none of us are safe."

A reporter who Taylor pointed at asked, "Two questions Chief. Is Travis Reynolds one of those suspects and do you think his attempt to fake his own death is evidence of guilt?"

Taylor had to think about the questions for a moment because they weren't easy to answer. "He's obviously the number one suspect in the death of Cameron Preston and he is being looked at with regards to the other cases. Why he would try to fake his own death, only he can answer that."

Taylor pointed to a national correspondent who asked, "Chief Taylor, you mentioned you have several suspects. Can you name them for us and is Nathan Miller one of them?"

"I don't want to name all of them because we don't want to tip them off but Nathan Miller is one of them. He has a warrant out of Miami for his arrest and we are currently looking for him."

The next reporter asked, "Chief Taylor, which cases is Nathan Miller suspected of and do you think he used his media persona to hide in plain sight so to speak?"

"I don't want to narrow down which cases he's a suspect in and if he thought being a fringe media member would protect him, I guess he was wrong."

A staple of Tampa area reporting asked, "I have a question for Agent Riley. Agent, I'm familiar with your work last year with the case in Webber, Iowa. Are you assigned here because there is something similar about these cases and the one in Webber?"

Riley stepped up to the podium. "No, I was already in Florida and I had just completed my last assignment and obviously this one is extremely important to the bureau so that's why I'm here."

A shouted question came from a male reporter, "Agent Riley, isn't your high profile addition to this investigation, and the death of the Deputy Chief of Police more evidence that this case has become a political liability?"

Evans moved toward the podium, "Agent Riley, let me take this one," his voice had an angry edge as he took her place. "We have seven people brutally murdered. None of them deserved to lose their life. This is a small community so we know the killer is operating right under our noses. I have a message for that person. We are going to find you. Florida has the death penalty, and one day, I'll be watching when you're sent to Hell, which is where you belong."

Taylor had not seen Evans so mad before, but he echoed what they were all feeling. She leaned toward the microphones and said, "This is a good place to end this news conference," she held her hands up to quell additional questions being lobbed in their direction. "Unless there is breaking news tomorrow, we will not be having a news conference because of Hurricane Walter. Between the loss of Brandon, the investigations, and the extreme weather emergency, we are just incredibly busy. Please bear with us, if there is anything to report, we will do so. Thank you."

Taylor, Evans, and Riley walked back toward the refuge of the police station beneath a cacophony of questions for which none of them frustratingly knew any answers for.

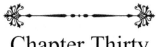

Chapter Thirty

Thirty minutes after the news conference, the front door to Taylor's house opened as she, Evans, and Riley stepped up onto the porch. When Taylor saw Abbie's smiling face, she held up plastic bags of Chinese food and quipped, "Let me guess, you're starving!"

"How did you know?" Abbie asked seemingly seriously.

"Wild guess," she made her way to the dining room table where she began dispensing the food to each of the four place settings.

Abbie walked in behind her and said, "It's so sad what happened to Brandon. He was always so nice."

"Yes he was," she gave Abbie a comforting hug.

"They're letting school out at noon tomorrow because of the hurricane," Abbie informed them.

Taylor asked, "Is Mrs. Davis able to pick you up then?"

"Yes."

"Alright, I want you to come home and stay. If the storm gets really bad we'll go to the storm shelter at the police station, okay?"

"Okay."

The four of them shared General Tso's Chicken and Wonton Soup, Fried Rice and Egg Rolls, while the conversation was steered away from the horror of Holt's murder and the investigation for Abbie's sake. When dinner was finished, Abbie excused herself and went to the bathroom. While they were in the kitchen cleaning up, Riley said, "I have an idea. It might not amount to anything but you never know. I think we should pay a visit to Kyle Stanton."

"He's in a coma," Evans stated the obvious.

"I know but he seems to be at the epicenter of all of our troubles."

"Are you channeling Andy O'Neil again?" He asked her.

Riley smiled, "Yeah, I guess I am."

Taylor shrugged, "Why not."

Suddenly Abbie was in the doorway. "Why would you want to see a guy that's in a coma?"

Taylor turned to her and asked, "Are you eavesdropping?"

"Didn't mean to."

Evans added, "I guess it wouldn't hurt to check on his condition."

Abbie offered, "It doesn't sound like it's going to help any."

Riley thought her comment was odd until she realized that Abbie probably had no idea how desperate they were for some kind of a break in the case.

Taylor's phone rang and when she saw it was the station, she was hoping they'd picked up Travis or Nathan Miller. She answered, "Chief Taylor."

It was Jasmine Fisher, the second shift 911 operator, "Chief, we have a situation at the Beechnut Tree Mobile Home Park."

"Oh, God, what?"

"We started getting calls about a fight so I dispatched units over there, then we just got a call about a stabbing so I've got an ambulance heading that way."

Taylor exhaled a frustrated groan, "Okay, Jasmine, I'm heading that way."

"Okay."

Taylor looked at Evans and Riley and told them, "A fight and a stabbing at the Beechnut Tree Mobile Home Park."

"Oh, good Lord!" Evans blurted out but his next thought was maybe this is something that might put them on the right track of the killer.

Taylor turned to Abbie and directed, "Stay home and keep the doors locked."

"I will," she assured her.

Evans and Riley rode with Taylor in her patrol car and three minutes later they arrived at the scene. At a few minutes past sunset, they could make out three patrol cars with their flashing red and blue lights, parked on the main road that ran through the park. Taylor pulled in behind the last police car and the three of them got out. Taylor could see dozens of people milling about, apparently spectators. It evoked memories of a year ago when apparently the seminal moment of their investigation occurred. The first police officer to spot Taylor was Brian Hennessey, the most experienced officer on the force. He came over to them and said, "Hey, Chief."

"Hey, Brian, what happened?"

He pulled a small notepad out of his breast pocket and referred to it, "We've got one transported to the hospital with knife wounds to the abdomen. Condition unknown but the paramedics were worried when they loaded him up."

"Who was it?"

"Tyler Gesicki, thirty-nine years of age."

"He's a plumber isn't he?"

"Yeah, that's his work van right there," he pointed to the white vehicle parked in the driveway of a mobile home two doors away.

"What happened?"

"According to his wife Katherine, it was just getting dark when their fourteen year old daughter Peyton was in the bathroom and she saw someone peeking through the blinds at her. She went and told her dad and he went storming out there. At first she said he didn't have a knife with him, then she admitted that he grabbed a kitchen knife on his way out. There was a fight and somehow he lost control of the knife and got stabbed with it."

"Do we know who it is?"

"You're going to love this, Blake Archer."

"Skylar's boyfriend!"

"Yep, he ran off when Katherine and Peyton started screaming and several people watched him run one street over to Skylar's house, jump in his old red pickup truck and tore out of here."

Evans muttered, "Red pickup truck again."

"Have we issued an APB?" Asked Taylor.

"Just did, for him and his truck."

"Good. You might alert Tampa PD, he lives there."

"Right away, Chief."

"Brian," she stopped him, "Did his wife and daughter go to the hospital already?"

"Yeah, they've already gone."

"Okay," Taylor turned to Evans and Riley, "I guess we're on the way to the hospital."

Five minutes later, they pulled into the parking lot of Delaney's small hospital. When they went inside, Katherine and Peyton Gesicki were seated all by themselves in the waiting room. Taylor, followed by Evans and Riley, walked up to them and introduced themselves, "Katherine, I'm Chief of Police Samantha Taylor and this is F.B.I. agents Evans and Riley. How is he doing?"

"He's in surgery but a nurse was just out here and said they're confident he'll pull through so we're very relieved."

"Oh, good," Taylor said, "Can you tell us what happened?"

"My daughter Peyton saw a man at the bathroom window and came running into the living room and told us about it. Tyler jumped up and grabbed a knife and ran outside. He apparently caught up with the guy at the back of the house. By the time Peyton and I got out on the back porch they were already fighting. Next thing I know, Tyler is yelling that he was cut, so Peyton and I started screaming and the guy ran off. We ran to Tyler and his shirt was soaked in blood. I called 911 and Peyton ran into the house and got a towel and we tried to stop the bleeding."

"Did you get a look at the guy?"

"Not a very good one, it was too dark. I could tell he was young and white and that's about it."

"Peyton, did you see the guy at the window?" Taylor asked.

"There was a gap in the blinds so I saw his eyes and maybe his nose but that's about it. He was right up against the window."

Katherine continued, "Some of the neighbors said it was Skylar Pittman's boyfriend but I'm not familiar with him."

"Did you know Skylar?"

"No. I knew who she was and would see her around but I've never met her. I heard her funeral was scheduled for Monday."

"Yeah it was pushed back from Saturday to Monday because of the hurricane."

"I feel terrible for that girl but if that was her boyfriend, he needs to be caught and pay for what he did. He could have killed Tyler!"

"I know," Taylor said, "We know where he lives so we should be able to get ahold of him soon."

"Oh good."

"Would you mind coming to the station tomorrow morning to give us a statement detailing everything that happened?"

"Not at all, do you need one from Peyton?"

"If she could just write one out, that should be okay."

"Alright, we sure will."

Taylor handed her a card and said, "If you need anything don't hesitate to call me."

"Okay, thanks."

"We hope Tyler gets better soon."

"Thank you."

Before they left, Taylor, Evans, and Riley all wished Tyler a speedy recovery and bid them farewell.

Once they were back in the car, Riley admitted, "I'm not up to speed on Blake Archer yet."

"Skylar Pittman's boyfriend," Evans began, "He's the one who reported her missing. Seemed genuinely distraught when her body was found. We confirmed that at least his phone was in Tampa during the hours that Skylar was murdered. He claimed he was home alone but we haven't been able to confirm it yet. He participated in a lot of Skylar's adult videos."

"Is it too much of a stretch to say that since he's not getting what he's used to because Skylar is dead, that he's out peeping in a young girl's windows?" Asked Riley.

"Apparently not," Evans answered.

"Is it possible he's our killer?" Riley asked.

"Before tonight I would have said, I doubt it. Now, I'm not so sure," Evans admitted.

Taylor added, "Well, he may or may not have been peeping but it's possible it was self defense."

Evans was a little surprised that Taylor would offer that as a possible scenario. "Running would seem to indicate guilt."

"Yeah," Taylor agreed, "He could be scared though."

"Bottom line, we have to add him to our growing list of suspects with Travis, Nathan Miller, and Tommy Dalton."

Taylor shook her head in dismay as she drove home, "I can't believe we haven't found Travis or Nathan Miller yet."

"I know," Evans agreed. "I hope we find them before there's another murder."

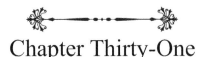

Chapter Thirty-One

Friday morning was hectic with preparations for Hurricane Walter's impending landfall later that day. Complicating matters was the lack of success in finding Travis Reynolds, Nathan Miller, or Blake Archer. By late morning Taylor, Evans, and Riley decided to eat lunch and then make the twenty-five minute drive to the county hospital to check on Kyle Stanton. At 1:30 P.M. Taylor parked her patrol car in the visitor parking lot of the three story medical facility. When they walked in through the automatic front doors, the three of them made their way to the information desk. Taylor spoke up to the middle aged woman behind the counter. "Hello, I'm Samantha Taylor, the Chief of Police over in Delaney and these are F.B.I. agents Evans and Riley."

"How can I help you?"

"We need to speak with someone with knowledge about one of your patients."

"Alright, what's their name?"

"Kyle Stanton."

The woman looked at Taylor with a peculiar expression and finally said, "Give me one minute," she picked up the phone and dialed a number. "Joanna, the police and F.B.I. are here about Kyle Stanton. Okay," she hung up and said, "The Director of Nursing will be right down."

"Thank you."

Two minutes later, a brunette in her forties wearing nursing scrubs walked into the lobby and introduced herself. "Hi, I'm Joanna Perkins, Nursing Director."

"Hi, I'm Delaney Chief of Police Samantha Taylor and these are F.B.I. agents Michael Evans and Emma Riley."

"What can I do for you?"

"We'd like to check on Kyle Stanton's condition and maybe ask a few questions."

"Oh sure, follow me," she turned and started walking toward the pair of doors that she had just come out of, "He hasn't had a visitor in over six months."

Taylor was stunned to hear that. "Wait a minute, you said he had a visitor six months ago?"

Perkins grinned, "Officially no but unofficially yes."

Evans interjected, "What does that mean?"

Perkins stopped walking and her expression became more serious, obviously being taken aback by Evans' abruptness. "I'm sorry, I just assumed all law enforcement knew about his visitor."

"No, we don't. Who was it?" Taylor was suddenly excited about the possibility of a lead.

"We don't know who it was."

"Someone was visiting this man and you don't know who it was?" Evans' voice displayed an uncharacteristically frustrating tone. "Do you know his reputation?"

"I think I better start from the beginning. Kyle Stanton was transferred here a year ago. He's been in a vegetative state ever since. The first few months he was in our ICU with various conditions that are common in comatose patients. For instance, he had a real problem with pneumonia. Anyway, when he became well enough to transfer to a long term care facility, there were no takers. Literally no one wanted him. It became a real legal, interagency, bureaucratic battle that continues to this day. So we moved him into a private room to free up an ICU bed and he's been there ever since. Late one night about seven months ago, the on duty nurse saw on a remote monitor that he had a slight uptick in brain activity. She went to his room but there didn't appear to be any change in his condition but right there on the table beside him was a cup of water. It was not there the last time she checked. She dismissed it as maybe one of the staff had done it without her knowledge. A few weeks later, that same nurse noticed the monitor showing an increase in Stanton's brain wave activity again. This time she rushed from the nurses' station and actually saw someone coming out of his room. She called for them to stop but they didn't and the nurse decided to check on Stanton rather than follow the person."

Taylor, Evans, and Riley all exchanged looks of astonishment and excitement. Riley beat them to the punch, "Can you describe this person?"

"I can't but the nurse that was on duty that night can. She's working upstairs right now."

Taylor told her definitively, "We need to talk to her right away."

"Okay," Perkins led the way through the doors and to the elevator.

Evans noticed the security cameras in the hall. While they entered the elevator he asked her, "Were you able to catch the person on video?"

"We sure did. That's how we figured out how they were getting in without coming through the front door and checking in at the nurse's station."

As the elevator ascended to the third floor, Evans asked, "And how was that?"

"Through the dock doors where deliveries are made. They still would've had to pass through a locked door to get to the third floor. They either worked here at one time and still had a key or they picked the lock, at least that's what the sheriff's department thought."

"The sheriff's department knew about this intruder?" Evans was almost shouting.

"Yes, they came out and viewed the video."

"You have video of this person?" Evans was furious but incredibly excited at the same time.

"Well, we did but not anymore. We only keep security video for six months. The person hasn't been back since. I think they knew we were on to them."

"Did the sheriff's department get a copy?"

"No. There didn't appear to be a crime committed so I don't think they took it very seriously."

As the elevator doors opened, Evans frustration overflowed and he spewed, "Fuck!" When he realized he'd startled the nurse he apologized, "Sorry."

Nurse Perkins led them to the third floor nurse's station where a thirty something year old nurse in scrubs was manning the desk. She introduced her co-worker. "This is Holly Whitworth. Holly, this is Police Chief Taylor and F.B.I. agents Evans and Riley."

"Oh," she seemed surprised.

Taylor started off the questioning, "Holly, before we talk about Kyle Stanton, can you tell us about this visitor of his?"

"Oh sure. I work the graveyard shift quite a bit and when Stanton was moved into his own room there were a couple of times when I did my rounds that I got a weird feeling that someone had been in his room. Nothing seemed disturbed and Stanton certainly was no different so I thought it was my imagination. Then one night I noticed on his monitor that we have here at the nurse's station, an increase in his brain activity. So I walked down there and I found a cup of water on his bedside table. I could have sworn it wasn't there earlier but again, I thought maybe I had missed seeing it or one of the staff had come in after me and left it there. Then a couple of weeks later, about 3:00 in the morning, his brain activity goes up once again..."

Evans interjected, "I'm sorry to interrupt but when was this?"

"Oh, six or seven months ago."

Taylor and Evans exchanged glances, each thinking the same thing. That is when Cameron Preston was shot and killed, their second victim and the first one that was definitely a murder.

Holly continued, "As soon as I saw the spikes in brain activity I quickly walked that way," she pointed down the corridor to her left, "His room is down that hall and around the corner on the right. By the time I turned the corner someone was coming out of his room. I said, excuse me, ma'am..."

"It was a woman?" Evans asked with excitement.

"I think it was more like a girl."

Riley couldn't help herself and jumped in, "Can you describe her?"

"Well, I never saw her face..."

Taylor emitted a frustrated growling sound and then asked, "How old do you think she was?"

"I'd say, twenties maybe, but she could've been younger, like I said I didn't see her face."

"What was she wearing?" Evans asked expectantly.

"A gray hoodie, jeans, and tennis shoes which were maybe blue, but I'm not sure."

"Did you see her hair color?" Taylor asked.

"No, she had the hood pulled up over her head. When I called to her she briefly stopped and almost turned my way but then it was like she thought better of it and immediately turned away and headed toward the end of the hall. There's nothing down there except the stairwell so I made an instantaneous decision to go in and check on Stanton rather than follow the girl. Since he was alright, and I guess from your reaction, I probably should have gone after her instead."

Riley asked, "If you didn't see her face, how do you know she was a girl?"

"Her size and her shape...I'm sorry. I'm such an idiot. I should've already told you, the way she walked would give her away in a second."

"What do you mean?" Asked Evans.

"Well, that girl obviously had Cerebral palsy."

Evans and Riley looked at Taylor's suddenly stunned expression but it was Riley that asked, "Why do you say that?"

"Well, being a nurse I'm familiar with that condition. She basically dragged her right foot behind her when she walked and she held her right hand up against her side kind of awkwardly. It was clear that she was neurologically affected on the right side of her body. That's another way I know it was a girl, her hands and fingers were feminine."

They were all stunned and quiet for a long few moments, each thinking the same seemingly impossible thing. Could that have been Abbie? Finally Riley asked, "Have you seen anyone else at this hospital with that condition?"

"No. I've been here four years and that was the first time. It's just not very common in a small community type setting such as this. I was employed in Miami before I worked here and we had CP patients there. It's pretty unmistakable."

Evans asked, "Did cameras pick up a vehicle this person was driving?"

"No, she must've parked on an adjacent street because after she walked out of the door, video showed her crossing the parking lot and out of the camera's view."

Taylor looked as though she was in a state of shock and even Evans had a look of confused disbelief on his face. When both were silent for a long few moments, Riley spoke up, "Could we look in on Stanton?"

Perkins told Whitworth, "Go ahead, Holly, I'll watch your station."

"Sure, follow me," Whitworth led them down the hall, around the corner, and into Stanton's room. There were wires and tubes, a heart monitor and a bag of fluids attached to his 6'6" frame that had obviously lost a great deal of weight.

The four of them stood around his bed but it was Riley who spoke first, "What's his prognosis?"

"He suffered extensive trauma to his cerebral cortex so after this long in a coma his chances of recovery are very low."

"You said his brain activity increased during the mystery person's visits?"

Whitworth nodded her head, "Yeah, we constantly monitor his brain activity with an EEG, a non-invasive method. There has been an occasional uptick but they're hardly detectable and so far non-sustainable."

"What would cause that?"

"That is a matter of debate within the medical community. We had a neurologist who speculated that Stanton knew the person that visited him but was only aware of them on an almost subconscious level."

Evans asked her, "You say the girl hasn't been back over the last six months?"

"Right. We changed the locks on all the doors and security installed a special lock on that back door that is apparently hard to pick if that's what she did."

"You said the sheriff's department knew about this, can you remember was it the sheriff himself?"

"Oh, no. It was a deputy and he only came out here once. I think he said at the time that this person apparently hadn't done anything wrong so there was no crime."

After a long period of silence, Taylor, still looking like she didn't feel very well, offered Whitworth her card and said, "If he gets a visitor of any kind or his condition changes will you please give me a call?"

"I sure will."

Taylor, Evans, and Riley left the room, went down the hall, took the elevator down to the ground floor, walked through the lobby and out through the front doors without saying a word to each other. The clouds that had been rolling in all day were now getting darker and moving faster and the wind had begun to pick up considerably. The leading edge of Hurricane Walter's outer bands had arrived. Taylor's experience told her the deterioration in the weather would begin to accelerate but that was not what was on her mind. When they were all back in the car she said, "Well, we know that person was not Abbie."

From the front passenger seat Evans glanced at Riley in the back but her expression was impassive. He said, "Let's talk this through."

Taylor looked at him with surprise, "You don't seriously think that could be Abbie?"

"I just think we need to talk about it, that's all."

Taylor looked into the rear view mirror and made eye contact with Riley but when she apparently didn't have anything to add, Taylor said, "Okay, let's talk about it."

"The girl she described could be Abbie," Evans began, "There can't be many people, if any, who fit that description in the whole county. She said she hasn't seen anyone with that condition here in four years."

"That doesn't mean it's her," Taylor argued, "This was seven months ago. Abbie doesn't drive, how did she get here?"

"You told me that Abbie had not gotten her driver's license yet because she needed to practice her driving skills since they were difficult for her to master but that she can do it."

"Okay, seven months ago, she was still living at home with her parents. What did she do, sneak out of the house in the middle of the night, steal her parent's car and drive here to visit a comatose career criminal? Do you realize how crazy that sounds?"

Evans steeled himself for the question he knew was not going to be well received by Taylor. "How certain are you that Cameron was Abbie's dad?"

Taylor looked at him like he was insane. "Are you fucking kidding! Are you saying that Kyle Stanton is actually Abbie's father?"

"No, I'm just asking the question. Sam, the stakes are so high, we can't overlook any possibility."

"Michael, you've been here for a week and a half. You know Abbie wouldn't hurt a fly."

"I know it seems impossible."

"It is impossible!" She yelled. She started the car and forcefully put it into gear, "We've got to head back."

While she drove Evans continued, "Sam, I'm going to ask you a tough question. Just understand it's because it has to be asked. Is there any way that Olivia would have kept a secret about being sexually assaulted?"

"No! Absolutely not!" Taylor was certain. "She always told me everything about her life. If that had happened, there's no way she would've kept that from me."

"If we didn't know Abbie was so nice and sweet, I could concoct a scenario for our entire case," Evans told them.

"Okay, let's hear it," Taylor responded angrily.

"Don't be mad at me, I'm just hypothesizing."

"Alright," despite saying she wasn't, she was furious that he would think Abbie capable of murder.

"Abbie was practicing her driving and accidentally strikes and kills Aaron Driscoll. Cameron, whether he is or isn't her father, begins to suspect her in the hit and run so she shoots him to keep him quiet. Olivia begins to suspect her in his death and Abbie kills her. She was the one who found her body after all. Next, maybe Darius Kelly killed himself or someone else exacted revenge on him for his part in attacking Stanton. Then Jonah Sutherland let someone into his house, somebody he didn't suspect would harm him. He gets whacked in the back of the head with a hammer and then bludgeoned to death. Anyone can kill with a hammer. Skylar was killed by Nathan Miller or maybe her boyfriend Blake. And then there was Brandon. He too let someone in his house that he trusted. Apparently a female. He had been a customer of Skylar, even if it was online, since she was eighteen. Abbie is almost seventeen."

Taylor couldn't believe what she had just heard. She defiantly said, "You've seen the crime scene photos of Abbie's parents. You saw Jonah Sutherland's body, as well as Skylar's and Brandon's. Do you really think Abbie is capable of that?"

Evans exhaled a heavy sigh. "No. I can't see Abbie harming anyone."

Taylor looked in the rear view mirror and asked, "Emma, what do you think?"

"Do you remember last night when we were discussing coming over to the county hospital to see Stanton?"

"Yeah."

"Abbie said something to the effect of, 'Why would you want to see a guy that's in a coma?' and 'It doesn't sound like anything that would help you.' I got the weird feeling that she was almost trying to talk us out of going."

"Are you taking his side?" Taylor blurted out.

"Sam, we're all on the same side. We're just trying to figure this out. My big case last year was a teenage girl who kidnapped three of her classmates and shot and killed my partner. No one suspected her. I've learned to have a very open mind."

"I'm going to call her," Taylor said, pulling her phone out and pressing the right contact number.

"I wouldn't tell her anything about this," Evans advised.

"No, of course not," she listened as voicemail picked up without a ring, "That's strange. It went right to voicemail, Abbie it's me. I'm just checking on you, the weather is turning bad already. Call me back ASAP."

Evans asked, "Does that happen very often?"

Taylor shook her head, "No. She almost always answers but if she doesn't, it rings a few times before voicemail picks up."

"Any chance the battery went dead?"

"She is constantly charging that thing."

Riley added, "The timing is odd."

Fighting a growing sense of fear and anxiety, Taylor thought for a brief moment then said, "I'm going to drive straight to the house and check on her. I told her to stay there."

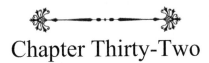

Chapter Thirty-Two

At 3:00 o'clock, Taylor pulled the patrol car into her driveway, still unable to reach Abbie by phone. By now, with the weather rapidly getting darker and windier, her level of worry had grown to a point where she almost felt sick to her stomach. She jumped out of the car and ran toward the front door with Evans and Riley trailing behind. When she got to the door, she grabbed the knob, preparing to insert the key but the door was unlocked. For a split second she was mad but it was just as instantly smothered by her concern for Abbie. She swung the door open and yelled, "Abbie!"

When there was no answer, that all too familiar feeling of dread, that had preceded so many tragedies, felt like a hand gripping her around the throat. She ran toward Abbie's bedroom with another yell, "Abbie!"

The lamp on the nightstand was on and sitting on the floor was Abbie's school backpack emblazoned with her name on it. Taylor grabbed it and unzipped the side pocket and her heart sank. Inside was Abbie's wallet and keys, something Taylor knew she wouldn't go anywhere without. She was looking around the bedroom for any clue about where Abbie might be when Evans appeared in the doorway. He asked, "Is her phone here?"

"I don't see it but her keys and wallet are. Dammit Michael, she wouldn't go anywhere without these."

Evans could hear the worry and panic in her voice, "Sam, we're going to find her. Why don't you stay here and start calling her friends. She could be with some of them and she might come right back. Emma and I will run over to her parents house in case she's over there for some reason."

"Okay, there's Lily and Ava and my God, she has so many friends," Taylor nervously scrolled through the contacts in her phone.

Riley met Evans in the hallway and she told him, "It doesn't look like she's anywhere else in the house."

"Let's run over to her parent's house and check."

When they were back in Riley's rental car she asked him, "What do you think is going on?"

"I wish the Hell I knew."

As she backed out of the driveway Riley stated the obvious, "It's awfully coincidental she's missing and not answering her phone right after we go to the hospital and find out about Stanton's visitor."

Evans shook his head in dismay, "How could that not be Abbie at the hospital? But how is it possible she could be a cold blooded killer?"

"You know, I didn't want to say anything in front of Sam but there's another possibility."

"What's that?"

"That it could have been Abbie at the hospital but someone else is committing the murders."

"I hadn't considered that," his mind raced with all of the potential connections between people necessary to make that scenario possible.

"A DNA test would resolve whether her father is Kyle Stanton or not."

"The only problem with that is it would take weeks to get a result not to mention that she's a minor with no immediate legal guardian."

"It would be interesting to see what her answer would be if we asked her though."

"If she refused that would be a red flag."

"We've got red flags all over the place."

Three minutes later Riley pulled into the driveway of Abbie's parent's house. With the rapidly darkening skies, they could tell there were no lights on inside the house and both Cameron and Olivia's cars were parked in front of the garage. Evans said, "Let's check the doors."

Riley headed for the front door and Evans went around to the back but the house was locked up tight. They knocked loudly but there was no response. They met back at the car and decided to return to Taylor's house.

Five minutes later they pulled into Taylor's driveway just as the first rain began to fall and it looked as though every light in the house was on. Taylor met them at the front door and she was clearly anxious and distressed. She told them, "I've called her ten closest friends and no one has seen her. I called it in and every officer on the force, except the third shift, is out looking for her."

Evans closed the front door behind them and said, "Why don't you call your friend at the state police and have them track her phone?"

"Yes! Thank you, Michael," she dialed his number and when he answered she said, "Cory, I've got an emergency. I've got a missing sixteen year old girl and I need her phone located."

"What's the number?"

"863-555-4782."

"Alright, Sam, I'll get right on it."

"Thanks, Cory."

"Abbie's parent's house is dark and locked up," Evans said.

"I was so frazzled I didn't think that if her keys were here she wouldn't be able to get in over there."

Riley asked, "Does she have any other family?"

"No, that's why she's staying with me."

Evans had a thought, "You could call your sheriff friend and have them look out for her and at the same time you could ask him about the hospital visitor."

"Good idea," she looked his number up in her phone and dialed it.

Sheriff Anderson answered, "Hello, Sam."

"Mark, I've got an emergency."

"What is it?"

"The sixteen year old daughter of my second and third victims is missing. She's the one who's been staying with me."

"What's her name?"

"Abigail Preston, she goes by Abbie."

"Does she have a license?"

"Not yet."

"Okay, describe her."

"She's about 5'3", maybe 115 pounds, light brown hair, and green eyes. She suffers from Cerebral palsy so she walks with a limp."

"I'll get the word out to my deputies right away."

"Thank you, Mark, but I have a question also. Do you remember about six or seven months ago getting a call from the county hospital about a late night visitor to Kyle Stanton?"

"No, it doesn't ring a bell but I can research it and find out for you."

"Yeah, when you get a chance, obviously finding Abbie is the top priority."

"I'm on it, Sam."

"Thank you, Mark."

"Bye."

Taylor hung up and began to pace, worried sick about where Abbie was and if she was okay. She knew beyond a shadow of doubt that Abbie wasn't running or hiding but could not help fearing the worst for the most beautiful soul that she had ever known. Seventeen minutes later her phone rang and she answered and held her breath.

Cory said, "The phone for the number you gave me has been turned off since 12:45 and the last place it was on was at your house, Sam."

Evans and Riley watched Taylor's expression and body language and knew it wasn't good news.

"Dammit," Taylor uttered, "Can you do me a favor and continue to track it and let me know if it comes back on?"

"We sure will, Sam, I'm sorry."

"Thank you, Cory," she hung up and told them, "Her phone's been off since 12:45 and the last time it was on was here."

Evans rubbed his face in his hands and said, "I was afraid of that."

"Dammit, Michael, somebody has her! They came in here and took her away!"

"Sam, we don't know that," Evans tried to calm her.

"Well, she's not on the run. Where would she go? She has no money and nobody has seen her!"

Riley jumped in, "If she was abducted, why would they take her phone but turn it off?"

With her anxiety at a fever pitch, Taylor said, "I don't know but I can't just sit here."

When she started heading for the door Evans called to her, "Sam, there's going to be hurricane force winds in the next hour or so."

"I know, that's why I need to be out there on patrol with my officers. There's going to be wind damage and high water. Besides, I have to keep busy."

Riley asked, "Do you want me to go with you?"

"No, you guys stay here in case she comes back."

Evans said, "I have an idea. One of us will stay here and the other can canvass your neighbors to see if they saw anything."

Taylor nodded, "Good idea. There's an extra rain slicker in the hall closet. Let me know what you find out."

"Okay, be careful, Sam."

Taylor opened the door and instead of commenting on the rapidly worsening wind and rain, turned and tearfully said, "Michael, if anything happens to her, I don't think I can take it."

"I know," Evans said sympathetically, "We're going to find her, Sam."

Taylor closed the door behind her and ran out into the growing storm, feeling guilty for having the fleeting thought that a deranged killer might end up more deadly than a monster hurricane.

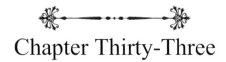

Chapter Thirty-Three

A half hour before the normal time for sunset, it was almost as dark as night. The rain was coming down in torrents and the wind was gusting up to seventy-five miles an hour. Taylor had already assisted in two high water rescues and Evans had updated her that he and Riley had not yet found a neighbor who had seen anyone around her house that afternoon. They speculated that most of the people who were not at work were hunkered down watching cable news coverage of the hurricane. As Taylor slowly made her way down an almost deserted Main Street, her phone rang. When she saw the name she screamed, "Abbie!" She swerved toward the curb and slammed on her brakes causing her patrol car to skid across the rain saturated street and smash into two parking space concrete bumpers. Her heart suddenly racing, she answered breathlessly, "Abbie!"

"Sam, listen carefully," Abbie said in a surprisingly calm voice.

"Oh thank God you're alive!"

"Sam, listen. I have to read a note to you from my kidnapper."

Her heart sank, her voice barely audible, "Okay."

"I am willing to exchange Abbie for you. It is you I want, not her. You are to immediately drive out to Abiaka Island, on Tommy Dalton's ranch, by yourself. If you don't come alone I will slit Abbie's throat. I can see anyone approaching the island, so if the police or F.B.I. follows you, I will slit Abbie's throat. You will be searched. If you bring a weapon I will slit Abbie's throat. You are to take the small motorboat from the dock to the island. Sam, please do as they say…" the phone disconnected.

"Abbie!" She was gone. "Oh my God!" Taylor screamed, her mind suddenly flooded with 'what if's' and 'what to do's.' She tried to think clearly and make the best decision but she knew she didn't have any time to spare. She knew she couldn't go out there with other officers because there would be no sneaking up on that island without advance planning and any delay put Abbie at further risk.

She didn't trust this person to uphold their end of the deal but if she brought anyone with her, it would almost certainly mean Abbie's immediate death and she couldn't risk that. She quickly made up her mind. She would head that way and wait fifteen minutes before she called Evans and Riley to follow her. That would give her time to secure Abbie's release or try and turn the tables on the killer. If her plan failed, maybe the agents could catch the perpetrator before they got away. She pulled away from the curb and drove east toward the highway that would lead to Dalton's Ranch. She thought, of course, Dalton's ranch! Travis, Nathan Miller, and Blake Archer probably didn't even know the island existed. They certainly wouldn't know the Dalton family's name for it. That could only mean the killer is Tommy Dalton! She thought about the possible reasons why Dalton would be committing these murders. He was a registered sex offender after all. He had a dark obsession with Skylar Pittman. He had the opportunities to commit the murders and a truck like his was spotted not far from where Jonah Sutherland was killed. And lastly, he was furious with her for talking to his wife and kids when he wasn't there. He even said she was going to be sorry for what she'd done. That's why Abbie's kidnapper said, 'It is you I want, not Abbie.' It had to be Dalton! He had completely fooled her early on, but now she had finally figured it out. She wondered about his wife and kids. Were they going to be there when she arrived? She could only hope and pray they were safe and away from the scene. She drove through sheets of wind driven rain, almost hydroplaning several times. She forced herself to slow down because she knew that if she wrecked and the car was undrivable, Abbie was almost certainly doomed.

Taylor watched the clock on the dashboard and when fifteen minutes had elapsed, she called Evans' phone and he answered, "Hey, Sam."

She tried to be concise and not emotional, "Michael, Abbie called me."

"Great! Is she alright?"

"No, she was reading me a note from her kidnapper. He wants to exchange Abbie for me."

"What?"

"Michael, I think the killer and Abbie's abductor is Tommy Dalton."

"Why?"

"The note Abbie read from said for me to come out to Abiaka Island. Tommy is the only one of our suspects who would know that name. I was told to immediately drive out there or they would slit Abbie's throat."

"Okay, where are you? We'll follow you out there."

"They said if anyone came with me or followed me they would kill Abbie by immediately cutting her throat."

"Okay, so we'll hang back and approach the ranch from a different direction and not go up the driveway with you."

"That's why I decided to give myself a fifteen minute head start."

"Dammit, Sam! That's too long! Slow down and let us catch up with you."

"I can't do that, Michael, this is Abbie's life we're talking about!"

"Sam, you can't trust a cold blooded killer!"

"I know, if it's a trap and I can't figure a way out, that's when you come in."

Evans yelled, "Emma! We have to roll now!" He continued, "Sam, at least slow down a little, a lot can happen in fifteen minutes."

The rain had gotten so bad she had to slow down even more anyway. She said, "Okay, I will. Be careful, conditions are terrible."

"Alright, we're leaving your house right now, Sam, please slow down!"

"Michael, I want to tell you a couple of things. Thank you for everything you've done to help me through this."

"Thank me when you see me."

"And, I had to make an instantaneous decision so if I'm wrong on my timing, just know that I did it to try and save Abbie. If we don't make it, kill that son of a bitch."

"Alright, just slow down and we'll get as close behind you as we can."

"Tell Emma thank you too."

"Okay, see you soon."

"Bye," she hung up and realized her eyes were full of tears. Two minutes away from the ranch her phone rang. It was Cory and she knew what he would say. "Hey, Cory."

"Sam, that phone pinged out at the Dalton Ranch for just a minute!"

"I know, I'm almost there."

"Oh, great!"

"How fast can you get State Police assets to the ranch?"

"In these conditions, at least thirty to forty minutes."

"Will you do so, it's an emergency. Our killer is there."

"Damn! Alright, who is it?"

"I think it's Tommy Dalton."

"Okay, consider it done."

"Cory, I want to thank you for all you've done for me."

"Hey, you can pay me back next time."

"Yeah, next time," she answered sadly, her voice breaking.

"We're on our way, Sam."

"Thanks," she hung up and realized those tears were now rolling down her cheeks. As she pulled through the open gate to the Dalton Ranch, she knew in her heart, she had said goodbye to those two men for the last time. As she drove along the sandy, gravel driveway, she tried to think ahead. She was instructed to take a motorboat to the island, which meant she probably wouldn't be searched until she got there. She made the decision that she would hide, as best she could, her service weapon on the boat. That way if things went badly and she made it back that far, she'd at least be able to defend herself. As she pulled into the clearing, she could see the Dalton's vehicles: the white SUV and the old red pickup truck. Taylor could not see through the darkness, rain, and trees, a vehicle that was hidden farther back into the woods. If she could have seen it, she would have recognized it. She parked in front of the dock, left her phone on the front seat, and pulled her hat down over her head as far as she could. When she opened the door and got out, the rain pelted her like stinging nettles and her yellow rain slicker fluttered and snapped in the fierce wind like a flag in a squall. She made her way down the length of the dock to where a twelve foot long, aluminum boat was being tossed back and forth in the choppy water. She lowered herself into it and stepped into about two inches of water on the bottom. She untied the rope and the wind pushed the boat away from the dock. She sat down beside the motor and yanked on the pull cord twice and it started up. She pointed the bow toward the lights, barely visible through the deluge, on the island a hundred and fifty yards away. The only things in the boat were two orange life jackets. She picked up one and placed it on the bench in front of her and tucked her 9mm service weapon underneath it. She remembered her training, that even a wet gun will fire. As she approached the dock on the island, she could see it was illuminated by a street light mounted high up on a metal pole. The only other vessel present was the white ski boat that she'd seen on her previous trips. She cut the motor off and bumped the tires encasing the dock. She grabbed one of the dock poles and wrapped the rope around it before tying a knot to secure the boat. She climbed up onto the wooden dock and shielded her eyes from the pouring rain to look toward the house. From her vantage point, it appeared to have a wraparound porch with overhead lights that illuminated outdoor furniture. There were four windows on one side of the house and a door flanked by four more windows on the other side. Leaning into the wind with the rain peppering her, Taylor walked along the dock and stepped off onto the row of pavestones that ascended the hill which the one story house was perched on. When she reached the house she stepped up onto the large porch, and when she was out of the rain, pulled off her rain slicker and tossed it aside. She wanted to show there was nowhere for her to hide a gun. She realized the closer she had gotten to the house, the slower she moved, perhaps subconsciously hoping Evans and Riley would catch up to her. She wondered how in the world they were going to be able to get to the island without a boat. Never before had she ever felt fear and dread like this. The front door was slightly ajar and Taylor slowly pushed it open with one hand and kept the other raised above her head. She called out, "I'm here! By myself!" She stepped into the doorway and looked inside. She froze. Standing eight feet in front of her was a person dressed in all black clothes, a black ski mask, and black gloves. In the person's right, gloved hand was a handgun pointing directly at Taylor. She was struck by the small size of the person. Maybe 5'4" and slightly built, but it was the eyes, large and dark, that were mesmerizing. They stood silently staring at each other, like two wild west gunfighters in a showdown. Only here, there was just one gun. Taylor forced herself to look past the black clad figure and there was Abbie, tied to a dining room type chair with duct tape over her mouth. Her hands were apparently tied behind the back of the chair and her ankles were secured to the legs of the chair with rope. On the other side of the room, Tommy Dalton was tied to another chair with rope, his mouth taped over as well. For some reason he was wearing only his underwear. While Abbie's eyes were surprisingly calm looking, Tommy's were wide and filled with absolute terror. Taylor knew then Tommy Dalton wasn't the killer.

The black clothed person pointed to the floor and Taylor knew what they wanted her to do. With both hands raised, she stepped into what looked to be a living room or a den and got down first on all fours and then lay flat on the hardwood floor. The dark figure walked behind her, yanked her hat off, and the next thing Taylor felt was the barrel of a gun pressing up against the back of her head. She held her breath, bracing for the next second to be the last of her life. The person grabbed Taylor's right wrist and pulled it roughly behind her back. Then the unmistakable sound of handcuffs clicked around her wrist. Next, her left arm was pulled back and the other cuff clamped tightly. With the gun still pressed to her head, the person began to search Taylor. The torso, legs, and even pulled her shoes off. It was a very thorough search. Taylor had the impression that it was as if a police officer was searching her. Next, a length of rope was tied very tightly around her ankles and Taylor knew she was totally at this person's mercy. She was forcefully pulled up into a seated position, her long legs stretched out in front of her. The person stood over her, slid the handgun into a hip holster and then slowly, as if with a dramatic flair, pulled the ski mask off of their face.

Taylor's mouth dropped open. There standing in front of her, was Officer Leah Thorson! All Taylor could do was shake her head in stunned disbelief.

Thorson grinned widely and exclaimed, "I love doing that!"

Taylor managed to utter, "Leah, why?"

"Kyle Stanton was my father," she watched as Taylor's face registered incredulity and then Thorson suddenly glared at her with an intense, menacing gaze and proclaimed, "My vengeance will breathe forever!" She paused to take a deep breath, as if composing herself, and continued, "I periodically went to visit him in the hospital, late at night when very few people were around. I made sure I limped so the security video would make it look like Abbie stumbling around in case your investigation ever went that far. I'm surprised you were smart enough to figure that out. Then that nurse caught me leaving his room which meant I would no longer be able to visit him. That really pisses me off. Tell me, didn't you suspect that maybe Abbie was Kyle Stanton's daughter out for revenge?"

"No." Taylor managed a defiant tone.

"Of course not Abbie, the golden child. You talk about her as if she walks around with a fucking halo over her head!" She paused as if to gather her thoughts and quell her emotions, then began again with what sounded like a pre-rehearsed theatrical style, "What we have here Chief is a horrible tragedy. Tommy, the ex-con, after hearing about the Mayor killing Cameron Preston, decided he wanted little Abbie for all kinds of twisted, sex offender reasons. So he murdered Olivia Preston to get her out of the way and just missed abducting Abbie that night. After he did eventually kidnap her and bring her out here he murdered his own family. Guess he got tired of being a family man. Then he raped and tortured and killed sweet, little Abbie in a most horrible way. Tommy will also have killed you after you arrived here but I followed you out here, per your instructions, and shot him dead, thus saving the day. I will be a hero, and the obvious next Chief of Police. I will be leading the news conferences from now on, and almost certainly fielding calls from talk shows who'll want to interview me. I can even see a book deal in my future. But most importantly, I will have avenged my father's death, although there's still a few others that need to pay for what they did to him. I've got some creative ways for them to die as well. I'll solve those cases too and arrest the guilty parties. So you see, all very perfectly logical reasons for doing what I've done."

"Leah, you can't seriously believe you'll get away with this."

"Oh, but I will bitch! Just like I got away with running over Aaron Driscoll and making it look like a hit and run. Stringing up Darius Kelly and making it look like a suicide. Shooting Abbie's daddy and planting the gun to frame Mayor Reynolds!" She laughed, "My father taught me how to pick a lock. I hid the gun and then called the tip line and put on a pretty good acting job if I do say so myself. I also sliced and diced Abbie's mommy. Who would've guessed that a middle school teacher would put up a better fight than all of those other losers. Of course, when you get whacked in the back of the head with a hammer like Jonah Sutherland, it's hard to put up much of a fight. And do you know why I killed that little whore Skylar? Because she was out there with her phone filming my dad being beaten to death. How sick is that? Do you know how I paid that filthy, fucking slut back? When I had her bound and gagged in that dark, scary warehouse, I used my flashlight to light up my face while I told her how I had killed everyone else and she was next. She was absolutely terrified. Crying and begging and praying. I laughed while I strangled her over and over. She'd pass out and then come to in a panic. I strangled her nine times. She woke up eight times!" Thorson let out a loud, diabolical laugh. "Then there was that stupid ass redneck Brandon. Actually drunk and horny enough to let me tie him to the bed. He thought he was going to get lucky, especially when I told him how kinky I was. Boy he got pissed off when I duct taped his mouth shut but it was too late. Imagine the terror he felt when I pulled out the bloody butcher knife. Now there was some real panic but I had him tied really tight. I told him in great detail everything I had done and why and what I was about to do to him. Before I began carving up his dick and balls like a Thanksgiving turkey, I had some fun with him by jabbing and sticking the knife into him. I stopped counting after a hundred. He was thrashing around and trying to scream but they were all muffled. Of all the victims, he suffered the most. Oh well."

Taylor couldn't believe what she was hearing. Thorson had to be some kind of sadistic monster. She felt compelled to ask her, "Why?"

"It's all part of my grand design. This ain't the result of some fucking whim! I've been planning this for a long time and it's going to work too. Don't believe it?" She walked over to the coffee table and picked up a large, ziplock bag with a blood stained butcher knife in it. She held it up where Taylor could see it. "The knife with Olivia and Brandon's blood on it will also have each of Tommy's family members' blood on it and sadly, Abbie's blood too. It will also have Tommy's bloody fingerprints on it. Put there after he's dead of course. I'm going to put Tommy's clothes on over what I'm wearing and then kill all six people in this house, including the kids, then put the bloodstained clothes back on him. I'm even going to wear his socks and shoes. I'll then burn these black clothes in the fireplace, make sure there's no blood on me, and then put my uniform back on. So you see, I've thought of every fucking detail!"

"My God, Leah, please don't kill the children," Taylor begged.

"Oh!" She dropped the bagged knife back down on the table and walked over close to Taylor, flashing her a fierce look, "So now you're concerned for children. What about little Leah? I never knew my mother. My father told me she was a schizophrenic, drug addicted prostitute. He told me she ran off but I suspect he killed her. I'm sure she deserved it. My father molested me from the time I was a baby. By the time I was twelve years old he was fucking me! I thought it was normal. Routine schedule: school, fast food, TV, my daddy fucking me, and homework. When he wasn't in jail that is. When he was incarcerated, I took care of myself. Yes, he could be mean and evil but he was my father. He loved me and I loved him."

Taylor felt sick to her stomach and was terrified for Abbie, Charlotte, Aiden, Vanessa, Tommy, and lastly herself. It was too much to process. They were all captive and defenseless against a truly maniacal evil. This woman, who she thought she knew, had to be stark raving mad. She knew their only chance was for Evans and Riley to show up and kill this woman. Keep her talking. "Where is Tommy's wife and children?"

"Locked in the bathroom," Thorson answered absentmindedly as she walked back over to the table and picked up Dalton's shirt and began to put it on. "Without a phone of course. I stacked some empty glasses against the outside of the bathroom door so if it opens they'll fall and break and I'll hear them. I made sure the mom has no doubt that if they come out, I'll shoot them."

"Leah, these children don't deserve this anymore than what happened to you as a child."

"Oh, Chief, you are so clever," she began to put on Dalton's pants, "You know as well as I that life isn't fair."

Taylor fought the overwhelming urge to cry, "Dear God, Leah, murdering children?"

Thorson pulled off her shoes and began putting on Dalton's hiking boots. "Collateral damage. The cost of doing business. Pick your metaphor, Chief."

Taylor knew in her heart that Evans and Riley would never get there in time. She cried, "Please God, no!"

Thorson slowly took the knife out of the plastic bag and looked at it reverently in her gloved hand, "It looks like God is the only thing that can save all of you now. It's not like I want to kill the kids but the adults, I couldn't give a shit. I must admit though, I am going to enjoy watching the horror on your face as I take this knife and slowly begin to slice away at the most tender and private parts of sweet, little, innocent Abbie…" she turned to glance at Abbie, as if to gauge her reaction, and froze. Abbie had finally wriggled her wrists free and held a black handgun out in front of her in both hands, a length of rope dangled from her left wrist. A second later, she pulled the trigger. BOOM! The deafening explosion shook the room. The bullet stuck Thorson in the left chest, spinning her around, and causing the knife to fly out of her hand. Before Thorson hit the ground, the knife landed upright, embedded into the wooden floor, wobbling back and forth. Thorson twirled around like a surrealistic ballerina and landed flat on her back.

Taylor, her ears ringing, watched in shock as Thorson gasped for air, with animalistic grunts and groans, and flailed her arms and legs in agony. A minute later, Thorson was no longer breathing. Taylor looked over at Abbie, who only then lowered the gun, pulled the duct tape from her mouth, and began untying the rope from her ankles. Taylor realized she had been holding her breath and when she exhaled, she could no longer hold back a flood of tears. A sense of relief like she had never felt before, could not keep her from crying.

Once Abbie had untied her legs, she walked over with her distinctive gait and looked down at Thorson, to make sure she was dead. She was. Still holding the gun at her side, Abbie bent over and reached into Thorson's right front pocket and pulled out a set of keys that had the handcuff key on it. When she stood up and looked over at Taylor, tears were beginning to well up in her eyes. "Sam, I'm sorry I lied to you. I've had my mom's gun on me the whole time."

"Oh my God, Abbie, you saved us all!"

Abbie awkwardly kneeled down and used the key to unlock the handcuffs. Once Taylor was free, they frantically embraced each other and sobbed in each other's arms. "I love you, Abbie!"

"I love you too, Sam!"

They cried and hugged each other until Dalton uttered a growling sound from his taped up mouth to get their attention. It seemed to snap them out of their emotional spell and Taylor tried to think straight. "Abbie, I'll free Tommy and you let his wife and kids out of the bathroom."

"Okay," she said, then shuffled that way.

Taylor untied her ankles and then got up and went over to Tommy and pulled the duct tape away from his mouth.

"Oh my God, I thought for sure we were going to die!" He watched as Taylor went around behind him and began tugging at the rope that he had tried without success to untie. "Thank God for Abbie!" Once she had freed his hands he began clawing at the rope around his ankles.

When Taylor heard the voices of Tommy's children coming she ran over and picked up a folded blanket off of the couch and hurried over and covered Thorson's corpse with it. She thought, "To hell with crime scene integrity, I don't want these kids to see Thorson's bloody body."

Just as Dalton got his legs untied, his children, nine year old Charlotte and seven year old Aiden, came running across the room and hugged their daddy. Dalton burst into tears and hugged his kids tightly. His wife Vanessa was close behind and she too joined the emotional family hug.

Coming back into the room, right behind Vanessa was Abbie, the gun still in her left hand, dangling at her side. Taylor walked over to her and said, "Let me hold onto that," Abbie handed the gun to her and they hugged again. Taylor was amazed but perplexed as well. She asked her, "Why did you take the gun and hang onto it?"

"I thought for sure the killer would come after me next, at least I was hoping so," she answered with a mischievous little smile, "Mom took me target shooting several times."

"That's why you were never afraid to be alone," Taylor slowly shook her head in awe. Leah Thorson had greatly underestimated Abbie and she had to admit, she had too. "Where did you keep it?"

"Duct taped to my lower back. I saw it in a movie. I just made sure I wore big shirts," she turned around and lifted her shirt up and sure enough, there were still two strips of tape stuck to her back. Taylor pulled the sections of duct tape from Abbie's skin and she chuckled, "That tickles."

Taylor was simply astonished by this young lady. Olivia frequently used to talk about how special Abbie was and Taylor had always thought she knew what she meant. Now it dawned on her that it was entirely possible that even Olivia didn't realize just how special this child could be. She had to tell her, "Your mom and dad would be so proud of you."

Abbie's expression suddenly transformed into one of sadness and she moved closer to Taylor and they hugged each other. Taylor thought this was the perfect time to bring up what she had been thinking for awhile. "What would you say if we made you living with me official and permanent?"

Abbie looked up at Taylor, her green eyes filling with tears and all she could do was nod vigorously.

Dalton, with his wife and children in tow, walked over and hugged Abbie as well. He told her, "I will never be able to repay you for saving my family. You are a hero!"

"I prayed a lot about it," Abbie told him and then smiled with a tear stained face and said, "You know it's kinda weird you hugging me in your underwear."

Everyone laughed and then Vanessa hugged her and said, "Thank you, Abbie, so much!"

Next, Charlotte and Aiden hugged Abbie as well.

Taylor watched these kids' expressions and how they looked up at Abbie as if they'd just met their idol. Although they certainly couldn't comprehend the monstrous evil that just had them in its grip, even at their young ages they understood something momentous had just happened, and it was all because of Abbie.

Taylor thought it was a good idea to get the kids away from the covered body of Thorson so she suggested, "Why don't we wait outside for the rest of the police to get here."

Dalton told them, "I'm going to get cleaned up and put some clothes on," before heading for the bedroom.

"C'mon guys, let's go outside," Vanessa put her arms around the kids to direct them toward the open doorway.

Aiden saw Thorson's gloved hand sticking out from beneath the blanket, pointed at it and asked, "Is that the bad woman?"

His mother didn't want to lie to him so she answered, "Yes, that's her."

Charlotte uttered the understatement of a lifetime when she said, "I think there was something bad wrong with her."

Taylor quietly agreed, "Yeah, there was," she put her arm around Abbie's shoulders and the five of them walked out of the front door onto the large, covered porch. For the next eight minutes they watched an incredible lightning show as the rain and wind lashed the island. Taylor knew that she had a newfound appreciation for life when the visual effects of a monster hurricane were actually beautiful.

Finally, Vanessa said, "Hear that?"

Even over the sound of the wind and rain, Taylor could hear what sounded like splashing. To her it sounded like a school of fish near the surface of the water. She walked to the edge of the porch, to have the light behind her and squinted into the night. Just barely visible through the darkness and rain was a person actually swimming in the lake. Coming ashore was Riley! As soon as she stood up on the shore, she turned around and yelled, "Michael, you okay?"

"Yeah," came his more distant reply.

Taylor smiled and shook her head. These two had swum a hundred and fifty yards in the middle of a hurricane to save everybody. She looked at Abbie, who was smiling broadly.

Vanessa said, "I'll get some towels," before heading back into the house.

Riley waited on Evans to make it to the grassy shoreline and even gave him a helping hand out of the water. Then the two of them walked through the rain, up to the porch and as they ascended the steps Evans said breathlessly, "It's good to see you're all okay."

With a big smile Abbie asked him, "You were coming to save me weren't you?"

"You better believe it, kiddo," he answered before the two of them hugged each other tightly.

Taylor hugged the soaking wet Riley and then Evans. She told them, "Abbie beat you to it."

As Abbie hugged Riley, Evans asked, "What do you mean?"

Vanessa came out with towels and gave them to Riley and Evans.

Taylor said, "Let me show you. Abbie, stay with Vanessa and the kids."

"Okay."

Taylor led Evans and Riley into the living room and lifted the blanket to show them the killer's face.

Evans was stunned. He said incredulously, "Thorson!"

Riley was shocked as well, "One of your officers?"

"I can't believe it!" Evans exclaimed.

"She's Kyle Stanton's daughter and she proudly confessed to every detail. She killed them all, including Cameron Preston."

"So she planted the gun in Travis' house?" Asked Evans.

"Yep, and she was about to kill every one of us with that butcher knife," she pointed to the knife which was still stuck upright in the wooden floor. The blade still stained with Olivia Preston and Brandon Holt's dried blood.

Riley asked, "What happened?"

"Abbie has secretly had her mother's gun on her the whole time expecting to be targeted next."

"So she's the one who took it," Evans could hardly believe it and then it dawned on him just as it had to Taylor. "That's why she was never afraid to be alone."

Riley added with wonderment, "She was using herself as bait!"

Taylor nodded, "She managed to get her hands untied just in time to pull the gun and shoot Thorson dead."

Riley uttered, "Oh my God."

"Then we wouldn't have gotten here in time," Evans sounded as though he had trouble even saying the words.

Taylor shook her head slowly as her eyes began filling with tears, "It would've been my fault. I waited too long."

Evans hugged her and said, "It's not your fault, Sam. It all worked out."

As Dalton came out of the bedroom area, Evans walked back outside and hugged Abbie again. He told her, "You know, you could have a career with the F.B.I."

As Taylor and Riley joined them on the porch, Abbie shook her head and said, "I know what I want to be."

"What's that?" Taylor asked.

"A teacher like my mom."

Taylor felt the all too familiar lump in her throat and once again fought a losing battle not to cry. She hugged Abbie and said, "That's perfect."

Across the lake, state police cars with flashing red and blue lights began arriving at the dock with a great sense of urgency. The cavalry had arrived but this time, it wasn't needed. A hero had already saved the day.

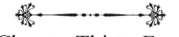

Chapter Thirty-Four

On Monday, the 25th at 12:00 P.M. the last news conference got underway. Even with the cleanup from Hurricane Walter in full force, all anyone wanted to talk about was how Abbie was able to save at least six people's lives by shooting Leah Thorson. At noon, Taylor, Evans, Riley, and Abbie were all standing in front of hundreds of media members and citizens looking to hear from the hero herself. Taylor began, "Good afternoon ladies and gentlemen. My name is Samantha Taylor, I'm the Chief of Police here in Delaney. To my far right is F.B.I. Special Agent Michael Evans. To my left is F.B.I. Special Agent Emma Riley and this is Abbie Preston," she put her right arm around Abbie's shoulders and they smiled at each other. "She is the daughter of our second and third victims, Cameron and Olivia Preston. I'm going to try my best to get through this without becoming emotional but I'm not making any promises because this has been a very trying time for all of us. First, I'm going to issue some thank you's and then I'm going to summarize our cases and I'm sure you'll have some questions. The first person I'd like to thank is Agent Michael Evans. Michael has been so important to me. He is my rock. I truly don't know that I could have gotten through all of this without him. Agent Emma Riley, I feel like I have a new best friend. Her instincts and insight were invaluable to me. And now Abbie. My classmate and dear friend Olivia was Abbie's mom. She used to tell me all the time how special Abbie was and I always assumed I knew what she meant. It turns out I never really understood just how special and wonderful she actually is. Because of my protectiveness of her, I was hesitant to bring Abbie to the news conference but there were some things that she wanted to say, so I knew there was no way I could tell her no. So Abbie, it's all yours."

When Abbie stepped in front of the podium, the clicking sounds of camera shutters resonated just like when the president comes out to make an important announcement.

"Whew! I've never had so many people listen to me before. I want to start by thanking Michael and Emma. I used to think that F.B.I. agents were like what you see on TV, but that isn't true. They are regular people just like everyone else. Michael is so smart and funny and he likes to tease me. Emma is so nice and even though she looks too young and pretty to be an F.B.I. agent, she's actually a badass," she allowed for the laughter to die down. "And now Sam. When I was growing up, Sam was always there. She was at every important event in my life. It was like having a second mom. I am so grateful to be adopted by a superhero like her. I love you," They smiled warmly at each other and Taylor didn't even mind the whole world seeing tears well up in her eyes. Abbie continued, "I have too many friends that I love to mention them all but I'd like to speak to the people who don't know me. When I'm around strangers I sometimes experience stares and ignorance. We need to stop judging each other about their handicaps and disabilities and try to understand what others are going through. I love who I am and I wouldn't change a thing. I guess I showed that just because you have a disability, it doesn't mean you can't do great things."

Taylor put her arm around Abbie and announced, "One at a time please, we'll take some questions."

A female reporter on the front row jumped ahead of the others and asked, "This is a question for Abbie. How did Officer Thorson abduct you?"

"Right before the hurricane hit, she came to the house when I was alone and told me that Sam had instructed her to pick me up and take me to the storm shelter at the police station. It seemed logical. On the way, she stopped and put me in handcuffs, took my phone and powered it off. She started driving toward the Dalton ranch, telling me all of the horrible things that she had done. I couldn't reach around behind me to grab the gun but even if I had, I wasn't sure I would've been able to get a good shot at her, so I waited for the right time. I knew I would only have one chance so I decided to be patient and make sure. When we got to the ranch, she told Tommy that she had a suspect that she wanted him to identify. When he got to the dock, she pulled her gun out and forced him to take us to his island. She locked his wife and kids in the bathroom and tied Tommy and I to chairs with rope. Then she forced me to call Sam and read a message that would get her out there. By the time Sam arrived, I had been working on untying my knots for quite a while. When Thorson said she was about to kill all of us, I knew it was now or never. I got loose, pulled the gun off of my lower back where I had it taped and aimed it at her. I had prayed a lot about being able to pull the trigger but when I heard her talk about the vicious things she had done, including killing my parents, and the horrifying things she was about to do, I knew in my heart I was doing the right thing. She was looking at the bloody knife and telling us what she was going to do with it. When she turned and saw me holding the gun, it was like she couldn't believe what she was seeing. There was no reason to hesitate so I shot her. One was all it took."

Numerous people yelled questions and Taylor said, "Raise your hands and we'll call on you."

The reporter Taylor pointed at asked, "Abbie, why did you have a gun on you to begin with?"

"My mom bought it for protection when my dad was killed and she took me target shooting many times. When she was killed, I was sure the killer would come after me next so I wanted to be ready."

The next reporter asked, "Abbie, you said you had the gun taped to your lower back, why did you do that, and where did you learn that from?"

"I saw it in a movie and it made sense in case I was searched. I prayed that Thorson wouldn't find it because I knew I was going to need it. She actually didn't even search me at all. I guess she never thought I'd be carrying a gun."

The next question was, "Abbie, does this make you want to have a career in law enforcement?"

She shook head, "No, I want to be a teacher like my mom."

Taylor spoke up, "Okay, I know you probably have a hundred questions for Abbie but I need to summarize our cases so we can get the most information for you," Abbie stepped aside and Taylor continued. "One person and one person only murdered all seven of our victims. That person was Leah Thorson, an officer with the Delaney Police Department and the daughter of Kyle Stanton. DNA tests will confirm that and we will release them as soon as the results are in. She admitted to me, Abbie, and Tommy Dalton that she was responsible for all of the killings. She ran down Aaron Driscoll, in the hope that it would be passed off as an unsolved hit and run. She then shot and killed Cameron Preston and then later planted the gun in Mayor Travis Reynolds' house, thereby falsely implicating him in the slaying. She then killed Olivia Preston and kept the murder weapon, a knife. She killed our next victim, Darius Kelly and made it look like a suicide. She bludgeoned our next victim, Jonah Sutherland, with a hammer and then falsely claimed she saw Tommy Dalton near the crime scene, trying to implicate him. Then she killed Skylar Pittman and tried to make it look like an accidental death. Lastly, she tortured and murdered in one of the most horrific ways our Deputy Chief of Police, Brandon Holt. Her motives were twofold as described to us in her own words. Aaron Driscoll, Cameron Preston, Darius Kelly, Jonah Sutherland, and Skylar Pittman were all murdered because they were at the scene of the assault of Kyle Stanton. Olivia Preston and Brandon Holt were murdered to further a plot she hatched which included killing me to become the next Chief of Police. She intended to kill Abbie and Tommy Dalton's family and blame it on him. Then she would kill him in what she would claim was self defense and blame all of the killings on him by planting and fabricating evidence. A truly diabolical plan conjured up in a very evil mind. I am heartbroken that my department employed such a person. Being a small police force meant the hiring process was not all that it should have been. That is going to change. Leah Thorson fooled everybody. No one saw what she really was. I won't go into the details here but, being the daughter of Kyle Stanton, especially with no mother around, shaped what she was to become," she pointed at a correspondent.

"Chief Taylor, you said the hiring process of your department was not all that it should have been with the hiring of Leah Thorson, but it doesn't end with her. What is the status of Officer Rebecca Daniels?"

"For those of you who don't know, another officer on our force, Rebecca Daniels, had a secret relationship with our former mayor, Travis Reynolds, and let him hide out in her home while he was being searched for after skipping bail. It's a little complicated legally speaking because Reynolds was hiding out from a false charge but she still has been deemed unreliable going forward and the decision has been made to terminate her employment with us. She simply would not be trusted going forward."

The next question asked was, "Chief Taylor, what is the status of the other suspects in this case?"

"Travis Reynolds turned himself in and obviously the D.A. has dropped the murder charge against him. Nathan Miller has been arrested by Miami PD on a warrant for solicitation of sex with a minor and Blake Archer was arrested by Tampa PD on a charge of assault with a deadly weapon."

A reporter had a question for Evans, "Sir, have you ever seen a case like this with so many difficulties?"

Evans took his place at the podium, "I don't recall a case where there were so many murders in such a short period of time. Not to mention the way the murders were committed and ultimately the incredible way it ended. To that point, I'd like to tell the people of Delaney, you are lucky to have Sam Taylor as your Chief of Police. As great as she is though, I think it's been proven, Abbie is the real superhero." He patted her on the shoulder as he stood aside and they exchanged smiles.

The next reporter had a question for Agent Riley. "I was there last year in Iowa for your missing girls case and I have a question for you. If your partner Andrew O'Neil were here, what would he say about this case?"

Riley stepped in front of the microphones thinking about the man she missed so much, and smiled fondly, "I think I know what Andy would say. He would say, 'Thank God for Abbie Preston."

About the Author

Robby (to his family and friends) was born in North Carolina and has lived in Texas since he was fifteen. *Maelstrom* is his second novel after *The Girls of Webber*. He lives in Hurst, Texas.

Printed in Great Britain
by Amazon